THE ENIGMA OF THE INVISIBLE

Unraveling the Shadows of the Inca's Curse

ECHO SABLE

Table of Contents

Chapter 1

The Brass Box

After returning from a clandestine mission at a foreign space base, I sought refuge within the confines of my home, vanishing from the world for two months. To the outside world, I was still abroad, my absence a carefully maintained illusion. I reached out only to a select few, ensuring my solitude remained undisturbed.

But my self-imposed isolation was destined to shatter. The catalyst? A peculiar box, sent by my friend from Egypt.

My friend, Mr. Jansen, is a distinguished water conservancy engineer known for his profound expertise. The Egyptian government enlisted his skills from the Netherlands to assist in an ambitious water conservancy project—one of the largest the world has ever seen. So monumental was this undertaking that it required relocating an entire ancient temple.

While orchestrating the temple's relocation, Jansen stumbled upon the box and entrusted it to me.

The box, a vessel of mystery, demands a detailed description.

Measuring approximately one meter in length, half a meter in width, and twenty centimeters in height, it is crafted entirely of brass. The lid seamlessly aligns with the box's midsection, yet opening it is no simple task.

The lock, a marvel of ancient ingenuity, defies modern comprehension. Despite our era's technological prowess, replicating such an intricate mechanism would be a formidable challenge.

The box's surface was an enigma, a hundred intricate grids meticulously arranged. Nestled within these grids were ninety-nine small copper pieces, each capable of sliding, each contributing to the mystery. The single vacant grid served as the only space where pieces could be maneuvered.

Each copper piece bore an embossed pattern, a tantalizing hint of a fragmented image. The task was to restore this image, aligning the pieces to transform the chaotic patterns into a coherent picture. Only then would the box's secrets be revealed — a reward for the patient and persistent solver.

Wang, knowing my penchant for the peculiar, sent this enigmatic artifact my way.

When the hefty brass box arrived, my curiosity was piqued.

I devoted days to deciphering its puzzle, but soon the complexity proved overwhelming, and I reluctantly set it aside, conceding its mystery for the time being.

Initially, I faced a daunting challenge: I had no clue what the original relief on the box was supposed to depict, leaving me without a reference point for reassembling the image.

Moreover, the complexity of the puzzle lay in its mechanics. The ninety-nine copper plates could not be freely removed; they could only be manipulated using the single vacant space, turning one piece at a time—a process requiring an intricate series of maneuvers.

With ninety-nine pieces in total, how could I possibly return each to its exact original position?

After conceding defeat in reconstructing the plates, I turned my attention to a careful examination of the brass box itself.

The other five sides of the box were adorned with reliefs—depictions of humans and animals, carved with bold, simplistic lines. Yet, these engravings were not of ancient Egyptian art. Their style bore a resemblance to Indian artistry, a curious deviation from the box's supposed origins.

On either side of the box, two copper rings were affixed, inscribed with words that defied translation into ancient Egyptian.

I penned a lengthy telegram to my friend, expressing my intrigue with the box and my inability to unlock it. I inquired whether mechanical force might reveal its contents, considering the box seemed out of place in an Egyptian temple. I also requested a detailed account of its discovery.

By evening, his response arrived:

"Ash, I strongly advise against using mechanical means to open the box. This artifact might be thousands of years old. Are we truly less intelligent than our ancestors? I suggest you consult my brother, a mathematician, who might calculate the probability of opening it. His contact is —. As for the box's discovery, it's a very tortuous story, which I'll share later. Sem Jansen."

Sem Jansen, my friend, known for his deliberate nature, left me curious with his mention of a "very tortuous story." If even he described it as such, the tale must be captivating indeed.

The fact that this mystery unfolded in the ancient land of Egypt only deepened the enigma, adding layers of intrigue to the brass box and its hidden secrets.

My curiosity about how Sem Jansen acquired the box overshadowed my interest in its enigmatic lock. Driven by a need to break the monotony, I urged him to recount the entire tale, hoping it would be an antidote to my boredom.

In tandem, I reached out to Sem Jansen's younger brother, Liam Jansen, a scholar at a local college. Upon receiving my call, he assured me he would visit when his schedule permitted.

By nine that evening, engrossed in research on ancient Egyptian bronze casting, I confirmed my initial suspicion: the relief on the brass box bore no resemblance to Egyptian art. Just then, Wilson ushered Liam in.

Liam Jansen, a young man in his mid-twenties, exuded a scientific air despite his pale complexion. Our introduction was marked by his polite, albeit slightly reserved, demeanor.

After I explained the intricacies of the box, he responded with a humble smile, "I'm afraid I may not be able to open it either."

I offered a reassuring pat on the shoulder, "It's alright if you can't. Think of it as a new hobby—an adventure waiting to unfold."

Together, we loaded the brass box into his car. With a wave, Liam departed into the night.

Days slipped by without a word from Liam Jansen, and my anticipation for Sem Jansen's story waned, allowing the mystery of the box to fade from my immediate thoughts.

Then, on the tenth day after Liam took the box, a change in the weather brought an oppressive humidity, the air thick and uncomfortable. At midday, as I lay napping, the shrill ring of the bedside phone shattered the quiet.

It's peculiar how the ring of a phone, always the same in tone, can sometimes convey a sense of urgency, as if heralding something significant. When the phone rang this time, I sensed just that.

I picked up the receiver without hesitation.

"Ash Morris? I—it's Liam Jansen," came the voice, slightly breathless.

"Yes, Liam Jansen," I replied, urging calm. "Take your time. What's happened?"

He inhaled deeply before speaking. "I've arranged the ninety-nine copper plates on the box into a relief painting."

I leapt from my bed, excitement coursing through me. "That's fantastic! Does that mean you've opened it?"

"Not yet," Liam Jansen admitted, his voice tinged with apprehension. "But I have this strange feeling that opening it might be... disadvantageous."

I chuckled, trying to lighten the mood. "Perhaps you've fallen under the spell of ancient Egyptian curses. But let me assure you, although this box was found in an Egyptian temple, it's certainly not of Egyptian origin."

Liam Jansen hesitated. "Don't other ancient civilizations have curses too?"

I laughed again, amused by his imagination. "I always thought mathematicians were dull, but you've got quite the creative mind!"

Embarrassed, he chuckled softly. "Alright. I'll call you once I've opened it."

I settled back against my pillow, anticipating his call within moments. But as time ticked by, I smoked through seven or eight cigarettes, and an hour slipped away with no word from Liam Jansen.

A growing unease gnawed at me. Yet, it seemed absurd to think he could have encountered trouble—after all, he was merely opening an old brass box!

As the minutes crept by, I found myself pacing the room, unable to shake the feeling that something was amiss. Why hadn't Liam Jansen called to share what he found? Even if he couldn't open the box, surely he would have reached out.

The day waned into evening, and after dialing his number for the tenth time with still no answer, dread settled in. Something was undeniably wrong.

Nearly five hours had passed since Liam Jansen's initial call informing me that he had successfully pieced together the image on the brass box. Since then, there had been an unsettling silence. What could have happened to Liam Jansen?

Despite reassuring myself that he was unlikely to have encountered any real danger, I couldn't suppress the worry gnawing at me.

His brother had provided me with his phone number, but Liam Jansen hadn't mentioned his address during his last visit. Growing increasingly anxious, I reached out to a friend who worked as a private detective for assistance.

This friend, along with his assistant, had painstakingly compiled their own phone directory, linking numbers to addresses. Within five minutes, they provided me with the information I sought: Liam Jansen resided on the fourth floor of No. 3 Bisan Road.

Bisan Road was known for its upscale residences, fitting for someone of Liam Jansen's stature. I set the phone down, prepared to visit him immediately.

But just as I reached the door, the phone rang again. I hurried to answer it, instantly recognizing the sound of Liam Jansen's labored breathing.

Alarmed, I asked, "What happened? Are you alright?"

His breathing was labored, each inhale and exhale weighed down by an invisible burden. I had to repeat my questions several times before he finally responded, "I-I'm in some trouble. Can I come see you? I'll be there right away!"

Despite his understatement of "some trouble," it was glaringly obvious that Liam Jansen was facing something far more serious. The usually calm and composed individual I knew seemed to have been completely unraveled.

"Of course, come over immediately," I replied without hesitation.

The call ended abruptly with a click, leaving me holding the receiver, pondering the gravity of the situation. What could have provoked such a drastic change in Liam Jansen?

Could it all be connected to the enigmatic box, a relic not native to Egypt yet unearthed in an ancient Egyptian temple? The mystery deepened, and with it, my concern for Liam Jansen's safety.

Bisan Road wasn't far from my place, so I expected Liam Jansen to arrive within ten minutes. But twenty minutes dragged by before the doorbell finally rang.

Hearing the chime, I dashed downstairs, catching Wilson's gruff inquiry, "Who is it? Who are you looking for?"

I quickly interjected, "Wilson, it's Mr. Jansen from last time. Let him in." Wilson, peering through the peephole, turned to me with a perplexed expression and said, "Is this really the same Mr. Jansen?"

Wilson wasn't usually prone to such hesitation, and my impatience flared. "Just open the door."

Without further protest, Wilson complied, and a figure stepped inside. I looked up, and froze in disbelief.

Could this really be Liam Jansen?

It was no wonder Wilson had been uncertain. Even I struggled to recognize the man standing before me as Liam Jansen.

Though of similar stature, Liam Jansen was nearly unrecognizable, shrouded in an ensemble more fitting for an Arctic expedition. An oversized coat with an exaggerated collar, gloves, a hat, and a scarf wrapped tightly around his face, all crowned by large black sunglasses, transformed him into a figure of mystery. His familiar presence was obscured beneath layers of winter gear, each piece adding to the intrigue of his sudden, urgent visit.

In such attire, he could visit an Eskimo village without fear of the cold. Yet today, with the return of the south wind, the air was oppressively hot and humid. I was comfortable in just a shirt!

I stood there, momentarily speechless. Then, muffled through the layers of his scarf, came Liam Jansen's voice—urgent yet unmistakable. "Have you been waiting long?"

I stepped closer, eyes fixed on Liam Jansen. "Are you feeling unwell?" His bitter laugh was unconvincing. "Not unwell, no, I'm fine."

His attire and demeanor said otherwise — no one "fine" would dress as he did on such a warm day. "You mentioned trouble on the phone. What's going on?"

He sidestepped away, almost as if wanting to maintain distance, and sank into the sofa without a word.

The air grew thick with tension. I moved toward him, probing gently, "What's troubling you? Are you cold? Why not take off your hat and glasses?"

Liam Jansen rose abruptly, his voice trembling, "Take it off? No! No!" His hands shook as he spoke.

Our acquaintance was relatively new, so I refrained from pressuring him. Instead, I offered, "You came here for a reason, seeking my help?"

"Yes," he admitted, "I need to ask you something."

I gestured for him to continue. "Alright, out with it."

His breath quickened. "How did you come by that brass box?"

So, it was indeed about the box. My mind raced as I replied, "Your brother sent it to me from Egypt."

Liam Jansen waved his hands frantically, "No! I mean, how did my brother find it? What's its origin?"

His face remained hidden, but his agitation was palpable. His nerves were frayed, bordering on hysteria. I ignored his question and pressed, "What happened with the box? Did you open it? What troubles did it bring?"

He ignored me, instead pleading, "Tell me, tell me where the box came from!"

I sighed, admitting, "I can't. Your brother hinted at a complicated story behind it but hasn't shared the details. I've sent him telegrams, but no response."

Liam Jansen, previously half-standing, slumped back into the sofa, muttering incoherently. His body shook violently, prompting me to suggest, "You seem unwell, Liam. Should I call a doctor?"

Suddenly, he sprang to his feet. "No, no need. I—I should go."

He retreated toward the door, facing me as he did. I had no intention of letting him leave—not when my questions had only multiplied. Liam's erratic behavior had deepened the mystery, and I couldn't let him slip away without answers.

I moved to intercept him, but Liam Jansen waved his hands, insisting, "You—there's no need to see me off, I can manage."

His hands were encased in thick gloves—a puzzling choice given the warm weather. The incongruity gnawed at me. I leaned in, sensing there was more beneath the surface. "You didn't come all this way just to ask a few questions, right?" I pressed, my curiosity blending with a growing concern.

"No—no—yes—just for that," he stammered, his words tangled and incoherent. I couldn't let him leave in such a state.

As Liam Jansen continued to retreat toward the door, an impulse drove me forward. I closed the gap in a few swift strides, reaching for his hand. My fingers closed around the glove on his right hand. "Why are you encasing yourself like this in such heat?"

His ensemble reminded me of the "man in a casing" from Chekhov's tales, and my tone conveyed curiosity more than alarm. Despite the strangeness of the situation, I hadn't fully grasped its gravity.

My action caught Liam Jansen off guard. In a swift motion, I pulled the glove from his hand, even as he tried to fend me off.

And then, time seemed to stand still.

Shock coursed through me like electricity, leaving me momentarily paralyzed.

Before me, Liam Jansen's hands remained in a defensive posture. His left hand still gloved, but his right hand—now exposed—was a sight that defied belief.

What I saw was not a living hand—it was skeletal, five finger bones bare of flesh, yet eerily intact, capable of motion.

In that moment, both Liam Jansen and I stood frozen in a tableau of disbelief, the air between us charged with the impossible reality of what lay before us.

Chapter 2

Horrifying Mutation

What lay before me was a pair of skeletal hand bones—a sight that defied all logic. A living person, yet his hand was nothing more than bones, able to move and shake in protest as if to guard its owner. I felt a wave of dizziness crash over me, threatening my balance.

Both Liam and I stood frozen in a tableau of shock, the moment stretching into eternity. Just as the room seemed to spin, Liam let out an eerie cry. He pivoted abruptly, using his skeletal hand to grip the door handle and fled, disappearing into the outside world.

I felt as though plunged into icy waters, trapped in a nightmare from which I couldn't awaken. I stood there, paralyzed, unable to muster the strength to pursue him.

It wasn't until the roar of an engine pierced the silence that I stumbled to the door, just in time to see Liam's car tearing away like a runaway stallion. It was a miracle he didn't crash at the corner.

I stood dazed, grappling with the surreal reality. Surely, my mind was playing tricks on me, I thought.

The spell was broken by a loud "thud" behind me. Turning, I found Wilson sprawled on the floor, eyes wide with terror.

"What happened, Wilson?" I demanded, rushing to his side.

His teeth chattered as he stammered, "I saw a ghost—a ghost."

"What ghost?" I pressed.

Wilson trembled violently, "That man... his hand was a skeleton..."

His voice faltered, trembling under the weight of unspoken horror. Yet, I needed no further explanation. Wilson, like me, had borne witness to the ghastly sight of Liam's skeletal hand—animated and eerily mobile, yet stripped of flesh. The memory of that horrifying image lingered, a haunting reminder of the unseen forces at play. It was clear that whatever trouble Liam faced, it was beyond ordinary comprehension. The calm before the storm had passed, and the true nature of his predicament was beginning to unravel before our eyes.

Trying to ground us both, I insisted, "You're imagining things. You must be mistaken. It's just a trick of the eyes."

Wilson looked up, his expression pleading. "Mistaken?"

There was no time for further debate. I bolted out the door into the drizzle, rain be damned. Leaping into my car, I fired up the engine with a sense of urgency. The tires screeched as I swung onto the road, desperate to catch up with Liam. The chase had begun, and I couldn't afford to lose him now.

I drove recklessly, heedless of the curious stares from pedestrians. Their opinions didn't matter — all that mattered was finding Liam and uncovering the truth behind the skeletal hand.

As I sped toward Bisan Road, my mind wrestled with the impossibility of what I'd witnessed. Even with Wilson as a corroborating witness, my rational mind balked at the bizarre reality of Liam's skeletal hand.

Had Liam been a chemist, I might have entertained the notion of an accident with corrosive substances. But he was a mathematician! And even if the flesh had somehow been stripped from his hand, how could the bones remain intact and functional?

The car glided over the rain-slicked streets, my thoughts a chaotic whirl akin to scenes from horror films like "Vampire Zombies" or "Frankenstein."

I arrived at Liam's residence, scanning for his vehicle but seeing no sign of it. Parking at the entrance, I hurried up the stairs to the fourth floor. Liam's home wasn't part of a high-rise but an old four-story building. I reached his door and found it shut, ringing the bell repeatedly without response.

Using a spare key, I unlocked the door—a simple lock, easily bypassed—and stepped inside.

The dim illumination from the streetlights revealed a scene of disarray. The living room lay in chaos. Flicking on a light, I dashed through the other rooms—a study and a bedroom—both equally untidy.

Liam was nowhere to be found.

In the study, I discovered the brass box, its lid ajar. As Liam was absent, I had little time to linger. I closed the lid with a decisive thud, noting the completed puzzle of copper pieces.

The relief they formed was both ancient and intricate, a testament to artistry lost to time. The scene depicted was unsettling: a gathering of skeletal figures—both human and animal—encircling a radiant object resembling fire, yet not fire. The realism of the skeletal forms was astonishing, considering the box's likely age of one to two thousand years. Such detailed anatomical knowledge from so long ago was remarkable.

Scattered on the floor were various ornaments, clues to the box's enigmatic origins.

Until now, I had doubted the box's cultural provenance. But the ornaments in the relief on the box's lid confirmed it—a masterpiece of Indian art!

Moreover, I became certain that this brass box was a relic of the Inca Empire, a civilization whose sudden and mysterious disappearance has puzzled historians for generations. Only during the Inca Empire could such intricate works of art have been crafted by an Indian nation.

Yet, one burning question seared through my mind: How could artifacts from the ancient Inca Empire find their way into the ancient temples of Egypt?

In all the explorations of the Inca Empire's history, there had never been a mention of any connection to Egypt. Under the circumstances, I couldn't delve deeply into this enigma. I was momentarily stunned by the implications. My immediate concern was that Liam's bizarre experience was undoubtedly linked to this box.

I reopened the lid, hoping for a clue. But the interior was pristine—empty and devoid of any trace or clue about its previous contents.

The priority was clear: I had to find Liam. He alone held the key to understanding the terrifying ordeal he was undergoing.

Switching off the study light, I made my way back to the living room. Just as I turned out the light, the sound of footsteps echoed up the stairs. They had a distinct rhythm—the unmistakable click of high heels on the floor. It was a woman's footsteps, instantly recognizable to anyone familiar with their sound.

Originally, I intended to open the door and step outside, but the approaching footsteps halted me in my tracks. Although I couldn't be certain the woman was here for Liam, I preferred to avoid any encounters in the stairwell. Given the unfolding mystery, I was unsure what role I would play and wanted to minimize involvement with outsiders.

So, I waited by the door, hoping to remain unnoticed.

Unexpectedly, the footsteps stopped right outside, and the doorbell chimed. I hesitated, unsure of how to proceed. Should I open the door to this unexpected visitor, especially with Liam absent? As I deliberated, the doorbell ceased, followed by the unmistakable sound of a key turning in the lock.

I quickly retreated behind the door, positioning myself just out of sight.

The door swung open, and the visitor hesitated, met by darkness. Then, a woman's voice called out, "Darling, you had the lights on just now. Why did they all go out suddenly?"

She was evidently a close acquaintance, perhaps even an intimate friend of Liam's, as she not only possessed a key but addressed him familiarly.

I remained silent, moving sideways to conceal myself behind a sofa. Just as I settled, the room was flooded with light. Peeking out, I saw a beautiful young woman, her expression a mix of concern and determination.

She appeared to be in her early twenties, clad in a stylish raincoat cinched at the waist. Her presence was commanding, exuding the vitality of youth. Despite the chaos, her eyes betrayed only a flicker of panic, and her set lips showed she was not easily intimidated.

Momentarily stunned, she called out, " Liam, Liam, what's the matter, what's the matter?" Her voice echoed as she hurried toward the study.

Before she reached the door, I emerged from my hiding place, addressing her, "Miss, what do you think might have happened?"

She spun around, her reaction swift and composed, far beyond what I anticipated. She didn't scream or panic, merely fixed me with a steady gaze.

I advanced, speaking again, "What do you think might have happened to him?" As I approached, she surprised me by grabbing my arm and, with a deft motion, sending me flying over her shoulder.

Clearly adept at judo, she had executed the maneuver flawlessly. My body sailed through the air, landing with a thud behind her.

Had I been an ordinary man, the impact might have rendered me unconscious. But I was no ordinary person.

Even in mid-air, I strategized, tucking my legs and absorbing the fall with practiced agility. I rebounded quickly, rolling into a defensive stance behind the sofa once more, ready for the next move in this unexpected encounter.

The girl exuded confidence. After effortlessly tossing me over her shoulder, she stood with her hands on her hips, clearly expecting to hear the satisfying "bang" of my landing.

But that sound never came. When she finally turned around, I was already hidden behind the sofa, watching her expression shift to one of disbelief.

I chuckled, rising from my hiding place. "Miss, I'm right here!"

She took a step forward, suspicion etched on her features. I quickly interjected, "There's no need for hide and seek. If you're a friend of Liam, then so am I!"

Her skepticism lingered as she replied, "I wasn't aware he had a friend like you."

"It's never too late to make new acquaintances," I responded. "Did you come here by coincidence, or did Liam ask you to visit?"

Though still wary, she began to explain. "Liam called me earlier this evening. He said he was in trouble, but I couldn't come right away, so I'm here now."

I nodded, acknowledging her explanation. "Yes, he's certainly found himself in an unusual predicament."

Her curiosity piqued, she pressed on. "What exactly is it? What happened?"

I sighed, the weight of uncertainty heavy on my shoulders. "It's hard to pinpoint right now, but I suspect it has something to do with that mysterious brass box."

Her eyes widened with recognition. "That brass box—"

She paused, scrutinizing me once more. But her doubt soon faded, and she approached, extending her hand. "So, you're Mr. Ash Morris? I'm Nora Lee—a friend of Liam."

We shook hands, and I remarked, "Miss Lee, your judo skills are impressive!"

Nora Lee smiled, a hint of pride mixed with regret. "Had I known who you were, I wouldn't have dared attack you—" Her smile quickly vanished, replaced by concern. "What sort of trouble has Liam encountered because of the brass box from the Inca Empire?"

Her words startled me, and I couldn't help but exclaim, "The Inca Empire? Are you certain this box is a relic from them?"

Nora Lee nodded decisively. "Yes, it's not surprising. Although the Inca Empire vanished mysteriously — a highly advanced civilization disappearing from the South American plains—many relics have been uncovered. Not only in South America but also in places like Mexico."

Her knowledge of the Inca artifacts intrigued me, and it seemed Liam's situation was intertwined with a much larger historical mystery.

At this point, I found myself scrutinizing Nora Lee with a mix of curiosity and skepticism. How could someone like her possess such knowledge about the ancient Inca Empire?

Sensing my hesitation, she addressed it directly. "No need to wonder too much. I'm a history student. At the University of Hamburg, I've studied under Professor P and Professor W, both of whom are experts on the Inca Empire."

Her explanation was reassuring. While I knew little about this enigmatic civilization, it seemed that Liam Jansen's current predicament was intertwined with the ancient mysteries. Having Nora Lee's expertise was undoubtedly beneficial.

I quickly shifted focus. "Liam has already opened the box. Do you have any thoughts on that?"

"What was inside?" Nora Lee inquired.

I led her to the study, reopening the lid. "See for yourself. When I arrived, it was empty."

She examined the relief on the box, her expression thoughtful and perplexed. After a few minutes, she pointed to a helmet depicted in the scene. "That's the monarch's helmet from the Inca Empire. The other ornaments suggest these are all leaders, but why are they skeletal? Why did they die?"

Her mention of death prompted me to interject, "Do you think the figures in this relief are all deceased?"

It was a logical question. Despite their skeletal forms, the human and animal figures in the relief were animated, with outstretched arms and uplifted heads, depicting vitality rather than death. The artist had clearly invested effort in bringing them to life.

Nora Lee hesitated. "I don't believe a person can live without muscles."

I coughed gently. "At least, Liam Jansen's right hand is like that."

Her eyes widened in shock. "What does that mean?"

"Liam Jansen visited me about half an hour ago," I explained. "He was bundled up, and I accidentally removed one of his gloves. His right hand—" I gestured toward the relief, "was just like the skeletal figures here."

Nora Lee's eyes grew even wider, yet she remained silent.

I sighed, understanding her disbelief. "I know. It's difficult to convey such things without witnessing them firsthand."

She offered a bitter smile. "Mr. Morris, are you sure you're not overly tense?"

I shook my head firmly. "Absolutely not."

"So you're saying Liam Jansen's finger bones defy gravity and remain intact?"

I sighed deeply. "Not only do they stay intact, but I also saw him use them to open my door and flee."

Nora Lee took a startled step back, processing the gravity of my words.

I reassured her firmly, "Miss, I'm completely sane. There's no need to think I'm deranged and shy away from me!" Nora Lee's breath quickened, indicating her rising anxiety. "If what you've said is true, then what on earth has happened to Liam?"

I shrugged helplessly. "We need to find him to get any answers."

Nora Lee's complexion turned ashen with worry. "Where could he have gone?" she asked.

"I don't know," I replied. "After leaving my place, he might've returned here or gone elsewhere. Since you're his close friend, do you have any idea where he might seek refuge?"

She hesitated briefly before answering, "He doesn't have many friends. Besides me, he's closest to Professor Lomono, who supervises his research."

I nodded, recognizing the name. Professor Lomono was a distinguished scientist, highly regarded in academic circles worldwide.

I pressed further, "Miss Lee, do you think if Liam Jansen were deeply troubled, he might turn to Professor Lomono, perhaps even before reaching out to you?"

Nora Lee flushed slightly, a hint of personal emotion in her response. "Liam and I are quite close. We were planning to marry this fall. I believe if faced with true danger, he would confide in me."

"But he came to me first," I pointed out. "That might be because the brass box came from me, or perhaps the situation was so overwhelming that he couldn't process it—"

Before I could finish, Nora Lee interrupted with a panicked cry, "So what about him now? Has he hidden away, avoiding me?"

I sighed, trying to calm her. "Miss Lee, let's not jump to conclusions. Let's visit Professor Lomono. He might have some insights."

Nora Lee demonstrated her pragmatic approach by first calling her home to ensure Liam Jansen hadn't sought refuge there. Satisfied with the response, she penned a note and placed it prominently for Liam, instructing him to stay put as we would come back for him. Her actions were a testament to her clear-headedness and determination to find Liam amid the unfolding mystery.

Together, we left Liam Jansen's residence. Outside, the rain had intensified, drenching everything in sight. My palms were slick with sweat, a mix of rain and anxiety. I wiped them dry before gripping the steering wheel, preparing for the drive to Professor Lomono's.

Driving up the mountain to Professor Lomono's residence was a harrowing ordeal. The rain-slicked, winding roads demanded every ounce of my concentration, yet my anxiety for Liam Jansen spurred me to push the car to its limits. Each twist and turn felt precarious, the ever-present threat of slipping into the valley below my constant companion. My grip tightened on the steering wheel as I navigated the treacherous path, the urgency to reach Liam overriding my fear of the looming abyss.

Despite the danger, I didn't ease off the accelerator. Nora, seated beside me, was wholly absorbed in worry for Liam Jansen, seemingly unaware of the near misses we faced.

Guided by Nora, who had visited the professor with Liam Jansen before, we navigated the treacherous route. Finally, we arrived at a sprawling garden house nestled on the mountainside.

By now, it was nearly midnight. A solitary light glowed from a corner of the house, a beacon in the darkness. Nora and I exited the car, the chill of the rain seeping through our clothes. Her voice trembled, whether from the cold or a mix of excitement and apprehension. "Look, there's a light on. Liam might be inside."

I nodded, sharing her hope. "Perhaps."

As I pressed the doorbell, my finger lingered on the button, the continuous ringing signaling urgency. I hoped the persistent chime would convey the need for immediate attention.

Nora stood beside me, peering inside the house. Her voice was a soft distraction from the tension, "Lomono is a bachelor. I never understood why he needs such a large house to himself. Oh, and there's his housekeeper — a peculiar fellow—"

Her commentary seemed less about Lomono and more a way to manage the anxious waiting. Her words filled the space, an attempt to make time pass more quickly.

Suddenly, a figure emerged from the house, moving swiftly through the rain without any protective gear. Tall and thin, the person approached the door, their gaze sharp and fierce.

Nora nudged me gently, whispering, "That's the housekeeper."

I quickly addressed him, "I'm sorry for the intrusion, but we need to see Professor Lomono!" The housekeeper's voice matched his harsh demeanor, grating and unpleasant.

"At this hour?" he barked in heavily accented English. Nora stepped forward, asking urgently, "Has Mr. Jansen from the university come by?"

The housekeeper's eyes snapped to Nora, his stare unnerving, causing her to instinctively recoil.

I didn't blame Nora for her reaction. The housekeeper's eyes were predatory, reminiscent of a vulture seeking carrion. It puzzled me why a respected scientist like Professor Lomono would employ someone so off-putting.

Chapter 3

Car Falling off a Cliff

The housekeeper's voice was sharp and dismissive. "No!"

But I pressed on. "We need to see the professor. Can we?"

Before the housekeeper could respond, a commanding voice echoed from the doorway. "Larry, let our visitors in."

Lights flickered on, revealing a tall, ruddy-faced man standing at the entrance. It was Professor Lomono. Larry, the housekeeper, grudgingly opened the iron gate, allowing us to enter. As we approached, Professor Lomono stepped aside, extending a warm handshake. "Apologies for the late intrusion," I offered.

Professor Lomono's smile was genuine. "I assume your visit is urgent."

"Has your assistant, Liam Jansen, been here?" I asked without hesitation.

Lomono's thick eyebrows arched in surprise. "Are you with the police?"

His assumption caught me off guard. Why would he immediately think of law enforcement? I pressed for an explanation, and Professor Lomono replied, "I fear he's in some trouble. He called earlier this evening. Larry took the call and mentioned Liam Jansen sounded anxious. Isn't that right, Larry?"

The housekeeper's sullen face loomed beside us as he affirmed, "Yes, professor."

Professor Lomono continued, "But he never showed up. After an hour, I had Larry call his home. No answer, correct, Larry?"

Larry's response was once again, "Yes, professor."

Larry's mechanical replies sparked a deep sense of distrust in me. I instinctively knew he was lying. If a call had been made to Liam Jansen's home, I would have known—I was there, and no phone rang.

Despite this, I held my tongue. A negligent housekeeper defying his duties seemed trivial compared to our larger concerns.

"It's nearing midnight now, and I fear something's happened to him," Professor Lomono mused.

I glanced at Nora, who seemed dejected, her gaze cast downward. We took our leave, with Larry shadowing us to the gate.

In the car, I sighed, "Where do we search for Liam Jansen now?" Nora shook her head, her sadness palpable. "I have no idea where else he might be."

"Then we may have no choice but to involve the police," I suggested.

Nora quickly interjected, "No! Remember Liam Jansen's hand—"

The memory of his skeletal hand sent a shiver through me. Nora continued, "I'm certain he wouldn't want anyone to know about that. Let's hold off on involving the authorities."

I nodded, agreeing with her logic. I turned the car around, and we began our descent down the mountain, the rain and darkness cloaking the path ahead.

We returned to Liam Jansen's residence with a flicker of hope that he might return, that somehow the night's mysteries would unravel with the dawn. Yet, as the hours slipped by in torturous anticipation, Liam Jansen did not come back.

Throughout the night, Nora's resilience shone through. Despite her anxious pacing and restlessness, she never succumbed to tears. By dawn, her beautiful face had grown weary and haggard. As we exchanged glances, I rubbed my hands together, breaking the silence. "Miss Lee, should we inform the police?"

Nora nodded silently, and I reached for the phone.

Just as I dialed the second "nine," the doorbell chimed unexpectedly. I abandoned the call, rushing to the door with hopes it was Liam Jansen. My hand hovered, ready to catch him if he tried to flee again.

But my hand froze in mid-air. The figure at the door was not Liam Jansen.

At first, surprise rooted me to the spot. Only then did I realize the absurdity of expecting Liam Jansen to ring his own doorbell. Our desperate hope had clouded our judgment. I withdrew my hand and peered outside, greeted by three figures: a uniformed police officer and two in plainclothes.

Turning back to Nora, I managed a wry smile. "It seems the police have come to us."

Nora's composed exterior began to crumble, her face paling. "What are you three doing here?" she asked, her voice edged with apprehension.

The police officer stepped forward, his tone straightforward. "Does Liam Jansen reside here?"

Nora's concern deepened. "What happened to him?"

The officer pressed on, "Miss, what is your relationship to him?"

Drawing a deep breath, Nora straightened, her voice steady. "I am his fiancée. This is Mr. Morris, a close friend. We waited for him all night, but he never returned."

The officer lowered his voice, a somber note creeping in. "Miss Lee, you'll need to be strong and prepare yourself for some difficult news."

Her voice trembled with fear and urgency. "What has happened to him?"

The police officer spread his hands, delivering the heavy news with a somber expression. "Early this morning, we discovered the wreckage of his car on the cliffside road leading to the mountain top."

Nora's composure faltered, and I quickly moved to steady her. Yet, her resilience shone through. She asked in a firm voice, "Is there any hope for him?"

The officer replied, "His car came to rest on a large rock, reduced to scrap metal. From my experience, in such a situation, survival is unlikely."

A peculiar note in his voice caught my attention. "Are you saying you haven't found his body?" I pressed.

The officer sighed deeply. "There's a sea below the cliff. The impact likely jarred the door open, and in such a shock, anyone would lose consciousness. The car was perched on the rock, and he probably fell into the sea."

Silence enveloped us. Nora buried her face in her hands, tears finally breaking through her brave exterior.

I wanted to offer words of comfort, but emotion constricted my throat, rendering me speechless.

The officer removed his hat in a gesture of respect. "He passed without pain. May he find peace."

With a sudden resolve, Nora lifted her head. "His body—?"

"The search is ongoing," the officer answered, "but the chances are slim."

Desperation drove me to ask, "Is there any chance he could have escaped?"

The officer looked at me solemnly. "Mr. Morris, even for someone experienced, escape would be near impossible under those circumstances."

His words struck a chord, reminding me that the police were likely more familiar with my reputation than I was with theirs.

I forced a bitter smile, unable to face Nora's grief-stricken form. Naturally, if Liam Jansen's car had plummeted off the cliff, escape would be improbable—he was a mathematician, not someone accustomed to daring escapades.

The officer placed a firm hand on my shoulder. "Mr. Morris, comforting Miss Lee is now your responsibility."

Before I could respond, Nora interjected, her voice steady despite the dryness. "I don't need comfort." Her words spoke volumes of her courage.

I turned to see her standing tall. Though tears glistened in her eyes, her sobs had ceased.

She took a deep breath, addressing the officer. "Could you take me to the site?"

The officer hesitated briefly. "Of course," he said, admiration in his voice. "A brave lady indeed."

"I'll come too," I added quickly.

Nora nodded, and together we descended the stairs. The police car waited at the door, and we climbed in, setting off toward the scene, the vehicle cutting through the rain-soaked morning with determined speed.

The sky was a somber gray, with a persistent drizzle that added a chill to the air. As we traveled in the crowded car, moisture quickly fogged up the windows, blurring the view of the outside world.

Despite the obscured scenery, I recognized the road we were on—it was the same route Nora and I had taken to visit Professor Lomono the previous night. I turned to the senior police officer and asked, "Did he have the accident on this road?"

The officer nodded. "Near the top of the mountain."

I concluded sharply, "Then he must have been heading to see Professor Lomono. The rain and slippery road conditions led to the accident."

Nora remained silent, her head bowed. The officer inquired, "Do Liam Jansen and Professor Lomono know each other well?"

"Liam Jansen is Professor Lomono's assistant and student," I explained. The officer sighed, shaking his head. "The accident site was just thirty yards from Professor Lomono's residence. After discovering the wreckage, we spoke with him. He and his housekeeper mentioned hearing what sounded like a car crashing but never imagined it was someone they knew."

Curiosity piqued, I asked, "Did Professor Lomono mention when he heard this sound?"

"Around two in the morning," the officer replied.

Two o'clock. Nora and I had left Professor Lomono's place around midnight. If only we had lingered on the road, could we have prevented this tragedy?

The weight of the situation settled heavily on my chest. Silence enveloped the car until we reached our destination.

I was the first to step out, approaching the edge of the cliff where several officers stood, pointing toward the sea. Looking down, I spotted the wreckage of Liam Jansen's car.

It lay about fifty meters below, precariously perched on an outcropping above the gloomy waters. Half of the vehicle hung over the edge, its door hooked on a corner of the rock, preventing it from plummeting into the sea.

The police officer handed me a telescope, and through it, the scene below came into stark relief. The license plate was intact, confirming the car's identity. But the vehicle itself was mangled beyond recognition—a mere heap of twisted metal. Faced with this sight, I reluctantly accepted the officer's grim assessment that Liam Jansen's survival was impossible.

I offered the telescope to Nora, but she declined, asking instead, "When will the car be lifted up?"

The officer replied, "We won't be retrieving the vehicle. Once you've seen it, we'll push it into the sea."

Nora fell silent. A thought struck me: even if Liam Jansen had been swept into the sea, could something of his remain in the car? It hadn't caught fire, so there might be something left to find.

Yet, with the windows shattered, discerning the car's contents from this distance was impossible.

I lifted the telescope from my eyes, studying the daunting cliff below. "I want to go down there," I declared, "to see if Liam Jansen left anything behind."

The police officer shook his head. "It's not advisable. The cliff is treacherous. Unless you're lowered by a rope, it's too dangerous."

I smiled reassuringly. "I'll manage."

With determination, I began my descent, grasping rocky outcrops and branches as I carefully made my way down. Ten minutes later, I stood beside the wreckage of Liam Jansen's car, my clothes now marked with mud.

Peering through a cracked window, I forced my way inside. The steering wheel was grotesquely twisted and broken. I rummaged through the small drawer in the dashboard but found nothing of significance, just a few scattered items.

Disappointment settled in. The mystery of Liam Jansen's disappearance—and his skeletal hand—remained unsolved. But then my gaze fell on the pristine steering wheel and the wooden dashboard, both conspicuously free of blood.

I pondered the implications: Could Liam Jansen have been ejected from the car without sustaining any injuries? If he was injured, why was there no trace of blood?

The lack of evidence left me perplexed. Two possibilities emerged: Liam Jansen was thrown from the vehicle without harm, or he wasn't in the car at all, and it was an empty vehicle that plummeted over the cliff.

If the latter were true, it suggested a deeper story.

I climbed back up the cliff, my mind racing. Without a word to the police officer, I took Nora's arm and led her away. Seeing the serious expression on my face, she whispered, "What did you find?"

I glanced back, noticing the officers discussing how to dispose of the wreckage. To them, it was an open-and-shut case of a tragic accident.

But I doubted that narrative. "There's no blood inside the car," I told Nora. "Maybe Liam Jansen wasn't in the car when it went over the cliff."

Nora halted, her eyes wide with shock.

Before she could respond, a car approached. I instinctively pulled Nora aside, recognizing the driver as Professor Lomono.

I waved frantically, calling out, "Professor! Professor!"

But despite hearing my cries, Professor Lomono didn't stop. His car accelerated, speeding past us without a second glance.

At that moment, I caught a glimpse of half a face peering out from the rear window of the car. It was brief, but unmistakable — the gloomy visage belonged to Professor Lomono's butler. As quickly as it appeared, it vanished, but I was certain of what I'd seen.

The sight of the butler, lying low in the back seat while Professor Lomono drove, struck me as suspicious. Why would the butler hide unless he didn't want to be seen? What was he trying to conceal from us?

As Professor Lomono's car disappeared from view, my mind churned with a flurry of questions. Why was the butler hiding? What role did he play in this unfolding mystery?

Nora's voice snapped me back to the present. "Mr. Morris, are you suggesting that Liam Jansen didn't die in the accident?"

I pondered the implications before replying, "It's hard to say definitively. Miss Lee, you mentioned that Professor

Lomono and his butler are the only ones residing at his house?"

Nora, still processing the situation, nodded, albeit with hesitation. "Yes, that's right," she confirmed.

I leaned closer and whispered, "Just now, the butler was watching us from the car's rear window. Did you catch that?"

Her eyes widened in surprise. "Really?"

"Yes," I affirmed, "and I have a plan that might shed light on Liam Jansen's mysterious circumstances. Can I count on your help?"

Nora, determination overcoming her earlier tears, nodded resolutely. "Yes, of course."

With a plan forming, I approached the police officer. I explained that to help ease Nora's distress, we intended to take a walk to the top of the mountain, suggesting they proceed without us and needn't wait to escort us back down. The officer consented to our request, and Nora and I began our ascent.

We walked slowly, deliberately, bypassing Professor Lomono's house until we reached the hill behind it.

At that moment, with the police officers no longer visible from our vantage point by the cliff, I stopped and turned to Nora. "Miss Lee, wait here for me," I said decisively.

Her eyes widened in alarm. "Where are you going?"

I pointed toward Professor Lomono's house. "I'm going to sneak in and have a look around."

Her voice trembled with concern. "What are you doing? The police are right near his house, and you're considering breaking in?"

I managed a wry smile. "Is it really a crime to take a peek? You never know what you might discover."

Nora pressed further, "What exactly are you hoping to find?"

I kicked at some pebbles, pondering the uncertainty of my plan. "Honestly, I'm not entirely sure. I have a vague theory, but it's shaky and needs more evidence. Right now, I'm just trying to follow any leads."

She persisted, "What is this theory of yours?"

I explained, "Liam Jansen was heading to see Professor Lomono. The police believe he went off the cliff before reaching the house, supposedly around 2 a.m., according to the professor."

"That's right," Nora agreed.

"But consider this possibility," I continued. "What if Liam Jansen actually did meet with Professor Lomono, and the car went over the cliff after he was no longer in it?"

Nora's gaze was penetrating, searching for the truth behind my words. "What makes you think that?"

I gestured back toward the cliff. "The car's wreckage didn't have any blood. If Liam Jansen had been injured in the crash, there would have been evidence."

Chapter 4

Cold-blooded Murderer

Nora persisted, "What exactly do you suspect Professor Lomono of doing?"

I shrugged, my hands open in uncertainty. "It's difficult to pin down right now."

She paused, processing my answer. "Alright, do you want me to 'keep watch'?" Her use of the term surprised me; it seemed she was more familiar with covert operations than I had assumed. Nora settled onto a rock, keeping a vigilant eye on our surroundings as I made my way down the hill, heading toward the back of Professor Lomono's residence.

Behind the main house stood a small stone building, likely a storage room. The door was locked, but a gentle twist of the knob was all it took to open it, and I stepped inside. The interior was dimly lit and cluttered with various odds and ends. Navigating through the mess, I found another door leading into the kitchen.

Cautiously, I stepped into the kitchen, only to immediately retreat and quietly shut the door behind me.

Despite my suspicions about Professor Lomono, I trusted Nora's assertion that only he and his housekeeper lived there — and both had recently departed. So, the bubbling coffee pot on the stove was an unexpected and troubling sign.

The presence of freshly brewed coffee indicated someone was in the house.

Sensing something was amiss, I crouched down and peered through the keyhole. My view was limited to the area around the gas stove.

Shortly, the sound of footsteps echoed through the kitchen — leather shoes clicking softly against the floor. Someone approached the stove.

The intruder reached for the coffee. My hand tightened on the door handle, ready to spring forward and confront the person. But what I saw through the keyhole stopped me cold.

The figure moved into view, but all I could see was their waist—a broad, solid frame suggesting a large man.

Just as I was about to act, the man turned. My eyes caught a glimpse of his midsection. He wore a distinctive white crocodile belt, its platinum buckle adorned with small rubies.

The rubies were arranged into a letter "B," which glimmered ominously as the man turned. In that instant, the letter seemed like it was written in blood, and I was paralyzed by the sight.

I couldn't muster the courage to push the door open, nor could I move an inch. I remained frozen, barely able to hold myself upright. Though I'd never seen such an opulent white crocodile belt or a buckle of such luxury, I'd heard whispers about them before — whispers of their infamous owner.

This belt belonged to a shadowy figure of unknown nationality and origin, a phantom with no trace in police files or intelligence dossiers. A true mercenary, he was reputed to kill without hesitation for the right price, even if it meant targeting his own flesh and blood. His methods were so clean and efficient that despite being suspected in many high-profile assassinations, no solid evidence ever pointed to him.

His "services" spanned a broad spectrum — from eliminating personal nuisances to taking out political adversaries. He valued nothing but money, with a heart as cold as stone and a mind sharp as a blade, particularly when it came to mechanics, where his ingenious devices often defied imagination. Years ago, an assassination of a world leader shook the globe. While the "murderer" was publicly executed, the real perpetrator, the cold-blooded

Braque, was rumored to have been soaring above in a personal aircraft at the time. Despite being brought in, the world's foremost arms experts found no proof of his culpability due to his high altitude, beyond the reach of conventional firearms.

Authorities worldwide understood one thing: if Braque was present, whether in the air or sea, he was involved. His brilliance allowed him to develop a singular weapon over years, using it just once, leaving no trace or clue behind.

Braque was the most dangerous man among billions, a figure so terrifying that seasoned detectives would rather confront a demon than cross paths with him.

And now, here he was, within my sight.

In the span of less than a minute, the situation had taken a dramatic turn. My initial suspicions had been confined to Professor Lomono and his enigmatic housekeeper, with the thought that Liam Jansen had somehow crossed their path. Driven by this suspicion, I had snuck in, hoping to gather any piece of evidence that could shed light on Liam's whereabouts. The atmosphere was thick with tension, and every shadow seemed to hold a secret. What had started as a simple investigation was quickly spiraling into something far more complex and dangerous.

This wasn't merely a suspicious house—it was a den of danger. My heart pounded with fear and concern. God! I had left Nora outside to "keep watch," unknowingly placing her in harm's way.

A chill ran down my spine as I prayed for Braque to leave the kitchen swiftly so I could make my escape and regroup with Nora. The gleam from his belt buckle was a constant reminder of the danger lurking mere feet away, a red beacon of threat that weighed heavily on my nerves. After what felt like an eternity, Braque finally turned and left the kitchen.

I exhaled a breath I hadn't realized I'd been holding and took a cautious step back. Despite my usual calm under pressure, the chilling legends surrounding the cold-blooded Braque had me on edge. My thoughts raced to Nora; if Braque found her, the consequences could be dire.

As I retreated, my foot collided with an empty metal bucket, sending it clattering loudly across the floor. The noise echoed like a gunshot in the silence.

In that moment, I knew panic was my enemy. If I let fear take over, I risked becoming another statistic, another victim of Braque's lethal efficiency. I forced myself to stay calm and sprang into action, leaping to the side of the door that led into the kitchen.

Just as I reached the safety of the doorway, the kitchen door swung open with a bang. I was hidden behind it, shielded from view. I didn't catch a glimpse of Braque, but within seconds, a series of rapid "chi chi chi chi" sounds erupted, accompanied by a brilliant display of crisscrossing firelight. It was as if a grand fireworks display had been set off just outside the kitchen.

But this was no celebration. The noise wasn't from fireworks. The sound and resulting destruction — a cacophony of metal and debris—were unmistakable. The air was filled with the acrid scent of gunpowder and the sharp crack of metal against metal.

Each flash was a bullet, its low sound and blistering speed a testament to Braque's deadly precision. In the span of ten seconds, I estimated at least fifty bullets had been unleashed, their lethal trajectory shredding everything in their path.

In the dimly lit storage room, the air was thick with tension. I had never encountered a weapon capable of unleashing such a relentless storm of bullets in mere seconds. It was undoubtedly another one of Braque's terrifying inventions—a testament to his twisted genius.

Ten seconds. That's all it took. Had there been a company of men inside, they would have met their end in that brief, hellish barrage. Yet, somehow, I remained untouched, a stroke of fortune that seemed almost divine. As soon as I kicked the iron can, instinct took over, propelling me towards the door with a desperate leap. The bullets rained down, filling every inch of the room with lethal intent, save for the small sanctuary by the door—the one blind spot Braque's bullets couldn't reach.

Though I hadn't glimpsed Braque's face, a chill swept through me, my skin slick with cold sweat. My thoughts raced to Nora, perched on the hillside not far from this deadly commotion. If the noise drew her near, the consequences would be dire, unfathomable.

I held my breath, forcing stillness upon myself as the room descended into silence. A sudden "bang" shattered the quiet—a dead cat, riddled with bullets, fell from above. It had been hit four or five times, a grim testament to the weapon's ferocity. From the doorway came a low, disdainful hum, followed by the heavy thud of the door closing.

Relief washed over me. The dead cat had unwittingly become my savior. Without it, Braque would have stormed in, his monstrous weapon ready to unleash its wrath. But now, convinced the noise was the cat's demise, he left, certain no one could survive his onslaught.

I peered through the keyhole, my eyes locking onto Braque's silhouette. In each hand, he held a peculiar firearm—crude, functional, devoid of any aesthetic grace. It was no product of a sophisticated arsenal, but rather a mechanical monstrosity, its complexity defying description.

Amazed, I watched as Braque stashed the weapons beneath his coat, picked up a coffee pot, and disappeared from view.

Throughout this ordeal, I had only seen Braque through the keyhole, never face-to-face. The infamous, cold-blooded killer remained a shadowy enigma.

As I stepped back, the world seemed to shift back into place. I had faced countless perils, stared down the barrels of machine guns, and yet, I knew that even with a gun to my chest, there was always a fleeting moment—a gap in time—where victory could be seized from the jaws of defeat.

But Braque was a different breed entirely. Cold-blooded and merciless, he offered no chances for escape. He killed with the ease of drawing breath, devoid of reason or purpose. Such a man instilled a fear that clung to the very core of one's soul, a primal terror that refused to be banished. His presence was a stark reminder that some dangers were beyond human comprehension, and in the face of such malevolence, survival was anything but certain.

With painstaking caution, I retreated from the storage room, ensuring each step was silent. Outside, the sky remained shrouded in a gloomy veil, yet to me, it was a sight of profound beauty. I had narrowly escaped bidding it farewell forever.

I crouched low, crawling through the thick grass, each blade a shield from the eyes that might watch from the house. Ignorant of Braque's presence when I arrived, I had been bold, but now, knowing the danger that lurked, I moved with the utmost care. Any window could be a portal for his gaze.

Reaching the hillside, I found Nora still perched on the large rock, blissfully unaware of the impending danger. I didn't waste any time with explanations. I grabbed her hand and pulled her down, my body a protective barrier as she collapsed against me.

Startled, she sprang up, but I hushed her urgently, "Crouch down quickly!"

My face, I knew, betrayed the gravity of our situation, prompting Nora to crouch beside me. Her voice was a soft whisper, "What did you find in that room?"

In that fleeting moment, a cascade of thoughts flooded my mind. Braque's presence here was no random happenstance. He was a harbinger of chaos, a plague-bringer whose very arrival heralded disaster. Normally, I would steer clear of such a menace, leaving heroics to the police. But this was personal, tied intricately to Liam Jansen, whose life had been upended by a seemingly innocuous copper box—a gift from me. His brother, Sem Jansen, was my friend, and that bond pulled me into this web of danger.

Yet, I couldn't fathom linking a ruthless killer like Braque to someone as innocent as Nora. When she inquired about the room, I chose deception. "Nothing," I told her. "It was indeed an empty house." I believed my lie convincing enough to pacify her.

But Nora's eyes betrayed her disbelief. She studied me with a knowing look, her silence speaking volumes. I added, lamely, "Miss Lee, indeed—nothing."

She smiled, a gentle curve that held no judgment, and suggested, "Well, since there is nothing, we should leave here."

Her words echoed my own thoughts. I resolved to shield her from the harsh truth. Knowing of Braque's existence would shatter her innocence, and I couldn't bear to darken her world with such knowledge.

Together, we retreated, vigilant and wary, casting glances back at the house. It sat in deceptive quietude, a stark contrast to the danger that dwelt within. If not for my own encounter, I too would have been fooled by its facade.

We skirted the house, leaving its ominous presence behind, and soon found ourselves back on the road. The place where Nora's car had plummeted off the cliff loomed ahead, now deserted save for a solitary police officer standing vigil. The emptiness of the scene struck a stark contrast to the turmoil churning within me.

As we approached, doubt gnawed at me. Should I inform the officer about seeing the notorious Braque at Professor Lomono's house? What purpose would it serve?

Braque hadn't committed any crime here, and the police would be powerless to act on mere presence.

Lost in these thoughts, I remained silent during our descent. Eventually, we reached a fork in the road, where a small street station offered several empty cars waiting patiently. Nora and I approached one of these vehicles. She opened the door, turning to me with a gentle resolve. "Mr. Morris, you don't have to see me off. I'll go back by myself."

Her words caught me off guard. "Where are you going?" I asked, bewildered.

Without meeting my gaze, Nora replied, "I feel very tired. I want to go home and rest."

I couldn't argue with her decision. Despite the brevity of our acquaintance, I recognized that Nora's mysterious ordeal, though distressing, hadn't broken her spirit. She possessed a resilience that was both admirable and unexpected — a strength far surpassing my initial impression of her.

Nora was unlike anyone I had ever met: confident, self-assured, and unfathomably strong. Yet, at that moment, I failed to fully grasp the depth of her fortitude. I watched as she climbed into the car, her departure leaving a lingering sense of awe. As her vehicle disappeared down the road, I hailed another taxi, instructing the driver to take me to the telegraph office.

Sem Jansen, occupied with his work on a massive construction site, was unreachable by phone. I resorted to sending an urgent telegram, succinct in its urgency: "Your brother suffered an extremely mysterious change because of the mysterious copper box. I need to know how you got the box and the real origin of the box. Call back quickly."

With the telegram dispatched, I returned home, my mind a turbulent sea of uncertainty. Reclining in my chair, I pondered the enigma before me.

What course of action remained? If Nora had been in the car when it tumbled into the abyss, then he was lost, and the mystery dissolved into tragic finality. Even with the story behind the copper box, unraveling Nora's fate seemed impossible.

Yet, intuition whispered otherwise. I believed Nora hadn't been in the car when it met its fate. This conviction, though unproven, offered a glimmer of hope—a slender thread to follow in the labyrinthine puzzle that awaited.

The mystery deepened with each unanswered question. What had Nora uncovered within that enigmatic box, and what drove him to possess something so mysterious? Where was he now? These questions spiraled outward, intertwining with the identity of Professor Lomono, his connection to Braque, and the reason for Braque's presence here.

As I pondered these layers, my sense of unease intensified. I felt like a blind man in a labyrinth, grasping for threads of understanding that continually eluded me. Rest was impossible with so many questions gnawing at my mind. I reached out to my network, inquiring about Lomono's true identity, only to receive consistent replies. Professor Lomono was a highly regarded scholar, his reputation beyond reproach. No one had ever questioned his integrity.

Some friends even advised against my suspicion, emphasizing Lomono's dedication to his mathematical pursuits and dismissing my doubts as futile. When questioning them, I discreetly omitted my encounter with Braque at Lomono's residence. Given Lomono's esteemed reputation, my claims would likely be met with disbelief.

Realizing that the key to Nora's fate might lie with Lomono, I resolved to confront the professor directly. I packed a delicate pistol and essential supplies, steeling myself for the possibility of facing Braque. Sleep claimed me eventually, though it was restless.

When dusk fell, I awoke and splashed cold water on my face, a ritual to sharpen my focus. The prospect of confronting Braque, a merciless killer, required unwavering clarity. A lapse in judgment could mean my end.

Just as I was about to leave, it struck me—I needed to inform Nora. The potential dangers warranted a contingency plan. If I didn't return in time, Nora should alert a few trusted friends. While I could have entrusted this to my loyal butler Wilson, an inexplicable impulse urged me to reach out to Nora instead.

Dialing her home, an anxious middle-aged man answered. His impatience was palpable as he questioned my identity and purpose. "Who are you? What do you want to talk to her about?" he demanded, his tone bordering on hostility.

His reaction puzzled me. "I'm a new friend of hers," I replied. "Is she there? Please let her answer the phone."

He sighed, exasperated. "If she were here, I'd have handed the phone to her. She hasn't returned since going out last night. It's worrying!"

A chill ran down my spine. "What do you mean she hasn't come back? She didn't return this morning?"

The urgency in his voice escalated. "What? You saw her this morning? Who exactly are you?"

I inhaled deeply, my mind whirling as memories and concerns collided. Something was amiss, and the stakes had just escalated dramatically.

The realization struck me like a bolt of lightning—Nora, with her impressive judo skills and unyielding spirit, hadn't been home because she had likely ventured to

Professor Lomono's house on her own. Her earlier expression of disbelief now made perfect sense. The thought of her confronting the cold-blooded Braque alone was unbearable.

Fear and urgency surged through me. Nora was brave, but Braque was a force of nature, a predator without conscience. Every second counted, and the stakes had never been higher. I had to find her before it was too late.

Panic surged through me, and I leaped to my feet. Morning had turned to dusk, and the time that had passed weighed heavily on my mind. The possibility of Nora confronting Braque alone for hours was too dire to dwell on.

The anxious voice of the middle-aged man on the phone—likely Nora's father—faded into the background as I ended the call abruptly. I rushed out the door, ignoring the puzzled stares of passers-by, driven by a singular urgency. My training in martial arts propelled me forward with a speed that startled those around me. In less critical circumstances, I would never risk such a spectacle, but I couldn't afford a single wasted moment.

I barely settled into my car before it roared to life, tearing through the streets with reckless speed. Red lights blurred past, and near-collisions became a blur of adrenaline-fueled reflexes. Traffic violations and the ire of other drivers were inconsequential compared to the looming threat over Nora.

In my mind, the scenario played out relentlessly. Nora, in her determination, had returned to Professor Lomono's house and encountered Braque. The thought of her in the clutches of a murderer gnawed at my sanity, driving me to the brink of madness.

As darkness descended, the road to Professor Lomono's residence became increasingly treacherous. The dense fog that enveloped the mountaintop obscured my vision, reducing visibility to mere yards. Yet, this veil of mist was a blessing in disguise, providing cover for my approach.

I parked the car at a safe distance, the engine's rumble fading into the night.

Chapter 5

⁂

The Professor's Confusing Identity

The instinct to rush headlong into Professor Lomono's house was overwhelming, but caution prevailed. Braque was a man who wouldn't hesitate to shoot at any perceived threat, especially at night. After parking the car, I navigated the thick fog with the stealth and speed honed by years of training.

Soon, two faint yellow lights pierced the fog—the gate lamps of Professor Lomono's estate. I halted, straining to hear any sound beyond the oppressive silence. Slowly, I moved forward, reaching the formidable iron gate. Just as I prepared to scale the wall, a figure emerged from the fog, materializing so suddenly that collision seemed inevitable.

We stopped simultaneously, mere inches separating us. The unexpected encounter left no room for evasion. My instincts screamed for action as I reeled back, eyes locking onto the barrel of a pistol aimed directly at me. A surge of adrenaline ignited every nerve, propelling me into a desperate leap to avoid what I believed was Braque's attack.

But instead of a gunshot, a familiar voice cut through the tension. "Young man, it's you!" Professor Lomono's voice, not Braque's, brought me back to reality.

I landed lightly, my heart still racing. There stood Lomono, pistol in hand, yet it wasn't the menacing weapon of a killer, but rather the cautious tool of a man caught in uncertain times. His eyes, filled with a mix of surprise and curiosity, met mine. The professor, renowned in academia, now seemed part of a much larger enigma.

"Young man, what are you doing here?" Lomono asked, lowering the weapon with unexpected ease.

Caught between truth and necessity, I opted for candor. "I'm here to visit you," I replied.

He shook his head, a hint of disapproval coloring his expression. "In such weather, in such a way?"

His words hinted at my covert intentions, but I met his gaze with unwavering determination. "Professor, when a young girl's life hangs in the balance, even if knives were raining from the sky, I'd be here without hesitation."

Confusion clouded Lomono's features, his mind seemingly sifting through layers of unfamiliar information. In that moment, I realized his brilliance extended beyond mathematics; here was a man capable of masking intentions with ease.

His voice betrayed genuine perplexity. "How can I help you?"

Seizing the opportunity, I acted swiftly. My hand gripped his arm, and with a deft motion, I disarmed him, slipping the pistol from his pocket.

The night was a tapestry of shadows and secrets, woven tightly around me as I moved with a swiftness that belied my intentions. In my mind's eye, Professor Lomono was a worthy adversary, a man of hidden depths. Yet, to my bewilderment, he offered no resistance. His eyes widened in astonishment as he exclaimed, "Young man, what are you doing?"

An unsettling dissonance gnawed at me. This frail, startled old man seemed far removed from the figure entangled in shadowy missions I had imagined.

Memories of earlier that day flashed before me — Braque's white crocodile belt, the ruby-encrusted buckle glinting ominously, his swift draw that could transform a man into Swiss cheese in mere seconds. The impressions were indelible, a grim reminder of the stakes.

With resolve, I pressed my gun to Lomono's side. "I mean no harm," I declared, "just seeking a slight edge in our negotiation."

Professor Lomono's voice trembled with incredulity. "Negotiation? Dear God, I've encountered a madman!"

A smirk curled my lips. "Enough games. Let's go inside."

Under the weight of my coercion, Lomono complied, opening the iron door that creaked with foreboding. We stepped into the well-lit living room, my gun unwaveringly trained on him. I settled on the long sofa, vigilance a constant companion.

I suspected a connection between Braque and Professor Lomono, a bond that might shield me from sudden hostility in Braque's presence.

Scanning the room, my voice cut through the silence. "Let's get down to business. Where is Miss Lee? Is she dead or alive?"

Ignoring my inquiry, Lomono erupted, "Insane! You must be insane!"

A sudden crash—a door flung open—sent adrenaline surging through me. Instinctively, I yanked Lomono's body to shield myself, anticipating Braque's lethal entrance, ready to fire without hesitation.

But it was not Braque. Instead, Professor Lomono's butler stumbled in, dumbstruck. Lomono's plea broke the tension. "Call the police, quickly!"

I countered with icy resolve. "The police? Not ideal for your companions, is it?"

Lomono's face flushed with anger. "What companions?"

"Cold-blooded Braque," I shot back, believing my revelation would unravel him.

Yet, Lomono merely blinked, then clasped a hand to his forehead. "My word, what are you saying?"

In a voice as deep as the mystery itself, I pressed on. "Professor, cease this charade. Braque, the killer, is here. Your true identity is not that of a mere scientist. I have no desire to meddle in your sordid affairs, only to reclaim Miss Lee and Nora. If they have perished, then I will seek vengeance."

Lomono's complexion turned ashen, disbelief etched into his features. "Are you... a writer of fantastical tales?"

Fury surged through me, igniting a reckless resolve. In a swift, unthinking motion, I brought the butt of my gun down on Professor Lomono's head. The thud was quickly drowned by the unmistakable whir of a phone dial being turned.

My gaze snapped to the butler, who had stealthily reached the phone. The dial rested on two nines, and panic prickled my skin.

"Stop!" I commanded, my voice slicing through the tension.

The butler froze, his hand suspended in a moment of indecision. "Put down the phone!" I ordered again, my voice a steely edge.

His eyes met mine, shadowed with defiance, yet he obeyed, lowering the receiver. The weight of my gun ensured compliance.

We stood there, the tableau of a standoff—each of us entrapped by our own trepidations. Professor Lomono and his butler, paralyzed by the unexpected turn of events, and I, wrestling with the implications of their actions. If they were in league with Braque, would they truly risk summoning the police?

The bullet-riddled storage room was irrefutable evidence of the danger lurking within these walls. Had I acted a moment later, the butler would have completed the emergency call.

The thought gnawed at me: Could it be that Professor Lomono and Braque were not entwined in the web I imagined? The notion was preposterous, given that Braque had freely roamed this house, even fetching a coffee pot from the kitchen.

I brandished my gun, demanding clarity. "Where is Mr. Braque? Why not invite him to join us?"

The butler's voice was a hushed murmur, "Sir, we truly don't know what you mean."

A smirk twisted my lips. "Perhaps a visit to the storage room will refresh your memory."

Professor Lomono's voice trembled with bewilderment. "Storage room? For heaven's sake, what are you after, you madman?"

His innocence was almost convincing.

"Let's find out," I retorted, a cold laugh curling from my lips. "We're going for a walk. All of us." With my gun pressed to Lomono's side, I gestured sharply at the butler. "You too."

The butler hesitated, eyes darting between us. "To the storage room — sir, surely you don't mean to shoot us there—"

A mirthless chuckle escaped me. "I was nearly killed there by your associates."

An unspoken exchange passed between Professor Lomono and his butler, their silence a heavy confirmation. "Move!" I barked.

The butler turned reluctantly, leading the way. Professor Lomono and I trailed him, a strange procession through dimly lit halls. "And turn on all the lights," I instructed, my voice laced with paranoia.

Despite having secured an advantage over Professor Lomono, the specter of Braque haunted my mind. His legendary marksmanship was the stuff of nightmares — seven shots, each a perfect hit on the seven of hearts from thirty meters. In the darkness, against such a foe, survival was a fleeting hope.

The housekeeper obeyed my command, illuminating every corner of the house as we moved forward. Despite the bright lights chasing away the shadows, I remained on edge, keeping Professor Lomono firmly positioned as my shield.

Reaching the kitchen without incident, I exhaled, feeling as though I had traversed a treacherous path. Everything was as I remembered from yesterday. The coffee pot, once gripped by the elusive Braque, sat untouched. This reassurance hinted that Braque, the cold-blooded enigma, was likely absent—had he been here, our confrontation would surely have transpired by now.

The housekeeper halted before the storage room door, glancing back at me. I was determined to extract a confession from Professor Lomono about Braque's presence and to unravel the mystery of Nora and Liam's whereabouts—all before Braque's potential return.

"Open the door," I instructed, and the housekeeper complied, flicking on the storage room light without needing further prompting. I gave Professor Lomono a rough shove, propelling him to stumble forward while shouting, "Look—"

But my words faltered, and instinctively, I reached out to steady Professor Lomono, preventing his fall. Silence enveloped us, our breaths the only disturbance save for a soft, unexpected meow.

A cat. In the storage room.

Ordinary enough, yet it froze me in my tracks. The black-and-white striped feline was eerily familiar — the same cat I had seen yesterday, its lifeless body riddled with bullets among the clutter. Now, it stared at us, very much alive, its meow a haunting reminder.

The storage room unfolded before us in all its mundane reality. Piles of forgotten items were draped in thick dust, untouched by chaos. There were no bullet holes, no shattered remnants—nothing to suggest the violence I had witnessed.

My mind spun, grasping at the surreal implications. Was this a dream, a trick of the senses?

Confusion clouded my thoughts, but slowly, clarity began to seep in. I steadied my breath, determined to unravel the truth hidden beneath this illusion.

My mind raced as I tried to piece together the puzzle. Despite the seemingly innocuous scene in the storage room, I knew what I had witnessed yesterday was no figment of my imagination. I was in the same house, and the events were too vivid, too real to dismiss.

Nearly twenty hours had passed since that harrowing encounter, ample time to meticulously erase evidence—a dusty storage room could be fabricated, bullet-riddled items removed, walls repaired, and a lookalike cat procured to maintain the facade. But if this was the case, it raised the question of Professor Lomono's true identity. His eagerness to conceal Braque's existence suggested deeper ties, rendering my situation perilous.

With a firm grip on Professor Lomono's arm, a singular thought propelled me: I must leave, and quickly. Many speculated that Braque acted alone, but I was now convinced of a larger organization backing him. Alone, I was no match for such a force. I needed to escape and discreetly contact the authorities. Professor Lomono's helpless demeanor was a masterful act, his cunning hidden behind a veneer of innocence.

"You mentioned the storage room," he said smoothly, gesturing to the room behind us.

Feigning ignorance, I replied, "Ah, I must have been mistaken. It seems very peaceful here."

Professor Lomono nodded, a glint of understanding in his eyes. "It's just that your arrival was quite...unsettling."

"When I leave, force might be necessary," I countered, my voice steely.

"That's entirely unnecessary," he assured me.

"I have no desire to harm anyone, nor to be harmed. You'll accompany me to the door."

He acquiesced, "Very well."

Guiding him through the garden's iron gate, I welcomed the thick fog that shrouded us. It was an ally, masking my retreat and complicating any attempts on my life. Once outside, I released Professor Lomono and vanished into the fog's embrace.

The haze enveloped me, and the grass thicket was drenched, each droplet soaking through my clothes as I waited, tense and alert. Minutes ticked by, and the silence remained unbroken. Through the mist, I glimpsed Professor Lomono at the doorway. His figure was swallowed by the night as he re-entered the house, leaving me to the shadows and the encroaching dread.

The air was soon punctuated by hurried footsteps, the housekeeper's voice reaching my ears. "Professor, should we call the police?"

"No need," Professor Lomono replied. "I don't know what unsettled the young man, but I doubt he'll return. Secure my pistol—it was fortunate there were no bullets tonight. I nearly mistook him for a thief."

Their voices faded, the door closing with finality.

I stood frozen, my thoughts in turmoil. Two possibilities unraveled before me: either Professor Lomono was indeed innocent, and I had misjudged him, but how then could I explain the appearance of the cold-blooded Braque? Or he and the housekeeper were aware of my presence, their words a calculated ruse. If so, they were formidable adversaries, their guile a testament to their cunning.

After a tense, silent vigil of thirty minutes, I slipped away, finding my car and descending the mountain.

Anxiety knotted in my stomach as I sped down the mountain, desperate to contact the secret police studio. Known only to a select few, this clandestine organization dealt with the most dangerous threats—figures like Braque. My urgency translated into speed, the car tearing through the fog-laden night.

But the rain-soaked road had become treacherous. As I navigated a steep descent, the car's speed spiraled beyond control. An ominous sheen caught my eye—a slick of oil, not water, glistened on the asphalt.

Someone had set a trap, a crude attempt at murder.

A derisive smile flickered across my lips. Did they truly think a bit of oil could thwart me? My confidence dimmed as I pressed the brakes pedal, only to find it depressingly loose. The realization hit hard—the enemy wasn't as inept as I first thought. They had sabotaged my brakes.

With the car gaining momentum, my options dwindled to one. I flung open the door and leaped out, bracing for impact.

The ground met me with a brutal embrace, my body tumbling across the greasy surface. A thunderous explosion shattered the night, mere yards from where I lay. My car, engulfed in flames, pierced the fog with a fiery glow.

Instinct kept me prone, the oily grime camouflaging me against the ground. The very substance intended to harm me now served as a shield, hiding me from prying eyes.

And then, through the haze and the flickering firelight, I saw him — the cold-blooded Braque. His face was obscured by the chaos, but the telltale ruby belt buckle glinted with malevolence.

His stance was unmistakable, exuding a chilling aura of ruthlessness and lethal intent. He stood as if carved from stone, a predator surveying his domain.

Destroying my Braquees, slicking the road with oil, and orchestrating a fiery crash were mere trifles for Braque. He lingered only briefly, his silhouette fading into the fog, leaving behind a scene of chaos. Twice now, I had encountered him, yet his true visage remained elusive, shrouded in mystery.

Not long after he vanished, the sound of an engine roared to life, piercing the night. I rose, surveying the smoldering remains of my car—a charred heap of metal, a testament to the narrow escape from death I had just experienced. If I had leapt out of the car ten seconds later, I would have been reduced to ashes.

As I stood there, the adrenaline began to recede, and with it came clarity. Braque's confidence was his Achilles' heel, a double-edged sword that could very well lead to his downfall. His belief in his own infallibility had already betrayed him twice.

Yesterday, his confidence in the lethality of his rapid-fire rifle had been misplaced; I had managed to evade his assault by mere chance, hidden behind the safety of a door. Tonight, he presumed my demise in the wreckage, failing to verify his success. In truth, I had escaped his grasp once again.

The task of confronting Braque seemed insurmountable at first, but now, a glimmer of hope ignited within me. I had glimpsed his vulnerability. If I could exploit one weakness, surely others would follow, unraveling his web of terror.

With renewed determination, I began the trek down the mountain, shunning the taxi stands I encountered. My appearance, streaked with oil and grime, would draw undue attention. Home was my immediate goal.

Though my pursuit of Nora and Liam remained unwavering, I realized the futility of acting alone. I needed allies, and the secret police studio was my best hope. Once home, I would reach out to them, enlisting their aid in this perilous endeavor.

The walk took nearly an hour, each step a reminder of my resolve. As I approached my building, the hall below was ablaze with light, an unexpected sight at such a late hour. Could it be that Wilson was still awake, awaiting my return? The thought quickened my pace.

Reaching the door, I fumbled for my key, anticipation and exhaustion mingling as I turned the lock and stepped inside.

Chapter 6

The Skeleton Spirit Returns

As the door swung open, Wilson's voice greeted me, "The master is back." His tone held a note of relief, yet something else lurked beneath it—anxiety, perhaps. For a moment, I hesitated, wondering who this unexpected visitor might be. Wilson approached, his eyes wide with surprise, and I realized why. My entire being was cloaked in a grimy layer of oil, the remnants of my narrow escape.

"Is someone here to see me?" I asked, urgency lacing my words.

Wilson gestured toward a sofa in the hall's shadowy corner. "Yes, a lady is waiting for you—" His voice quivered, betraying a tremor of fear.

A lady? Curiosity piqued, but Wilson's whisper halted my thoughts, "I—I'm afraid."

"Afraid of what?" I demanded, bewildered.

He leaned closer, voice dropping to a conspiratorial whisper, "Her attire is like the skeleton spirit from before."

"Nonsense!" I chided, brushing off his superstitions, though his grip on my sleeve lingered. "Be cautious," he urged, even as I shook free, striding toward the mysterious visitor.

From behind the high-backed sofa, only an arm was visible, resting on the armrest, shrouded in the room's dim light. "Who is it?" I called, moving closer.

"Mr. Morris, please don't come any nearer," a voice warned. It was unmistakably Nora's.

The revelation stopped me cold. Nora. The very person whose absence had nearly cost me my life. Yet here she was, cloaked in secrecy. What was she up to?

Ignoring her plea, I pressed on. "Nora, is it really you? Have you contacted your family? Where have you been—"

As I approached, Nora sprang from the sofa, retreating with a cry, "Don't come closer, don't come closer."

The sight of her stunned me. She was clad in ill-fitting clothes—trousers and a long coat—her hands gloved, her head swathed in dark silk scarves, entirely obscuring her features. Indoors, at this late hour, she wore black glasses. The resemblance to Nora's earlier apparition was uncanny.

A chill crept over me, electrifying my nerves. "You—you—what is going on?" I stammered, pointing at her, the words barely escaping my lips.

Her voice, steady and controlled, replied, "Mr. Morris, there's no need for questions. I've found Nora's whereabouts. It's over."

I took a step forward; she mirrored it backward. "No," I insisted, my tone firm. "This isn't over—it's just beginning. What happened to Nora? What happened to you? You must tell me!"

Nora's voice rose, sharp and insistent, "I said it's over. Don't meddle in what doesn't concern you. You've done enough for us. You must not involve the police!"

Her words hung in the air, a plea and a warning wrapped in mystery. The gravity of the situation weighed heavily on my shoulders as I stood there, caught between the urge to help and the ominous secrets that loomed like shadows in the room.

"Why?" I demanded, urgency slicing through the tension in the air.

Nora inhaled deeply, her voice steady yet evasive. "Because it's over, why cause alarm?"

A cynical smile tugged at my lips. "Over? Miss Lee, why the disguise?"

She shrank back, voice trembling. "I—I caught a severe cold, that's all."

"No!" I pressed, conviction hardening my tone. "You've suffered the same fate as Nora, haven't you? What happened? Why won't you tell me?"

With each word, I edged closer, and Nora retreated until the wall halted her progress. Fear etched into her features, she pleaded, "Don't come near! Don't come near!" Ignoring her protests, I reached out, intending to calm her with a reassuring grip on her shoulder.

In my haste, I forgot Nora's mastery of judo.

As my hand touched her shoulder, she deftly pivoted, seizing my wrist and sending me sprawling to the floor with a resounding thud. Even as I fell, instinct kicked in and I snagged her sleeve, the fabric tearing away in my grasp.

Nora's scream pierced the air as she bolted.

Confusion clouded my mind. A torn sleeve seemed trivial, yet her reaction was anything but. Driven by the need for answers, I pursued her. She blocked my path with an arm, and in the ensuing struggle, another sleeve tore free.

My breath caught in my throat as I beheld the truth. Emerging from the sleeve was not flesh and blood, but bone — a complete arm skeleton, gloved at the hand, somehow animate and connected to Nora's shoulder.

Paralyzed by disbelief, I watched as she swung the skeletal arm, fleeing into the night.

A loud crash jolted me from my stupor — Wilson, collapsing to the floor in shock. His complexion was ashen, mirroring my own. Rising shakily, he muttered, "We need to move. We can't stay here."

"Don't talk nonsense," I snapped, though my voice lacked conviction.

I peered into the darkness outside, but Nora had vanished. Pursuit felt futile, so I retreated, ascending the stairs in a daze.

Under the cascade of hot water, I sought to cleanse not just the grime from my body, but the chaos from my mind. The shower alternated between scalding and cold, a futile attempt to shock my thoughts into coherence.

Yet, as the steam enveloped me, my mind remained a tumultuous storm, fragments of the night's revelations swirling without resolution.

Despite the hot shower and fresh clothes, my mind remained a tangled web of confusion. The bizarre transformation of Nora and Liam haunted my thoughts. What could have possibly stripped away their flesh, leaving only bones? Was it their entire bodies, or merely their arms? The notion was absurd, leading me to chuckle despite myself. Could skeletons truly speak, think, and move with such agility? The very idea bordered on the fantastical.

Yet the mystery surrounding them overshadowed even the enigma of Braque. The connections between Braque, Professor Lomono, Nora, and Liam teased the edges of my mind, but the puzzle pieces refused to fit. I paced restlessly in my study, my thoughts leaping as erratically as my movements. The frustration was palpable.

This was unlike anything I had ever encountered. Even the "Blue Blood Man" incident, with its extraterrestrial visitors, seemed plausible by comparison. Humanity had long speculated about life on other planets. But "skeleton spirits"? Could such a thing truly exist?

As dawn broke, Wilson's knock pulled me from my reverie. He handed me a telegram, its delivery a glimmer of hope. It was from Sem Jansen.

I tore it open eagerly, only for disappointment to settle in. Sem Jansen seemed blissfully ignorant of the gravity of the situation. His message dismissed Nora's peculiarities as mere eccentricity, unworthy of concern. He complained about the complexity of acquiring the brass box and casually suggested I join him in Egypt, as he was weary of belly dancing.

Frustrated, I shredded the telegram, cursing Sem Jansen's carefree attitude. Damn his belly dancing! His brother might be dancing a macabre "bone dance," yet here he was, lost in frivolity. The irony was too bitter to ignore, and my anger surged with every torn piece of paper that fluttered to the ground.

Yet, the message did prompt a moment of clarity. The brass box from the ancient Inca Empire held the key. Understanding its history could unravel the mysteries enveloping Nora and Liam. Egypt beckoned — a place where answers might lie.

But could I abandon Nora and Liam in their plight? Their actions suggested a desire for distance, yet I believed it stemmed from a sense of my helplessness. But I refused to accept that. I had accomplished feats as grand as sending Saturnians home; surely, I could aid them in their strange ordeal.

I went downstairs and hastily finished my breakfast. As I drank my coffee, I decided to wait three days. If Nora and Liam didn't show up, I would rush to meet Sem Jansen.

At that time, I believed there was no connection between Nora, Liam, and Braque. After all, if Nora had been to Professor Lomono's house, how could she have gotten away and come to me?

I thought my judgment was sound, but I didn't realize I was making my third mistake. The first was not keeping Nora, the second was not keeping Nora, and the third was assuming there was no connection between Braque, Lomono, and Nora and Liam. My discovery of Braque here was just a coincidence—or so I thought.

While drinking coffee, I called Lieutenant Colonel Jack, head of the police secret studio, and informed him that the internationally renowned assassination expert, the cold-blooded Braque, was in the area.

Lieutenant Colonel Jack's voice was excited but not shocked. I explained how I found Braque, mentioning Lomono and his housekeeper, but I omitted Nora and Liam.

As a seasoned secret worker, Lieutenant Colonel Jack didn't talk much. He listened with a series of "hmm"s and then simply said, "Thank you."

After talking to Jack, I felt relieved, having handed Braque's matter over to the police. Now, my focus was to find Nora and Liam.

Finding two people in a big city isn't easy, but it shouldn't be hard to spot individuals dressed like Nora and Liam.

I contacted several private detective friends and asked them to deploy their teams to track down these two people. Then, I went out to investigate who Nora and Liam usually interacted with, hoping to find them through my efforts.

However, I found no leads after a whole day.

That night, I was exhausted, not because I hadn't slept the previous night, but because I made no progress throughout the day! Nora and Liam, those two enigmas—I could call them that—still eluded me.

Despite my fatigue, I slept poorly that night. The next morning, I wandered around aimlessly until Wilson handed me the morning paper. I sat down to read out of boredom. Suddenly, my eyes landed on a small piece of news I would normally overlook.

It was a mundane "whereabouts of people" update, but it gave me an unexpected jolt. The headline read:

"Internationally renowned mathematics professor Lomono goes to Egypt for investigation."

The headline was innocuous, the text even more so: Professor Lomono had boarded a plane to Egypt the previous night.

What could a mathematician possibly need to investigate in Egypt? The question stirred something in me, a faint thread connecting disparate events.

The brass box originated in Egypt. Nora's accident followed its opening. Could there be a link between him and Professor Lomono? And now, Professor Lomono was in Egypt.

An invisible thread, tenuous yet tantalizing, seemed to weave through these events, hinting at a larger tapestry.

My mind was still clouded with confusion, but this news crystallized my resolve: I, too, would journey to Egypt. There, I would meet with Sem Jansen and keep a watchful eye on Professor Lomono. But first, I needed to hear from Nora and Liam.

The day slipped by in a haze of fruitless searching, my detective friends reporting the same lack of results. Frustration gnawed at me as I returned home, weary and despondent. I skipped dinner, collapsing onto my bed, thoughts swirling aimlessly—until the phone rang.

The clock read 11 p.m., the day having vanished in contemplation. I answered, and was met with rapid, panicked breathing on the other end.

"Who? Who?" I urged, heart pounding with anticipation.

The breathing paused, then Nora's voice came through, tinged with fear. If I could have reached through the line to him, I would have. But his presence was as intangible as the voice I heard.

"Mr. Morris, please," he pleaded. "Don't meddle in our affairs anymore. Don't send people to find us."

I knew I had to tread carefully. This was my chance to locate him, and I couldn't afford to scare him off. Calmly, I laughed and replied, "Find you, Mr. Jansen? Perhaps you're imagining things."

"You call it imagination," Nora retorted. "I spoke with acquaintances today; everyone asked where we were, mentioning some private detectives. Who else but you?"

His use of "we" confirmed my suspicions: Nora and Liam were together.

"That's good," I remarked. "You two must have had quite the funny time."

His tone turned coarse, frustration seeping through. "Funny? We are avoiding everyone, hiding in the wilderness—" Abruptly, he fell silent, realizing he had said too much.

"Where are you?" I pressed gently. "I need to meet with you urgently."

Nora's laughter echoed through the phone, a chilling and unsettling sound that sent a shiver down my spine. "No, I won't tell you," he said, his voice carrying an eerie edge. "And I won't trek a long distance to call you again. You don't need to bother looking for us."

I tried to keep him on the line, calling out, "Hello" repeatedly. "Then how can I explain to your brother? He'll be here in a few days," I lied, hoping to elicit a reaction.

The pause that followed was fraught with tension, and I knew my words had struck a chord. Finally, Nora responded, his voice tinged with uncertainty. "No, no, he won't come."

I pressed on, my tone gentle and sincere. "You and Nora may be facing extreme difficulties. Why don't we meet and discuss how to solve them together?"

Despite my overtures, Nora remained resolute. "No, no," he insisted. "If my brother does come, tell him that if he returns to Egypt and stumble upon that brass box again, not to open it!"

The line went dead with a decisive click, leaving me alone with my thoughts, my calls of "Hello" unanswered. I had gleaned no concrete clues, yet the conversation had not been entirely fruitless.

Nora's words hinted at a location outside the city—perhaps an isolated island. Earlier, I had discovered that Nora possessed a small yacht, which was now missing from the dock. It seemed likely that he and Nora were secluded on a deserted island.

With this fragment of information, my mind churned, restless and unsleeping. I retreated to my study, seeking distraction in the pages of a book. Blindly, I pulled a volume from the shelf, resolving to read until sleep overtook me or dawn arrived.

The book I chose brought a wry smile to my lips: a "Primary Color Tropical Fish Atlas" from Japan. Once, I had been enamored with breeding tropical fish, and this book was a relic of that passion. Now, its presence felt both absurd and strangely fitting.

As I thumbed through the pages, an idea—a wild, improbable notion—sprang to mind. My fingers paused on an image of a fish: a transparent catfish. This fish, seven centimeters long and half a centimeter wide, had all its internal organs concentrated in its head. Its body was mostly bone, arranged in neat, visible lines due to its transparency.

The sight of the transparent catfish, commonplace and inexpensive, sparked a sudden inspiration. Could it be that Nora and Liam's transformation was akin to this fish, their bodies somehow rendered transparent, leaving only the visible structure of their bones?

Two Transparent People

The picture of the transparent fish was mesmerizing, the photograph capturing the surreal image of a fishbone swimming through water. It was a strange, ethereal sight, reminding me of the eerie vision of an arm bone waving and a hand bone opening a door.

As I stared at the image, a realization took root. The muscles of the transparent fish allowed light to pass through unhindered, rendering them invisible to the human eye. Could it be the same for Liam and Nora?

Perhaps their muscles had become transparent, invisible to the naked eye because they no longer blocked light, turning them into living specters — transparent people.

The notion felt audacious, bordering on the absurd, yet it resonated with the bizarre happenings I'd witnessed. It seemed an unlikely truth, yet one that aligned with the facts:

no one could move freely without their muscles, and yet their muscles were unseen.

My heart raced with the implications. It was an incredible, shocking discovery, yet it left me with more questions than answers. Why had they become like this?

In my daze, I remembered to read the fish's description. The text noted this transparent fish's origins in South American streams, recently bred successfully in aquariums. A peculiar trait was highlighted: an intense self-fear, causing it to avoid other fish, even if it meant starvation.

Two points from the description seized my attention. First, the fish hailed from South America, echoing the origins of the brass box from the Inca Empire — a civilization that vanished mysteriously after achieving great heights in South America.

Second, the fish's self-fear mirrored Liam and Nora's behavior. Their fear was understandable; imagine gazing at a mirror only to see a skeleton staring back, devoid of flesh and life. The terror of touching muscles you can't see would be overwhelming.

Their visits to me were cries for help, yet fear chased them away. Their nerves must have been stretched to breaking point, grappling with an existence that defied reality.

I knew with certainty that Liam and Nora were on one of the outlying islands. Searching each island by foot was impractical, so I leveraged my connections with the international police. A helicopter search, equipped with aerial photography, was our best shot. The police, understanding the urgency, had already prepared the helicopter, needing only a word from me to launch the mission.

Arriving at the airfield at dawn, I briefed the pilot: we'd scour every island until we found them. With ample fuel reserves, we began our airborne search, my eyes glued to a long-range telescope. Each deserted island was scrutinized, our camera capturing every detail from above.

By afternoon, the helicopter returned twice to refuel. Doubts crept in—could Liam's yacht have ventured this far? Yet, we continued, circling each island, careful not to fly too low and reveal our presence.

As dusk descended, and fuel waned, just when hope seemed lost, my telescope caught sight of a medium-sized yacht beside a solitary island. The name "Quaternion" emblazoned on its stern leaped out at me. This was no ordinary name; it was a nod to the mathematical concept coined by the Scottish mathematician Hamilton, perfectly fitting for Liam, a mathematician himself.

Finding the yacht sent a surge of excitement through me. I instructed the pilot to veer away, lowering an inflatable rubber boat into the sea. I leapt onto it, and the helicopter retreated, leaving me alone amidst the vast ocean.

Darkness enveloped the sea as I paddled toward the island. The silhouette of the isle remained visible, guiding me. Silently, I navigated around the island, drawing near to the yacht. It lay abandoned, confirming Liam and Nora were ashore.

Concealing my boat between two rocks, I climbed onto the island. The terrain was rugged, the silence profound. What seemed a tiny island from afar revealed itself to be a challenging maze of caves and dense underbrush.

I moved with stealth, the darkness my ally, masking my presence. As I ventured deeper, a distinct scent caught my attention—the unmistakable aroma of burning food. I halted, pinpointing its origin, and crept forward.

Through the shadows, a tent materialized beside a stream. My heart raced with anticipation. Here, amidst the isolation, lay the answers I sought—the mystery of Liam and Nora could soon be unraveled.

I stood motionless, my heart pounding in my chest. Just a few steps forward, and I would confront the only two transparent people in the world—Liam and Nora. I inched closer to the tent, careful not to make a sound, until the rough canvas was within reach. Inside, Liam's voice broke the silence.

"Nora, what are you thinking about?" he asked.

I froze, not daring to move and risk alerting them. My presence needed to be revealed carefully. If I startled them, the shock could drive them to panic.

In response, Nora's voice emerged from the tent, calm yet contemplative. "Liam, you may not believe it, but I'm not thinking about our own predicament."

"Then what are you thinking about?" Liam inquired.

"I believe I've solved one of history's great mysteries," Nora replied. "But I'm afraid that if I reveal it, no one will believe me. No historian would accept my conclusion."

Liam sighed, a mix of disbelief and admiration in his voice. "Even now, you're still wrapped up in history?"

A bitter smile colored Nora's words. "I can't help it. Somehow, I want the world to know that I've uncovered this historical enigma."

Liam's voice carried a note of resignation. "What great mystery have you unraveled?"

With excitement, Nora explained, "The Inca Empire—the civilization that once thrived on the plains of South America. An Indian tribe established the Inca Empire, the most advanced ancient civilization of its time. But then, mysteriously, everyone vanished, leaving behind only ruins. To this day, no one has comprehended why. What could have led such a sophisticated society to disappear?"

Liam's response was tinged with skepticism. "And what do you propose happened?"

"The answer is clear," Nora said. "The people of the Inca Empire suffered the same fate as we have."

Liam's voice was laced with dread. "Nora, are you saying we're going to die?"

Nora's tone softened, resigned yet philosophical. "Liam, death is inevitable for everyone. It's the one certainty in life. Alas, we can't escape it."

Silence enveloped them, a shared understanding in their quiet.

Nora continued, her voice heavy with contemplation. "We are modern people, our nerves sturdier than those of ancient times. Yet even we are shaken to our core. Imagine the ancient Incas—how they must have felt. To them, it was likely the apocalypse. A horrific mass suicide, wiping out the Inca Empire in a blink. An entire civilization, gone."

Liam remained silent, absorbing the weight of her words.

Nora's voice carried the authority of a scholar, as if she were presenting at a historians' conference, unraveling the mystery of a lost civilization. "Some of the Incas didn't succumb to panic or mass suicide. They created that brass box and etched into it—"

Liam interrupted with a sharp cry, "Don't mention that devilish thing!"

Nora halted, leaving the contents of the brass box shrouded in mystery. She resumed, "On the box's surface, they carved a relief of their fate — all living creatures reduced to mere bones."

A shiver ran through me, confirming my earlier suspicions. Nora's words corroborated the horrifying truth: their muscles hadn't vanished but had become invisible to the human eye.

Liam's voice rose in agitation, "Stop talking! I can't bear it anymore!"

His cries echoed before he suggested, almost desperately, "Turn on the light. Maybe we've returned to normal."

Nora dismissed the hope, "No, don't dream."

But Liam persisted, "We became like this suddenly. Maybe we can revert just as quickly. Turn on the light, let's see."

His voice was laden with desperate optimism. I heard the rustling of movement, and then light flooded the tent. I pressed my eye to a slit in the canvas.

What I saw defied belief. Under the lantern's glow, two skeletons were visible—one seated, one crouching. Cold sweat seeped from my hands as I gripped the tent rope, my mind reeling at the sight.

The skeletons were unmistakably human, their gender discernible by the structure of their pelvises. The seated skeleton was Nora, the crouching one Liam.

I watched as Liam's skeletal fingers moved near his arm bones, but they never touched. Of course, they couldn't; just like us, their muscles were intact, merely rendered invisible, like crystal.

Despair colored his voice, "I see nothing. No muscles, no nerves, no blood, no hair! Why can't the bones be invisible too? Then we'd be truly gone."

Nora's jawbone moved rapidly as she spoke, "If only that thing hadn't disappeared."

"Don't mention that thing!" Liam shouted, his voice a mix of fear and frustration.

The scene before me was surreal, a living nightmare. The brass box held a power beyond comprehension, and its legacy had ensnared Liam and Nora in its ancient grip.

At that moment, I noticed the only distinction between Liam and Nora and mere skeletons: their eyes. Within the vacant sockets, two solitary, black eyeballs remained, a haunting reminder of their humanity amidst the skeletal remains. The sight was unnerving, yet it made sense. If their eyes were transparent too, they wouldn't be able to see anything at all.

After a tense silence, Liam muttered, "Why do you keep bringing up that thing?"

Nora responded with a bitter smile, "I'm just wondering if prolonged or repeated exposure to that mysterious light would make even our bones invisible."

Liam lay down, resting an arm bone on Nora's delicate neck bones. In the lantern's glow, their skeletal forms lay intertwined, a poignant reminder of their plight. Their skeletal state meant they wore no clothes, understandable given their sudden and terrifying transformation. Once an engaged couple, now faced with an uncertain future, they clung to each other, seeking solace in their shared misery.

If I could see their muscles, the scene would be intimate, even romantic. But now, it was a stark tableau of two skeletons side by side. This reflection sparked a sobering thought: beneath our visible muscles, we're all destined to become bones. Why, then, do we burden ourselves with conflict and emotion?

Liam's sigh broke the silence. "Blow out the light."

Nora leaned forward, and through her ribs, I glimpsed the tent's interior—bones and nothing more. The tent went dark, and I retreated, pondering my next move.

I had found them, but what should I do? If I revealed myself, would I only add to their distress? In their shoes, I wouldn't want to face anyone. A letter, perhaps? But that would likely shock them further.

As I sat there, ideas eluding me, I shifted focus to piece together their perplexing ordeal. Liam had opened the brass box, unleashing a mysterious light that rendered him transparent. Nora's transformation followed, but the how and why remained a riddle. Where had Nora met with

Liam? And why did the same fate befall her? Their journey to this island was shrouded in even more mystery.

All I knew was that everything that happened to Nora occurred within a single day after she parted ways with me that morning.

Additionally, I was aware that the object emitting the mysterious light was no longer with them.

I was desperate to ask them about it and its current whereabouts, but I didn't dare reveal myself for fear of disturbing them.

I quietly approached the tent once more, hoping to overhear more of their conversation, knowing they wouldn't be able to sleep.

Sure enough, not long after I hid beside the tent, I heard Liam's voice again. He sighed and then said, "You make sense."

"What do you mean?" Nora asked.

"If we could expose ourselves to that light again, maybe we'd become completely invisible. It might be better than this half-existence," he replied.

Nora sighed. "Yes, but that thing is at Professor Lomono's house. How can we get there? I can't bear to cover up and blend in with the world again."

I was taken aback by what I overheard. It confirmed my suspicions: the incident was indeed connected to Professor Lomono. My earlier deductions hadn't been wrong. After leaving my place, Liam must have gone to see Professor Lomono. And during the time his car plunged off the cliff, he wasn't inside it.

Where was he then? Could it be that he was at Professor Lomono's house?

Liam's voice broke my train of thought. "I'll try again," he said.

"Don't go," Nora pleaded, her voice trembling with fear. "Last night, when you went to the city to make a phone call, I was terrified until you returned! I can't imagine what would happen if people discovered us."

Liam's response was laced with a bitter smile. "At least three people know our secret already. Ash Morris, Professor Lomono, and that stone-faced man, Braque."

Nora sighed, "Do you think they'll spread our story?"

"I doubt it," Liam replied.

When I overheard this, a wave of terror washed over me. The tension was unbearable; if anything unexpected happened again, I feared I might scream out loud.

It turned out that Liam and Braque had also crossed paths!

Their meeting must have happened at Lomono's residence, confirming a connection between Professor Lomono and Braque. My visit there hadn't unearthed any evidence, but it was clear that Professor Lomono's abrupt trip to Egypt was no mere coincidence.

Nora continued, "If we were sure about becoming invisible, we might risk it. But for now, we're stuck here."

"The food you brought back last night will last us a month," she added. "No one will find us."

Liam sighed, resigned to their situation. "It seems that's our only option."

Their conversation faded into silence.

I lingered, straining to hear more, but when no further words came, I quietly backed away. As I retreated, I resolved not to disturb them. They had enough provisions to last a month, and I would ensure they stayed put by discreetly disabling Liam's yacht. A small sabotage would render it inoperable.

I returned to the shore and disconnected two wires from the yacht's motor. Liam would be none the wiser about the damage, his yacht stranded and unable to sail.

With this act, I bought time — time to unravel the mystery fully and understand why Professor Lomono had traveled to Egypt. If my efforts over the next month didn't alter their circumstances, I would face them again, armed with knowledge and a plan.

Chapter 8

Death of an Intelligence Agent

As I paddled slowly in the rubber boat on the open sea, the vastness of the ocean surrounding me, my mind was a whirl of thoughts. I wasn't heading back home—returning by boat would be impossible given the island's distance from the city. Instead, I drifted with the current, waiting for the dawn and the helicopter I knew would come to retrieve me.

Sure enough, as the first light crested the horizon, the familiar thrum of helicopter blades sliced through the morning air. I had drifted far enough that the island was no longer visible. Firing a signal flare, I watched as the helicopter zeroed in on my location, a lifeline descending in the form of a long rope. As I was hoisted aboard, I was taken aback to find Lieutenant Colonel Jack, the head of secret operations, waiting for me inside.

Our interactions had been minimal, our exchanges never exceeding three sentences. I had never warmed to

Lieutenant Colonel Jack. If ever there was a man born to be a spy, it was him. His face was strikingly ordinary, yet curiously nondescript — a chameleon who could blend seamlessly into any crowd. Though a genuine English immigrant in Australia, his appearance was so adaptable that he could pass unnoticed among Orientals. He never spoke first, preferring instead to study you with a dispassionate gaze, as if you were just another commuter on a tram.

Sitting across from him, I shrugged and broke the silence. "Lieutenant Colonel, I assume our meeting here isn't coincidental."

"Of course not," he replied, his face as unreadable as ever. A peculiar thought crossed my mind: Lieutenant Colonel Jack and Braque were cut from the same cloth. Liam and Nora had described Braque as "a strange man like a stone," and Jack seemed no different. The only variance lay in their allegiances — one engaged in illegal assassinations, the other in legal ones.

I pressed on, "If it's not by chance, then it must be deliberate?"

Jack's voice was deep and steady. "Yes, I knew you'd board the helicopter near here, so I came to thank you."

"Thank me?" I echoed, curiosity piqued.

Jack nodded. "Yes, for providing us with information about Braque."

His words caught me off guard. "Lieutenant Colonel, discussing sensitive matters in any setting isn't advisable, wouldn't you agree?"

I had informed the secret police unit about Braque out of necessity. My dislike—a thin veneer over my deep-seated fear of Braque — drove me to it. I expected confidentiality, not casual conversation. Even in the helicopter, with only the pilot as witness, Jack's indiscretion baffled me. How could a seasoned intelligence officer be so reckless?

Jack's sidelong glance was piercing. "Ash Morris, are you afraid?"

A wave of anger surged within me, uncharacteristic but undeniable. I rarely lost my temper, but Jack's provocation—his blatant disregard for discretion and his insinuation of my fear—struck a nerve.

Jack must have seen the anger etched on my face. He gestured coolly towards the pilot. "In front of him, we needn't keep secrets."

I scrutinized the young pilot, noting his stern demeanor and tightly pressed lips. It was clear that today's driver was new, yet his silence was resolute.

The helicopter soared over the ocean, carrying with it a tension that was palpable, a reminder of the intricate web of secrets and allegiances that bound us all.

Lieutenant Colonel Jack continued with a steely gaze. "He's one of our top intelligence officers. His brother lost his footing and fell from a rooftop yesterday while tracking Braque."

The emphasis on "falling" was telling. But I knew it wasn't an accident; Braque had orchestrated it. A chill ran through me, and Jack's presence now made sense.

A chill ran through me. Jack's presence now made sense.

Before he could make his request, I shook my head. "No, don't expect me to join your operation. I have my own responsibilities, and intelligence work is the government's domain. I'm just a civilian."

Jack replied, measured and calm, "Our working group is an extension of the police, not a spy agency."

I remained firm. "I have urgent matters to attend to, which might require me to leave immediately. Let's leave it at that."

Jack fell silent, but I felt an intense gaze on me. The young intelligence officer was staring, his intentions clear.

I preempted him. "Focus on your instruments, not me. Otherwise, you might find yourself in danger before Braque even has a chance."

Chastened, the young officer turned away, disappointment etched across his face. But my decision was firm; Liam and Nora needed my undivided focus. Their plight demanded all my attention. I would either restore them or make them completely invisible.

The rhythmic drone of the helicopter filled the silence until we landed. As I stepped out, ready to leave, Jack stopped me. "Ash Morris, won't you say goodbye?"

I turned and shook his hand, his grip firm and unyielding. "Aren't you curious why Braque is here in the East?"

I shook my head. "I'm just an ordinary civilian. That's none of my concern."

Jack's eyes were cold. "You're no mere civilian. You're nothing but a despicable cowardly rat with a special international police certificate!"

His words stung. My expression hardened. "How dare you insult me?"

Lieutenant Colonel Jack released my hand with a dismissive "Puh," his arrogance fueling a fire I could no longer contain. In a burst of impulse, I lunged forward, delivering a swift kick to his backside. The impact lifted him a few feet off the ground before he crashed back down, a spectacle witnessed by the entire heliport.

The heliport buzzed with the activity of senior and junior officers, a stronghold of local law enforcement. Jack's influence within the force was substantial, his authority unchallenged—until now. My audacious act left the crowd frozen, their eyes locked on me in disbelief.

Before Jack could recover, three towering armed policemen charged toward me. I crouched, ready to confront them, but Jack, already on his feet, halted their advance with a sneer. "Ash Morris," he spat, "I'll remember your kick."

I retorted with equal ferocity, "And I'll remember your words."

Turning away, I made my exit. The tension was palpable, and though some officers seemed eager to impede me, Jack's intervention held them at bay.

The anger coursed through me as I left the heliport, my steps deliberate and unyielding until I flagged down a taxi, retreating to the solitude of my home where sleep eventually claimed me.

When I awoke, afternoon light filtered through the window. My thoughts drifted to the enigma of the brass box and its elusive contents.

Liam, I surmised, had only sought Professor Lomono for counsel that night, suggesting the mysterious object capable of rendering muscle tissue transparent was hidden in the professor's residence.

With Professor Lomono in Egypt and Braque under police scrutiny, I pondered the object's fate. Surely, a visit to the professor's home would unravel the mystery. Just as I prepared to leave, the phone rang, its timing uncanny.

Answering, a pleasant female voice announced a long-distance call from Paris. I hesitated; since Mr. Nelson's death, I had no ties to Paris. The calm voice that followed, however, was unmistakable. "It's your Excellency," I replied, astonished.

His name was legendary, revered even beyond my late friend Nelson. "I heard you declined Colonel Jack's invitation," he said, his tone steady, probing.

Inwardly, I cursed Jack's cunning—seeking Parisian intervention. "Jack's invitation was no more than an insult," I replied tersely. "He called me a despicable big rat."

"No, he said you are a despicable rat, not a big rat."

"What's the difference?" I shot back.

"And so, you kicked him hard?"

"Yes, but my kick was not heavy," I corrected, feeling the absurdity of the debate.

"Let's leave it there," he sighed."I wonder, if Nelson were alive, how would you choose?"

Silence enveloped me as I mourned my friend, the weight of his absence pressing heavily on my heart.

"Nothing more, I wish you happiness," the voice on the other end was ready to sever the connection.

I interjected quickly, "Wait, you called me long distance just to wish me happiness?"

"I hope you are happy."

"What else do you want?" My voice edged toward a shout, frustration bubbling over.

"If you're inclined," he replied calmly, "I suggest you reach out to Lieutenant Colonel Jack once more and inquire how his exemplary intelligence officer came to fall from a towering building."

A sigh escaped me, laden with resignation. "Fine, I'll contact him. But he'd better not provoke my anger again."

"I doubt he will," the voice assured, maintaining its steady, authoritative cadence.

I set the receiver down, a knot tightening in my stomach, before dialing Jack's direct line.

The call connected, and I wasted no time. "Is this Jack?"

"Yes, Ash." His tone carried the weight of expectation, as if he'd been anticipating my call.

"Spare me the pleasantries," I said coldly, "How did your prized intelligence officer plummet from a building?"

Jack's response crackled with restrained fury. "Could you come to headquarters for a detailed report?"

"No," I snapped, "Tell me over the phone."

Jack hesitated, then relented. "The officer didn't die immediately upon impact. He uttered a few words—words that left us baffled."

I dismissed him flatly, "If those brilliant minds of yours find it baffling, so will I. Save your breath."

"You're a—" Jack's voice rose, but I cut him off.

"A despicable rat!" I finished for him.

"Big rat!" he retorted before the line went dead with a simultaneous slam of receivers. A strange sense of relief washed over me; rejecting his overtures was a small victory, a refusal to be drawn into a confrontation with Braque.

I turned away, but my heart skipped a beat as I noticed the handle of my study door turning slowly.

Who could it be? Wilson would never enter unannounced. Had someone truly dared to breach my sanctuary? The loud conversation moments ago should have deterred any intruder, unless they were either deaf or possessed an audacity to rival my own.

In a heartbeat, my instincts kicked in—I needed to hide.

I swiftly maneuvered to the door, taking up a strategic position I had relied on before. It was the same spot that had saved me when Braque unleashed a hail of bullets in the storage room, a refuge that offered immediate concealment.

The beauty of this location was twofold: once the door swung open, it would shield me from immediate view. Anyone stepping through would find nothing but an empty room. Even more advantageous was the secret door beside me, leading discreetly to my bedroom. A clever contraption allowed me to surveil the study from behind this hidden barricade, transforming my retreat into a vantage point.

With my back pressed against the wall, I deftly triggered the mechanism to silently open the secret door. I was poised, ready to slip away soundlessly if the situation demanded it.

The door handle twisted, a slow, deliberate turn. My mind raced—who dared to intrude? It defied reason, this audacity. I angled my head to the side, anticipating a glimpse of the intruder through the widening crack.

Two seconds after the lock clicked, the door eased open, inch by inch. As it swung wider, I peered through the narrow slit. Half a finger's breadth revealed nothing.

No one stood outside.

My heart skipped. Had my eyes deceived me? I blinked and rubbed them, straining for clarity.

The door continued its arc, now more than half a meter open. I peered through the widening gap, scanning the corridor beyond.

Nothing. No presence, no shadow—only the unsettling emptiness of an unoccupied hallway.

In that perplexing moment, I grappled with my confusion. Could it have been the wind? What kind of wind possesses the strength to twist a door handle? My mind churned with questions, each more bizarre than the last. Whatever was unfolding, it was beyond any experience I'd ever encountered.

I took a cautious step back, pressing my back against the secret door. In an instant, I was inside the hidden alcove, peering through the specially crafted glass that allowed me to observe the study undetected. The glass was a marvel—transparent from my side, yet seamlessly blending with the wallpaper from the study's perspective.

From my concealed vantage point, I watched the study door swing fully open, yet still, no figure emerged. My bewilderment deepened, and a part of me considered stepping back into the room to investigate.

But then, the study door slammed shut with startling force, as if an unseen hand had yanked it closed. There was no one there—no shadow, no presence. The chill that crept into my heart intensified, spreading like ice through my veins. I clamped my jaw to keep my teeth from chattering in the eerie stillness.

Courage wasn't the issue; fear was absent. It was the sheer strangeness of it all, the inexplicable and charged atmosphere that had every nerve in my body strung tight, like a bow ready to release.

I held my breath, listening intently. The room was silent, save for the echoes of my own thoughts. Could it possibly have been a peculiar wind? My rational mind clung to this possibility until reality shattered it.

Before my eyes, the chair at my desk creaked, the cushion visibly sinking as if someone had settled into it.

There was no wind, no logical explanation for such a phenomenon. Yet here it was, unfolding in front of me—a scene that defied all reason and sent a shiver down my spine.

Chapter 9

Invisible Enemy

Someone is sitting in my chair—yet the seat appears vacant. I'm not blind; my eyes scan every corner of the study, yet I see nothing where this presence should be.

Initially, my thoughts spiraled into chaos, but clarity soon emerged. There is indeed someone here, a presence I can sense but not see. Who is this unseen intruder? An invisible man—a transparent figure lurking in my study.

Is it just one person, or is my study filled with these unseen beings? Could it be Liam or Nora? Perhaps both? I was on the verge of stepping out to confront this mystery when a pen on my desk suddenly lifted, twirling in the air. It was the invisible hand that spun it, a gesture reminiscent of a gunslinger showing off his revolver. This habitual flourish didn't fit Liam or Nora, and it confirmed my suspicion: the invisible presence wasn't them.

This person—a transparent man—was beyond my identification. Billions of cells in his body failed to reflect light, rendering him invisible. There, in plain sight, yet unseen, he loomed.

Unsure of my next move, I remained hidden behind the secret door, observing. The invisible man didn't linger in my chair long before standing. Where he moved next, I couldn't discern.

The balcony door creaked open, and presumably, he stepped outside. Minutes ticked by before the door swung open again. A yellow rose floated into view, twirling gently as if held to an unseen nose for its scent.

If the rose met his nose, this transparent man was exceptionally tall—a stature typical of Westerners. Could he be a Westerner?

The chair cushion sagged again under unseen weight. A piece of paper rustled; the pen danced across it, writing in English. It was like witnessing a scene from a film with spectacular special effects.

I strained to catch a glimpse of the writing, but the language was unmistakably English. Then, my Spanish sword-shaped letter opener rose, pierced the letter with a sharp "slap," and embedded itself deeply into the table, its hilt wobbling.

The opener, normally blunt, had been driven in with extraordinary force. The invisible man possessed formidable strength.

The study door opened and slammed shut with a resounding "bang."

Quickly, I slipped out from behind the secret door, peeking through a crack. Within minutes, the main entrance opened and closed with the same force. Wilson emerged from the kitchen, bewildered by the sound.

The invisible man had vanished, leaving behind only questions and a sense of unease.

I quickly made my way to the balcony door, slipping behind the curtains to peer down at the street below. Everything appeared normal, unchanged from the usual hustle and bustle, and unsurprisingly, the invisible man remained elusive. I retreated back into the study, my attention drawn to the ominous message left behind.

The words on the paper sent a shiver down my spine: "You can escape this time, but you can't escape the next time!" There was no name, no signature, just a stark warning laced with lethal intent.

I pulled the letter opener from the table, folded the paper swiftly, and tucked it into my bag. My hand reached for the phone, dialing Lieutenant Colonel Jack's number with urgency.

"Lieutenant Colonel Jack? Ash Morris here."

"Big Rat, what's going on?" he replied, his nickname for me tinged with our usual banter.

"Get Braque's file ready. I'm on my way."

"Welcome, welcome!" His voice, icy moments ago, warmed with the eagerness of a Hawaiian welcome.

"Like you had a choice, old fox!" I quipped, ending the call and slipping out the back door.

Before leaving, I instructed Wilson to vacate my residence and stay with a friend temporarily, ensuring his safety. I avoided using my own car, changing transportation multiple times en route to the secret working group's headquarters. Tracking me would be difficult, but considering the invisible threat, I couldn't be sure. How does one spot an unseen shadow?

The secret group, led by Jack, operated discreetly from the top floor of a commercial building, masked as an import and export company. It was a front I'd only visited once before. Pushing open the door—crafted from the finest bulletproof glass — I was immediately met by two operatives.

"The boss is waiting for you," they murmured.

"Boss" was Jack's codename. Without a word, I followed them to a row of filing cabinets. One of them nudged a cabinet aside, revealing a hidden door. A sequence of button presses later, the door opened to reveal Jack behind a massive desk. The operatives retreated as I stepped inside, the door closing silently behind me.

Jack greeted me with open arms, his demeanor welcoming. "What made you change your mind?"

I shrugged, extracting the paper from my bag. "Do you have samples of Braque's handwriting?"

Jack nodded, a knowing glint in his eye. "Police worldwide have copies of his handwriting—love letters he penned to a woman. It's ironic, really. They call him cold-blooded Braque, yet those letters are as fervent as a sonnet."

I unfolded the paper, holding it out. "Take a look. Who penned these two sentences?"

"Braque!" Jack exclaimed, scrutinizing the handwriting. "I can tell at a glance."

Lieutenant Colonel Jack was an expert in this field, and his words left no room for doubt. My worst fears were confirmed. I sank into a sofa, cradling my forehead, momentarily speechless.

The invisible intruder in my study was none other than the murderer Braque.

Braque was already a perilous figure, but now, transformed into a transparent man, his threat level had multiplied exponentially. Once elusive, Braque was now as intangible as a ghost, lurking unseen and striking without warning.

Jack observed me silently, sweat trickling down my forehead and stinging my eyes.

"I don't understand why you're so rattled, Ash," Jack remarked, his tone almost dismissive. "You were never like this before."

I met his gaze, my voice steady. "Rattled? I wasn't afraid initially. I simply had no intention of confronting Braque. But now, it's not just me you need to fear too."

Jack's expression remained stoic. "Let me correct you, Ash. Fear is not an option for me."

I chuckled, a grim edge to my voice. "That's because you haven't encountered Braque in his current form."

"What's happened to him?" Jack queried, leaning forward.

I exhaled slowly, gathering my thoughts. "First, tell me how your intelligence officer met his demise."

Jack hesitated, then retrieved a document, handing it to me. "Read for yourself. This is the account of his final moments, word for word."

The record was meticulous. The dying officer had expended his last energy to relay his experience, though anyone unfamiliar with the situation might struggle to decipher his meaning.

"I sensed someone trailing me — yet I couldn't see him — he was so near, I felt his breath — suddenly, he shoved me—I couldn't fight back, couldn't see my assailant, but the force pushed me over—tell Lieutenant Colonel Jack, I—failed to complete my mission—tracking Braque—"

The officer had been an exceptional operative, his dedication unwavering even in death.

I returned the document to Jack, who was impatient for answers. "What do you make of this?"

I spread my hands wide. "He's been explicit. The person who pushed him was invisible."

Jack massaged his temples, exclaiming, "Oh, Ash Morris, spare me the material for a fantasy novel. I need—"

I cut him off, my tone firm. "I'm not spinning tales here, Jack. I'm stating the facts. The invisible assailant is Braque. Cold-blooded Braque is now the invisible Braque."

I locked eyes with Jack, absorbing the gravity of the situation. After a pause, he asked, "Ash, is he completely transparent?"

"Completely," I confirmed. "When he left the note on my desk, I only saw the pen moving—nothing else."

"Not even two black dots?" Jack probed further.

Confused, I asked, "Two black dots?"

He clarified, "His eyeballs. Could you see them?"

I shook my head. "No, nothing." Jack leaned back thoughtfully. "I assumed the transparent man was just someone our eyes couldn't perceive—not some fantastical creature from the fourth dimension."

I nodded in agreement. "Exactly. As far as we know, Braque is just an ordinary invisible man. Whether he might evolve into something more, becoming untouchable as well as unseen, remains unknown."

Jack considered this. "Even if what you're saying holds—"

I interrupted him, raising my voice. "Everything I'm saying is true."

He waved a hand dismissively. "No need to shout, Ash. It's just us here—" He paused, scanning the room with a wary glance, then gave me a rueful smile, acknowledging the possibility of unseen listeners.

I returned his smile, albeit grimly. "You believe me, or you wouldn't be looking around like that."

Jack's expression turned serious. "But science claims true invisibility is impossible. If light passes through the eyes, they can't see."

"I know," I said, "but Braque can see. Maybe not clearly, but enough. His slow movements suggest his vision might be blurred, but he sees."

We both fell silent, the weight of our predicament settling around us. Jack finally broke the silence with a sigh. "How did he become invisible?"

"I have some insight," I admitted, "but it's intertwined with my friends' secrets. What I can tell you is that his invisibility stems not from modern science, but from an ancient artifact."

Jack chuckled wryly. "An ancient artifact, like a magical ring?"

"I wish I knew," I replied, "though if I did, I might be invisible myself."

I stood, ready to leave. Jack asked, "You're leaving?"

I shrugged. "What's my alternative?"

"You'd be safer with us," he suggested.

I shook my head. "Don't worry, I can change my appearance."

I retrieved a finely crafted nylon fiber mask from my bag, slipping it on. Turning back to Jack, I asked, "Do you recognize me now?"

I had transformed into a dark-skinned, troubled middle-aged man. Jack gaped, then said, "Ash, I just thought of something."

His expression showed he was onto something, so I pressed, "What's your plan for Braque?"

"If Braque is invisible, he won't be wearing clothes," Jack speculated.

"I agree," I nodded.

Jack snapped his fingers, "If we spray him with thick colored liquid, his silhouette will be revealed."

I couldn't help but laugh, the absurdity of the idea hitting me.

Jack frowned. "You think it's impractical?"

"Possible, yes," I conceded, "but first, you'd need to locate him. Then, you'd have to immobilize him, and that's not accounting for his rapid-fire capabilities."

Jack stood, meeting my gaze. "It's difficult, not impossible."

I nodded. "Yes, but finding someone you can't see in the first place is a monumental challenge."

Jack continued to gaze at me, digesting the bizarre turn of events. "Ash, I've heard tales of your fearlessness. Why such a retreat this time?"

I was momentarily at a loss, reflecting on past encounters. "Yes, I've faced many threats, even the Saturnians. But the difference is, I could see them. Braque is invisible. I can't see him at all!"

As I gestured wildly, my hand unexpectedly struck something solid—a sensation like brushing against an arm. Yet, there was nothing visible within reach.

Startled, I recoiled, a scream escaping me. Jack, hearing the impact, paled visibly. He quickly grabbed a bottle of blue ink, hurling it across the room. It shattered with a splash, blue ink splattering the floor.

He drew his gun, and I instinctively hefted a chair, ready for confrontation.

In that instant, a strange calm descended over me. Braque was here, following me even to this place. But he had no visible weapon—nothing hovered in the air that could harm us from afar.

If it came to hand-to-hand combat, I was confident of my advantage, thanks to my rigorous martial arts training.

I split the wooden chair, tossing half forward as I shouted, "Fire!"

Jack was visibly shaken, the composure he had honed over years of special operations now frayed. His panic had led to gunfire, and one errant shot had nearly struck me.

As his subordinates burst through the door, drawn by the gunshots, they narrowly avoided becoming unintended casualties. Seeing them, Jack ceased firing, and we exchanged tense looks. "He must have been hit, right?" I ventured.

The intelligence officer who had stumbled in regained his feet, eyes wide with confusion. "Who? Who left?" he asked, bewildered.

Others crowded at the doorway, their expressions a mix of concern and disbelief at the scene before them. Jack barked out, "Get out quickly, close the door!"

Reluctantly, they obeyed, casting puzzled glances our way as they retreated, sealing us back in the room.

Jack retrieved another pistol from his drawer, tossing it my way. I caught it and positioned myself against the wall, ensuring Braque couldn't approach from behind.

In a steady voice, Jack called out, "Braque, are you still here?"

The room remained silent, the tension palpable.

"Braque," Jack continued, trying to coax a response. "don't think I'll shoot if you speak. Your mission in the Far East is already a failure; there's no need for bloodshed."

Still no answer.

Jack pressed on, "Being invisible can't be easy. How will you manage come winter?"

I nearly laughed at the absurdity, the surreal situation tinged with dark humor. Jack's words seemed almost dreamlike.

I took a steadying breath. "Jack, he's gone."

Jack shook his head. "No, I feel he's still here."

"Why?" I asked, my voice low.

"Intuition," Jack replied. "I just know."

I shrugged, considering the risk. "If he's still here, maybe he'd be willing to talk if we put down our weapons."

Jack hesitated, the danger of such an action clear. Braque could seize a gun at any moment.

Holding my weapon, I scanned the room for any sign of movement—perhaps an object displaced, or a subtle sound. If Braque's vision was impaired, as we suspected, he might inadvertently reveal himself.

But five minutes passed with no indication. I broke the silence. "Jack, he might have slipped out when the door opened. Braque on his own is not the threat. It's his inventions, his weapons. Without them, he's just flesh and bone. He wouldn't risk staying unarmed."

Jack shouted another warning to Braque, emphasizing the limitations his invisibility imposed on his career as an assassin. "Braque, whether you're here or not, listen up. Your days as a professional killer are over. You can't wear clothes without revealing yourself, and without clothes, you can't carry weapons—"

Before he could finish, I shouted, "Be careful!" and fired a shot into the room. My bullet struck a filing cabinet just as a crystal paperweight was hurtling toward Jack's head.

With quick reflexes, Jack blocked the projectile with his gun handle. It was then that the door swung open, clearly Braque's doing. Jack and I instinctively aimed our guns at the entryway but held our fire. Firing would risk hitting Jack's team, who were in the line of fire.

In our moment of hesitation, the door to the outer room opened on its own. Jack's agents, focused on us, missed the eerie sign of Braque's departure.

Jack and I exchanged a glance, relief washing over us. "He's gone," we breathed in unison.

Jack quickly secured the door, his expression turning grave. He made several urgent phone calls, repeating the same cautionary message: "The situation is dire. Do not act recklessly, or we can't ensure his safety."

After the calls, Jack sat heavily, wiping sweat from his brow. "Ash, I misjudged you earlier."

I remained silent, then said, "You're afraid too, aren't you?"

Jack paused, searching for words. "It's not fear, exactly. It's... there's no vocabulary for it. It's like being in a dream, where traditional skills and courage seem useless—"

His words trailed off, capturing the surreal sense of vulnerability we both felt. After a moment, I asked, "What's Braque's mission?"

"Assassination," Jack replied. "The leader of a new Southeast Asian nation is set to pass through here during an overseas visit. Braque intends to assassinate him, likely under orders from a neighboring country that wants to destabilize the region."

I nodded, piecing it together. "Braque's been bought off by that neighboring country?"

"Exactly," Jack confirmed. "The dictator there recently approved substantial foreign exchange — no doubt Braque's payment. I've already warned the visiting head of state to be cautious, better stay in his own country and don't move, but—"

Chapter 10

❧

Becoming Transparent

Jack sighed heavily as he finished explaining the precarious situation. I mirrored his sigh, understanding the unspoken truth: How do you thwart an invisible assassin?

I lingered for a moment before announcing, "I'm leaving now."

Jack's face reflected his concern as he asked, "Braque might be waiting outside. How do you plan to avoid his surveillance?"

I reached into my bag, retrieving the nylon mask. Pulling out a lighter, I set it aflame in Jack's ashtray. Braque had already seen this disguise, rendering it useless.

Next, I produced two more masks from my bag, handing one to Jack. "Don't worry about me. Focus on your own safety. This might come in handy."

With the other mask in place, I headed for the door. I stopped beside an intelligence officer of similar build and glanced back at Jack.

He caught on quickly, instructing the officer, "Swap clothes with this gentleman."

The officer blinked, puzzled by the odd command, but complied without question. We exchanged clothes swiftly, transforming me into an entirely different person. I exited the building, trying to appear at ease, humming softly as I merged into the bustling city crowd.

As the workday ended, the streets filled with people. I navigated through the throngs, using the dense crowd as a shield. In this sea of humanity, even Braque, invisible as he was, would struggle to keep track of me.

Returning home was out of the question. Instead, I contacted the manager of the import-export company where I served as the nominal chairman. I instructed him to prepare a yacht with all necessary equipment and have it waiting at a designated dock.

I needed to find Liam and Nora. I needed answers about how they, and Braque, had become invisible.

The situation had escalated beyond my concern for their "self-preservation" mindset. Understanding Braque's transformation was crucial. If the situation demanded it, I would consider undergoing the same process to combat this deadly threat.

To give my manager time, I ducked into a movie theater. A science fiction film was playing, but its fantastical plot seemed trivial compared to my reality. I drifted into a brief nap, waking as the credits rolled.

Exiting the theater, I took a meandering route, ensuring I wasn't being followed. Satisfied that I'd evaded any potential tail, I hailed a taxi and made my way to the dock.

By the time I reached the dock, night had fully descended, enveloping everything in darkness. The yacht awaited, prepared as instructed. I removed my mask and approached. My manager, visibly anxious, stood waiting on board.

I offered him a brief directive: "Don't mention this to anyone."

He nodded silently and disembarked, leaving me to navigate the swift yacht out to sea.

The island's location was etched in my memory. Guided by instruments, I soon arrived near its shores. Cutting the engine, I paddled silently, securing the boat among the rocky outcrops.

Liam's yacht was still moored there. I moved quietly towards their campsite. The night was pitch-black, the atmosphere tense. As I neared the tent, I overheard Liam's heavy sigh.

Nora's voice followed, "I think it might be from outer space. Maybe you'll be surprised—"

Liam interrupted with a pained moan, "Stop talking! Stop talking!"

Nora sighed softly, "Be brave!"

Her resilience was impressive. I approached the tent entrance and spoke firmly, "Miss Lee is right, Liam. You need to be brave!"

My sudden appearance startled them, eliciting screams. The tent's far end bulged as they recoiled, but they couldn't flee with me blocking the exit.

I quickly reassured them, "Don't be afraid. I'm Ash Morris. I found you yesterday. Even if I can't see you now, I understand your situation. I'm definitely your friend!"

Liam's voice trembled, "What do you want from us?"

"I'm here to ask for your help," I replied.

His teeth chattered as he echoed, "Help you?" I responded urgently, "Yes, I need your help."

Nora's voice, though fearful, was steadier. "Mr. Morris, since you know our situation, how can we assist you?"

"You need to listen carefully and dispel your doubts," I advised. "So far, only three people know your situation. I'm one of them, being here with you."

Liam asked, "Who are the other two?"

"One is Professor Lomono, currently in Egypt, so he poses no threat. The other is Braque, a notorious murderer. His profession is killing."

Liam began to sob quietly in the tent, while Nora remained composed.

A renowned psychologist once noted that women often exhibit greater calmness in extraordinary situations. I found this observation true now — real women can be remarkably composed. Those who scream often are not necessarily less calm; they simply choose to express vulnerability. Ironically, these women can be as strong as bulls.

I pressed on, "Braque's situation is marginally better than yours. He's a fully transparent man, which is incredibly dangerous. We know a Southeast Asian head of state has already been targeted."

Nora inquired, "Then what can we do to help you?"

"I need to know your story — everything you've experienced," I urged.

Silence fell as Liam and Nora considered my request.

Liam's voice had steadied somewhat, though it still carried the weight of his ordeal. "Then—what's the use?" he asked, uncertainty lacing his words.

I sighed, trying to convey the seriousness of the situation. "Understanding your experience can help me piece together the entire story. It might enable us to deal with Braque or even find a way to reverse what's happened to both of you. I need you to share everything in detail."

After a brief silence, Nora encouraged him, "Liam, you start. It happened to you first."

Liam hesitated before agreeing. "Alright, I'll go first. Mr. Morris, please don't come in."

"Of course. I'm outside the tent and won't intrude. You have my word," I assured him.

Liam's voice quivered as he recounted, "Ever since I received the box from you, I spent hours each day assembling the picture from its ninety-nine pieces. That afternoon, I finally succeeded. I called you before opening the box."

I nodded in acknowledgment, though he couldn't see. "I recall. When I asked about the box's contents, you mentioned not knowing but promised to tell me after you opened it."

He paused, his breath hitching with emotion. "But I never made that second call. After I hung up, I opened the brass box. The moment the lid lifted, a flash of light blinded me."

He hesitated again, gathering his thoughts. "It was a peculiar light, like a net weaving around me. When I looked inside, I saw a fist-sized mineral radiating this strange glow."

"Did you see it clearly? It was a mineral?" I pressed, intrigued.

"Yes," Liam confirmed. "It resembled tin, lightweight and emitting that eerie light. I was astonished. While I know of minerals that glow, they're rare and precious, like radium. Holding it, I worried about radiation damage and quickly returned it to the box."

His voice shook as he relived the fear. "When I put it back, I noticed my hands—just bones were visible. My flesh was there, but unseen. I thought about my face, rushed to a mirror—and fainted."

I sighed, empathizing with his shock. Discovering such a transformation in oneself would be horrifying.

"I was unconscious for two hours," Liam continued. "When I awoke, I realized my entire body—muscles, hair, blood—had become invisible. What had I become? Was I even human anymore?"

He paused, regaining composure. "Eventually, I deduced the light from the mineral caused this. I sealed it in a metal box, donned clothing, sunglasses, and gloves to appear normal, then contacted you, bringing the mineral along."

"I intended to ask for your help, but when I saw you, fear overwhelmed me. I worried you'd treat me as a monster. I fled, but you'd already pulled off my gloves—"

His voice trembled, the memory raw. I listened intently, understanding the immense psychological and physical toll this had taken on him. Liam's transformation was terrifying, yet his story might hold the key to unraveling the mystery and finding a way forward.

Liam continued, "After leaving your place, I thought of Professor Lomono. I trusted him and decided to seek his help. However, when I arrived, I encountered a strange man with him—Braque."

"When I saw them, the same fear gripped me as when I saw you. I wanted to flee, but Braque lunged and caught me. In the struggle, my hat fell, and my glasses shattered."

"I heard Braque and Professor Lomono shout in shock, then switch to a language I couldn't understand. Braque held me tight, demanding I explain my situation to Professor Lomono. I lied, saying I'd discarded the mineral."

"Braque locked me in a dark room, pressing me to reveal where I supposedly threw it. I gave him a random location, and he left. I remained imprisoned in darkness until Nora arrived."

He paused for breath, and I prompted Nora, eager to learn more. "Miss Lee, how did you find Liam?"

Nora replied, "It was simple. I noticed something was off when you left Professor Lomono's place, so I followed my instincts and came here."

I couldn't help but express my concern. "But the murderer, Braque, was there!"

Nora's voice remained composed. "Yes, upon entering, someone aimed a gun at me. He didn't shoot, perhaps because I'm a woman. He questioned me, and I explained I was searching for Liam. He said I arrived just in time and suggested I persuade Liam to reveal the mineral's true location — the one that could render human muscles transparent."

She continued, "After that, he shoved me with such force that I couldn't resist."

I nodded, understanding the peril she faced.

Nora described the confrontation. "I didn't know his identity then. I turned to see a man with a face as hard as stone pushing me into the dark room where Liam was held."

"Inside, I couldn't see Liam, only hear his terrified breathing. I called out, but he remained silent. I rushed toward him as he tried to flee. I caught up easily, but during our struggle, a box fell from his coat."

"When it hit the ground and opened, a powerful light blinded me, and I saw him—" Nora, though strong and brave, paused to catch her breath.

I whispered, "So, you also—"

Nora smiled wryly. "Yes, I became like him. But I wasn't sad. Knowing we shared the same fate was comforting. We were in love, and now we could rely on each other. It was better than him enduring it alone."

I was silent, absorbing her words, before asking, "How did you escape?"

Nora explained, "You may find it hard to believe, but after a while, under that strange light, Liam and I calmed. We embraced and gathered strength. I approached the door and listened. Can you guess what sound I heard?"

Curious, I replied, "What sound?"

Nora recounted the startling moment. "I heard laughter—Braque was laughing. It was a harsh, grating sound, like rocks clashing together."

Both Nora and I were taken aback. Could someone as cold and calculating as Braque actually laugh? It seemed almost inconceivable for a professional killer, a man devoid of warmth, to find joy.

She continued, "Not only was he laughing, but he was also calling out Professor Lomono's name. Summoning my courage, I held the door handle and pushed it gently. It wasn't locked. I signaled Liam, and we both approached."

Nora's excitement rose as she recounted, "I swung the door open. The burst of light from our room startled Braque. He looked confused, reaching for a weapon. But I didn't give him that chance—"

I chuckled, "You knocked him down?"

Nora nodded, "I threw him into the room, grabbed Liam, and locked Braque inside. We escaped to the beach and used Liam's yacht to reach this island."

I believed her story. Though Nora seemed delicate, her judo skills were formidable. Her ability to surprise and overpower Braque was impressive. I mulled over the implications. "In that room, Braque must have been exposed to the mysterious light, rendering even his bones invisible. He became truly invisible."

Nora theorized, "Perhaps the prolonged exposure to the light made him that way."

Liam broke his silence, addressing me with urgency, "Mr. Morris, now that you know everything about us, can't you help us? Can't you find a way to restore us?"

I sighed deeply. "As you mentioned, it's easy enough to become transparent like Braque if we can locate the mysterious object again."

Liam protested, his voice trembling, "No—no—what kind of life is that? Wearing a bit of clothing or holding an object makes people scream. Even if unseen, it feels like being perpetually exposed—"

I couldn't suppress a smile; his words echoed Jack's earlier musings about Braque. While Braque might be unfazed by permanent invisibility, his true threat lay in his unparalleled marksmanship and crafted weapons. Yet, as an invisible man, his ability to wield them was severely compromised. Imagine a gun floating mid-air, a spectacle that could betray his position.

For Braque, invisibility was more a hindrance than an asset. Though clever, he could disguise himself with clothes, masks, and wigs, the psychological impact of seeing nothing in the mirror would likely unsettle him.

I reassured them, "Don't worry. I'll do everything I can to help. Only I know you're here, and I won't tell anyone. I can supply you with essentials and food. For now, it's best to stay hidden and let people believe you've vanished."

Liam groaned, "How long do we have to wait?"

I sighed, unable to provide an answer.

As I paced, Nora suddenly spoke up, "Mr. Morris, I have some clues."

Intrigued, I stopped. "What clues?"

Nora explained, "The brass box and its contents are relics of the Inca Empire. The mysterious object might explain the sudden disappearance of the Inca people. But why were these items found in Egypt?"

I shook my head, "I have no idea. It's beyond imagination."

Nora continued, "I've pondered deeply. The brass box was likely crafted under the Inca leader's directive. Though there's no historical evidence of contact between the Inca and Egypt, someone must have traveled extensively with the box, seeking a solution to save them—"

I listened as her excitement grew. "This person was tasked with finding a way to save the Inca people. He ultimately reached Egypt."

Her theory was fascinating, suggesting a historical quest that spanned continents, driven by desperation and hope. It added a layer of mystery to the ancient artifact, hinting at untold stories and lost knowledge. Our challenge now was to uncover these secrets, seeking both a solution for Liam and Nora and a way to neutralize Braque.

I had to admit that Nora's inference was quite reasonable, and I encouraged her to continue.

Nora went on, "I believe that man found a way to save himself in Egypt!"

Her confidence was striking, and it gave me pause. I immediately thought of Professor Lomono. Hadn't he traveled to Egypt as well? Was he following the same line of thought as Nora? Did he intend to find a way to restore Braque, or perhaps to discover how to manipulate invisibility at will?

Liam interjected, "If he found a way to save himself, why didn't he return?"

Nora answered, "That was many years ago. Journeying from South America to Egypt was itself a miracle. Returning would have been impossible. Even if he could, it would be futile. The people of the Inca Empire couldn't bear what happened and chose mass suicide."

"So, what you mean is—" I prompted.

"I mean," Nora clarified, "if we visit the site where the brass box was discovered, we might find records of all this!"

Her suggestion was electrifying. "You're right! I need to go immediately. The brass box was found in an ancient temple, scheduled to be submerged due to a water project. Professor Lomono is already in Egypt, likely with the same goal!"

Liam asked anxiously, "You're going to Egypt? Who will look after us?"

I considered this. "There's an old man in my family, Wilson. He practically raised me. I'll ask him to deliver food and supplies. Is that okay?"

Liam hesitated, "This—"

Nora, decisive as ever, said, "Okay, we can trust him."

Their different personalities were evident. Liam was cautious and hesitant, whereas Nora's inner strength shone through, despite their shared ordeal.

I stood up, offering reassurance. "Don't worry. Wait for my good news."

"If you find anything, return as soon as possible," Nora urged.

I paused before replying, "Of course."

The pause was due to uncertainty — I couldn't guarantee results from my trip to Egypt.

Leaving them behind, I made my way to the beach. As I stood there, the vast, dark sea stretched out before me, a stark reminder of Earth's countless mysteries. In the grand scheme of the universe, our planet seemed minuscule. The notion that we earthlings could ever conquer such vastness seemed utterly foolish.

Eventually, I boarded the speedboat and left the island.

Back in the city, I avoided my home, opting for a hotel. I contacted Wilson, entrusting him with Liam and Nora's care. Then, I called my manager to arrange the necessary documents for my trip to Egypt.

The following day, I stayed in, contemplating a visit to Professor Lomono's residence to check for the mysterious object. Ultimately, I decided against it.

The reason I chose not to visit Professor Lomono's residence was twofold: firstly, the risk of being discovered by Braque was too great; secondly, the mysterious glowing mineral posed a threat — exposure could render me invisible like Liam Jansen and Nora Lee.

On the morning of the third day, I made my way to the airport. My manager had efficiently arranged everything for my departure. Just five minutes before boarding, I called Lieutenant Colonel Jack, briefly informing him of my impending long journey.

Once on the plane, I closed my eyes, grateful for the opportunity to rest. The past few days had been exhausting, and I hoped to catch up on much-needed sleep during the flight.

The journey itself was uneventful. During a stopover, I sent a telegram to Sem Jansen, notifying him of my arrival in Cairo and requesting that he meet me. I also mentioned my purpose—his brother's situation—and asked him to gather all available information on the brass box.

I allowed myself to relax until the plane approached Cairo, where the vast desert and iconic pyramids came into view below. The sight stirred me fully awake, knowing I needed to remain vigilant for whatever awaited in Egypt.

Upon landing, I navigated through customs and soon spotted Sem Jansen, who waved enthusiastically. His genuine happiness to see me was obvious—a welcome reprieve from the loneliness of living abroad.

However, I couldn't mirror his joy. The gravity of the situation weighed on me, with its serious implications and unpredictable developments.

As Sem Jansen approached for a handshake, I noticed a peculiar man standing behind him. This man was notably short, no more than 150 cm, with a dark complexion and a disproportionately large head. His brown hair and eyebrows framed a face of quiet intensity. His clothes were ill-fitting, and he nervously fidgeted with a hat in his hands.

The man accompanying Sem Jansen piqued my curiosity, and I couldn't resist asking, "Who is he?"

Sem Jansen patted the man's shoulder and introduced him as a friend. "He helped me acquire the brass box," Sem Jansen explained. "You mentioned in your telegram that you wanted to know everything about it. Is it a valuable antique? I went through quite a bit to get it out of Egypt!"

Given the Egyptian government's strict regulations on antiquities, it was impressive that Sem Jansen managed to transport the box. It seemed the adage "money can move the gods" held true here.

I gave a wry smile. "It's a long story. But first, I'd like to hear yours. What's your friend's name, and what language does he speak?"

Sem Jansen admitted, "His name is quite unusual, and I can never remember it." He then turned to the short man, switching to English. "What's your name? Tell this gentleman."

The short man stood stiffly, yet when addressed, he seemed to draw himself up with a sense of pride. "My name is Sopa Michibo Oig," he declared, adopting a noble demeanor. "I am the last generation chief of the Sopa tribe."

Chapter 11

The Sacrificial

Chamber in the Sura Temple

Upon hearing him introduce himself, I couldn't help but frown. Either my understanding of geography and history was too limited, or he was delusional. There was no known "Sopa" tribe in Egypt, nor did his name seem authentically Egyptian.

I kept my thoughts to myself as Sem Jansen elaborated, "He said his name means 'the eagle on Michibo Peak.' You can call him Yige. He considers you a friend and offers you this familiarity."

We continued our conversation as we walked to the car Sem Jansen had arranged. Once settled inside, I asked, "Mr. Yige, what ethnic group does your Sopa tribe belong to?"

Yige's expression turned somber, "This—I don't know. By the time I was born, only seven of us remained. By the time I was sixteen, the others had passed, leaving me the last of the Sopa tribe."

I gave a wry smile, "So you declared yourself the chief of the Sopa tribe?" Yige looked affronted, and I realized I'd blundered.

With dignity, he replied, "Sir, I am the chief of the Sopa tribe. My family has always led the Sopa."

Quickly, I apologized, "Please forgive my earlier comment."

Yige shook his head, "I don't mind. The Sopa tribe once possessed great wealth, fertile plains, and majestic mountains. Now, I am all that remains."

Despite his broken English, there was an earnestness in Yige's voice that made me believe he was sincere.

Sem Jansen leaned over and whispered, "His tribe's legends are grand tales. He claims their peak rivaled the Roman Empire."

I studied Yige closely. My skepticism wasn't just because I'd never heard of the Sopa tribe but also because I wondered how he was connected to the brass box.

My question was soon answered. After arriving at the hotel and settling in, Yige asked, "Mr. Morris, Mr. Jansen mentioned you've opened the box?"

I hesitated, "You could say that. Do you know what's inside?"

Yige shook his head, "I don't, but according to our tribal legends—"

Sem interrupted, exasperated, "Oh boy, another legend from your tribe!"

Yige persisted, "Our legends are true!"

Sem sighed, "True or not, you're the last of your tribe. Refusing to marry outside means your lineage ends with you."

Yige's face went pale, visibly shaken.

I quickly intervened, recognizing Yige's pride had been wounded. "Even if Yige were gone, the Sopa's glorious history and beautiful legends would endure."

Yige grasped my hand, his eyes filled with gratitude. "Thank you, thank you!"

Sem Jansen threw up his hands, "Great, now there are two lunatics."

I smiled bitterly at Sem Jansen, "Mad? If you knew the full truth, you might join us."

Sem Jansen, knowing I wasn't one to joke about such matters, looked concerned. "What truth?"

I shook my head, "Not yet. I must discuss some things with Yige first. You brought him to me because the brass box came from him, right?"

Sem Jansen nodded, "Yes, Yige is a peculiar case. The box seemed unremarkable except for its intricate lock."

I gestured to Sem Jansen, "Hold off on judgments about Yige. First, give me a rundown of what happened."

We conversed in our dialect to keep Yige from understanding. He simply watched us with wide, curious eyes.

Sem Jansen settled into his seat, somewhat resigned, and began to explain. "It's unclear when exactly Yige first appeared at the construction site, but since his arrival, he's claimed that the Sura Temple contains seven sacrificial chambers meant solely for the Sopa tribe. Supposedly, no one but the Sopa tribe is allowed to enter these chambers."

I listened intently. The Sura Temple, nearly 3,000 years old, is one of Egypt's most ancient temples. It had become a significant obstacle to a massive water conservancy project. Plans were initially made to relocate the temple, preserving it intact. However, the exorbitant costs led to the abandonment of this plan, sealing the temple's fate to likely be lost.

Sem Jansen continued, noting Yige's concern over the temple's destruction. "He wanted to retrieve something left by his tribe in the sacrificial chambers before it was too late."

I nodded, "So you accompanied him?"

Sem Jansen explained, "Few believed his stories, and even fewer dared to traverse the tunnels allegedly filled with ancient spells. But my curiosity and skepticism of such spells led me to join him, and that's how we found the brass box."

I patted Sem Jansen's shoulder, signaling that his part in this saga was appreciated. "You've done more than enough. You should return to work. The rest will be between Yige and me."

Sem Jansen eyed me, intrigued. "You opened the box, didn't you? What's inside? Is it like Yige said—a treasure chest with a 'transparent devil'?"

The term caught me off guard. "Transparent devil?"

Sem Jansen nodded, gesturing towards Yige. "That's what he calls it. It's a tale akin to Aladdin's lamp. Once opened, a transparent monster supposedly emerges."

Stunned, I turned my gaze to Yige. Though he couldn't follow our conversation, he seemed to grasp the subject matter from our demeanor. He murmured, "Really, this is true."

I approached him, placing a reassuring hand on his shoulder. Turning back to Sem Jansen, I said, "Legends from any culture are often beautiful stories. They deserve respect, not ridicule."

Sem Jansen chuckled, eyes twinkling with skepticism. "Do you truly believe he's the chief of the Sopa tribe?"

I nodded. "I believe it. I want to visit the secret sacrificial chambers of the ancient temple with him." Sem Jansen shook his head, recalling his own experience. "It's a dreadful place, like a vision of hell. After going there once, I have no desire to return."

Nonetheless, I was resolute. "But I must go. There is a mystery I need to solve."

Sem Jansen sighed, then offered, "Alright, I also need to visit the construction site. We can fly back together on the engineering department's small plane. It's much more convenient and spares us a bumpy ride."

I knew the "small plane" Sem Jansen referred to was likely an old model from the early World War II era. The pilots—often thrill-seeking adventurers from Europe or America—took risks flying these outdated machines for high wages, indifferent to their own safety and that of their passengers. Such planes and their pilots were notoriously unreliable.

But urgency overruled caution. Eager to reach the ancient temple, I accepted Sem Jansen's offer. He promptly called the Ministry of Water Resources to arrange our flight.

Meanwhile, I took Yige to the hotel balcony, overlooking Cairo's bustling streets. The city exuded an air of mystery; even without a specific mission, one could feel its enigmatic allure. Cairo's atmosphere was palpable, drawing one into its ancient secrets.

In a hushed tone, I asked, "Yige, has the legend of the transparent devil been part of your tribe for long?"

Yige's eyes sparkled with a peculiar light. "Do you believe it, Mr. Morris? Do you truly believe it?"

I nodded, "Yes, I believe it."

Yige's response was heartfelt, "Mr. Morris, you're the first outsider to believe in our legend. Mr. Jansen mentioned you have the box. Did you open it?"

I sighed, "Yes, and the transparent devil emerged." Yige seemed momentarily stunned, stepping back until he reached the balcony's edge. His face turned so pale I feared he might fall. I quickly grasped his arm. "Calm down. I need to know—why did you sell the brass box?"

Yige's face flushed with embarrassment. He stammered, "I learned the temple wouldn't be preserved. It's a relic of my clan. I'm the last one left. You see, I have no money, so I..."

"So you sold the box cheaply, and Mr. Jansen was the only buyer?" I interjected.

Yige lowered his head, "Yes. He paid 60 Egyptian pounds, enough for me to live on for a while."

I sighed, "Yige, do you not believe in your tribe's legends? If you truly believed a transparent demon was inside, would you sell it for 60 pounds?"

His shame was palpable. "It's not that I don't believe. I just needed money. The box was the only thing I could sell. The sacrificial rooms have many murals, but the tunnel is terrifying, so no tourists visit. Worse, no one believes me anymore. No one at all."

Tears welled in Yige's eyes.

Hearing about the murals in the sacrificial chambers reignited my interest. Though uncertain of success, I felt I'd uncovered part of the story. Visiting the seven chambers could illuminate many mysteries. The journey ahead might hold the answers to questions that had long eluded us.

Sem Jansen appeared at the balcony door, announcing, "Get ready. In 20 minutes, a plane from the Ministry of Water Resources will take us to the construction site. I've arranged everything. We'll all fly together."

I shrugged, acknowledging the lack of rest. "No rest for the weary, I guess."

Sem Jansen chuckled, "If you want to rest, you'll have to wait two days for the next flight. Why not take in Cairo for a bit?"

I quickly declined, "No, let's deal with things first. Maybe later."

Sem Jansen, respecting my focus, then asked about his brother. "How's my nerdy brother doing?"

I suppressed the urge to tell him the truth about Liam Jansen's situation. Knowing Sem Jansen's tendency to react impulsively, revealing the secret would likely lead to widespread panic. Instead, I offered a reassuring lie, "He's doing well. He and a lovely girl named Nora Lee are planning to marry."

Sem Jansen sighed wistfully, "Really? My little brother's getting ahead of me. I sometimes regret choosing a career in water conservancy—it keeps me too nomadic."

I knew he was jesting. Despite his words, Sem Jansen loved his job and the freedom it brought. We left the hotel and sped to the airport in Sem Jansen's car, arriving in a swift thirteen minutes.

At the airport, we hurried towards a grass-green twin-engine plane—an outdated model, just as I expected.

As we approached, a man who appeared to be the pilot was casually inspecting the plane. Spotting us, he called out, "Sem, you're late."

Sem Jansen replied with a grin, "Right on time. Any issues with the plane today?" The pilot, already clambering aboard, yelled back, "Just pray!"

Sem Jansen grimaced, "I'd rather pray than take the road; it's dreadful!"

I said nothing, climbing into the plane. Inside, the cabin was basic, with seats that had seen better days. Two individuals were already seated at the front—one wearing an Egyptian round hat.

The co-pilot, an American chewing gum, briefly assessed us and muttered, "Seven people," before heading to the cockpit.

The plane roared to life, shuddering as it sped down the runway and took off. Despite the plane's age, the pilot's skill was evident.

Seated next to Sem Jansen, I observed our fellow passengers. Sem Jansen pointed out, "The man in the round hat is a Ministry of Water Resources official, here to greet and host important guests. The person with him is likely significant."

I responded nonchalantly, "Is that so?"

My words must have carried, as the two in front turned to face us.

The official quickly averted his gaze, but the person beside him continued to stare.

I found myself staring back, caught off guard by his intense scrutiny.

Sem Jansen nudged me, curious, "Hey, what's up? Do you know this person?"

I didn't immediately respond to Sem Jansen's question. Instead, I leaned forward, cautiously greeting the man in front of us. "Professor Lomono, nice to meet you, truly a surprise."

I was aware that Professor Lomono was in Egypt, but encountering him on this rickety plane was unexpected. Had I known he would be aboard, I might have reconsidered my travel plans. The professor's association with Braque, the notorious "murder king," was unsettling.

Such connections marked him as a potentially dangerous individual.

With someone like Lomono on the plane, the situation felt precarious. As I spoke, I was already strategizing how best to handle this unexpected development.

Sem Jansen remained oblivious to the tension. He seemed delighted by the encounter, standing to introduce himself. "Ah, the renowned Professor Lomono! What an honor to accompany you to the construction site. My brother, Liam Jansen, speaks highly of you in his letters. He's your student."

Professor Lomono's demeanor was as unyielding as stone. His gaze briefly met mine, then Sem Jansen's, before finally fixing on Yige. Yige's smile was forced, apprehensive. Lomono approached us with his large briefcase.

He stopped before us, and my nerves heightened. Yet, Lomono ignored me, directing his attention to Yige. He spoke in a peculiar language I couldn't place, despite my extensive study of languages.

Yige's response was immediate, his face lighting up with joy. He replied in the same enigmatic tongue. The exchange left me anxious, as I was aware that Lomono's objectives in Egypt were likely aligned with mine.

The language barrier only added to my unease. I couldn't decipher their conversation, which might hold crucial information about the brass box and the secrets tied to the Sura Temple. I needed to remain vigilant, ready to adapt to whatever revelations this unexpected encounter might bring.

Chapter 12

Journey to the Desert of Death

Securing Yige's assistance could be the key to success. However, my concern was whether Yige would choose to help me or side with Professor Lomono, given their shared language and apparent connection. The possibility of Yige abandoning me was unsettling.

Despite my anxiety, I couldn't interject or decipher their conversation. After several minutes, Yige shook his head repeatedly, seemingly refusing Lomono's request. Lomono's anger was palpable as he turned to me, speaking in English. "Ash Morris, has this man promised to guide you to the seven secret shrines in the temple?"

Lomono's direct and uncompromising approach took me by surprise. I nodded, "That's correct."

His demand was blunt. "I want you to relinquish your request."

Anticipating conflict, I was taken aback by Lomono's aggressive stance. I quickly weighed my options and replied, "I see no reason to do that."

Lomono barked, "Because I intend to take him to the seven sacrificial chambers, but this 'donkey' claims he's already committed to you."

Yige interjected with indignation, "Sir, I am not a donkey. I am Sopa Michibo Oig!"

I recalled that Yige's name meant "the eagle on Michibo Peak," and it was clear he took pride in it. Lomono's insult had struck a nerve, as Yige likely faced frequent ridicule, with few recognizing him as a tribal chief.

But I treated him as a friend, and that was my advantage.

I placed a comforting hand on Yige's shoulder. "Yige, the one who calls you a donkey is the true wild donkey here!" Yige's gratitude was evident. Turning to Lomono, I asserted, "Yige is honorable. He's committed to me and won't break his word."

Lomono sneered, "Fine. If you don't want him to guide you, I can ensure he guides me."

I stood firm, "As I said, I'm not abandoning my plan to visit the sacrificial rooms."

Lomono's tone turned ominous, "You'll regret this." Before I could respond, Sem interjected, "Are you really Professor Lomono?"

Lomono shot him a glare, then faced me again. "I'm giving you one last chance. Do you agree?"

I prepared to stand my ground, uttering, "No." But as I began to rise, I caught sight of a German-made military pistol in Lomono's hand—a formidable weapon, expertly handled. I resumed my seat, feeling Sem's tense grip on my hand. "What's happening?" he whispered.

I replied with a bitter smile, "Isn't it clear?"

Sem's expression grew grim, and he fell silent.

The situation was stark. Lomono, a trained firearms expert, had drawn a deadly weapon. I glanced at the Egyptian official with the round hat, noting his slack posture and drooling mouth — he appeared to be in a drugged slumber. Lomono must have anticipated using force and neutralized the official beforehand.

The cockpit door remained shut, ensuring Lomono's actions would go unnoticed, allowing his identity as a prominent mathematician to remain concealed. The chilling realization that Lomono intended to eliminate both Sem and me struck hard, sending a shiver down my spine.

Sem, visibly distressed, was trembling. I pointed to the large pistol in Lomono's hand, attempting to reason with him. "That will make a lot of noise. Aren't you worried about alerting the pilot?"

Lomono's response was a sinister smile. "Indeed, which is why I'll avoid using it. Now, stand up!"

Despite my uncertainty about his intentions, Lomono's authoritative tone and the presence of the weapon left me little choice. I complied, rising slowly from my seat. Lomono stepped back, instructing, "Open the door!"

Shocked by his demand, I hesitated, "You—"

"Open the door!" Lomono reiterated firmly.

Reluctantly, I moved toward the door. As it swung open, the high-altitude winds surged into the cabin, nearly dragging me out. I staggered back, clinging to the seat for stability.

Glancing at Sem and Yige, I noted their ashen faces. Lomono's voice cut through the chaos, "Ash Morris, this is the final step. You and your friend, jump!"

Having anticipated this, I maintained a semblance of composure. Sem, however, was overwhelmed, exclaiming, "Jump? No!"

"Sem, be quiet," I commanded. Though he appeared ready to protest further, he sank back into his seat. I turned to Lomono, stating, "Professor, we're over the desert. Jumping means certain death."

"Precisely," Lomono replied coldly. "That's my intention."

I countered, "Professor, I'd prefer to face your gun than certain death in the desert."

Lomono's grip tightened on the pistol. "Do you doubt I'd shoot?"

"I'm sure you would," I acknowledged, "but the gunshot would alert the pilot. Imagine the scandal—a world-renowned mathematician caught in such a predicament."

My words seemed to penetrate Lomono's icy resolve, leaving him momentarily contemplative.

Pressing my advantage, I proposed, "I'll jump with my friend." Sem interjected, "Ash, have you lost your mind?" I continued, "But you'll allow us to use parachutes."

I had noted earlier that the cabin contained seven parachutes. Lomono eyed them skeptically, "That means you might live."

Pointing out the window, I argued, "We're above a desert. With no water or food, our survival odds are slim—around 50%."

Lomono's expression remained grim. "Yet, there's still a chance you'll survive."

I spread my hands diplomatically. "Yes, this is a negotiation. A 50% survival chance in exchange for avoiding gunfire. It's a fair deal. Even if we make it, you've already secured what you wanted."

Lomono considered my words, weighing the risks against the potential fallout of a gunshot. It was a tense standoff, but I hoped logic would prevail, allowing us a slender chance at survival amid the vast desert expanse.

Lomono seemed convinced by my words. By the time we were struggling out of the desert, he might have already gotten what he wanted. A grim smile appeared on his face, one that made people's hair stand on end. "Alright," he commanded, his voice as sharp as the desert's edge, "you two, parachute down."

Sem's voice trembled with defiance. "No, Ash, we won't survive this."

I met his gaze, my voice steady, unwavering. "If we don't jump, he'll pull the trigger."

"But if he shoots," Sem argued, "the pilot will be alerted."

I shook my head, urgency creeping into my tone. "He'll kill the pilot and take control himself. A few more lives mean nothing to him."

Sem's skepticism was palpable. "How do you know he can fly a plane?"

I sighed, a weighty exhalation of truth. "You don't know the kind of man he is. To someone like him, piloting a plane is as simple as driving a car. I wouldn't be surprised if he could steer a submarine."

Sem's eyes flickered to the shifting sands below, his face blanching to a ghostly hue. I tossed him a parachute, commanding, "Take your chances. Quickly!"

As I strapped on my own parachute, I turned to Yige, my voice laced with a mix of hope and desperation. "Yige, my friend, remember this: your integrity is the hallmark of a true leader. I pray we meet again."

Emotion rippled across Yige's face, tears brimming in his eyes. I hoped my words would sway him, preventing Lomono from discovering the temple's secret sacrificial chamber. Sem had been there once before, and if we could escape into the desert, we might still reach the treasure first.

Yige's reaction suggested my words had struck a chord. But whether he would resist Lomono's threats? Only the heavens could say.

Sem was already securing his parachute when Lomono's voice cut through the tension. "Jump!"

Panic flared in Sem's eyes as he turned toward me. My response was cold, calculated. "Focus on your parachute lever. Pull it once you see mine deploy."

He nodded, a grim smile on his lips. I could feel Lomono's pistol trained on my back, a constant reminder of our peril. With a swift motion, I pushed Sem out of the plane, following him into the void.

The door slammed shut behind us with a resounding "bang." Amidst the chaos, a strange laughter bubbled within me. Was it madness, or the satisfaction of outwitting Lomono? Perhaps both.

As Sem and I plummeted earthward, I bet the cockpit crew couldn't have missed our dramatic exit. Surely, they would investigate, uncovering the unconscious Egyptian official and Lomono, pistol in hand, a monstrous figure of menace.

Though the pilot might comply under duress, once on the ground, Lomono would face the aftermath—a thought that served as my first trump card.

My second trump card was Yige. Would he lead Lomono, who had demeaned him, to the temple's secrets? I doubted it.

Clutching these hopes, I knew they meant nothing if I didn't survive. I banished all thoughts save one: the ground rushing up to meet me. At 600 feet, then 500, and finally 400, I yanked the parachute's cord. Relief surged through me as the canopy unfurled, slowing my descent and sealing my fate with the desert below.

Immediately, I saw Sem's parachute blossom like a flower in the morning sky. Above us, the plane wobbled dangerously before leveling out, proving my suspicions right. The pilot had realized Lomono's treachery but was coerced by the cold threat of a German-made pistol.

Once the parachute opened, the dizziness vanished, replaced by a serene sense of flight. The stillness of the day gifted us the perfect descent, as if we were gliding through the clouds themselves.

Minutes later, Sem and I landed on the vast desert canvas, rolling across the sand before freeing ourselves from the parachute straps. Sem approached, despair etched on his face. "We could be hundreds of miles from the desert's edge!"

I shook my head, trying to inject hope into his weary eyes. "Don't lose heart. As long as we avoid the scorpions' sting, we stand a chance of reaching your workplace."

"I need to get back to Cairo first!" Sem exclaimed.

His plea met my stern gaze. "Ah, Cairo. Where a grand hotel awaits, with its soft beds, whiskey on ice, soothing music, and luxurious baths, right?"

Sem nodded eagerly. "Precisely."

My grip tightened on his shoulders. "Forget those comforts, Sem. If you dwell on them, you'll lose the strength to escape the desert, leaving nothing but bones behind."

My words widened his eyes with shock. I released him, drawing a rough map in the sand. "Cairo to the construction site is about 900 kilometers. We've flown 600. Heading back means more distance. Forward, it's 300 kilometers to the site."

Sem groaned, "Three hundred kilometers!"

I offered a wry smile. "Perhaps less than 300 miles."

In the unforgiving embrace of the desert, a mile is not just a measure of distance but a testament to perseverance and survival. Two hundred miles can break a spirit in ways one hundred ninety-nine and a half cannot. That last half mile is a cruel mirage, convincing the weary traveler they're lost in the heart of the desert, sapping their will until they succumb at its very edge. Those who have traversed these sands know this truth all too well.

Yet I had no time to explain this to Sem. Words were a luxury we couldn't afford; in the coming days, we might not even find a drop of water. We moved, step by determined step, towards the construction site—and the temple that held my unspoken quest.

Sem, at first, filled the silence with complaints and questions about Professor Lomono. I offered him no answers, only a terse command to keep quiet. The desert was no place for idle chatter.

As the sun dipped below the horizon, darkness cloaked the land, and I lost track of the miles we'd walked. All I knew was that if we were heading in the right direction and kept pressing on, we would reach the construction site the day after next.

Along the way, hope lingered like a distant star: a plane might spot us, a convoy might cross our path, or perhaps an Arab on camelback might offer salvation. And then there was the elusive promise of an oasis, a haven in this barren expanse.

Sem's desire to rest grew with each step, but I urged him forward, pushing through the night until exhaustion forced us to halt. The desert's nocturnal chill seeped into our bones, and without fire, Sem's pallor deepened, his vitality nearly extinguished.

We sat in the oppressive silence, surrounded by the vast emptiness of the desert night, and waited for the dawn. The darkness felt eternal, yet the promise of a new day lingered on the horizon, a whisper of hope in this desolate expanse.

The next morning, the sun rose from the east, spreading its warmth like a comforting blanket over the barren landscape. It revived us slightly, infusing a bit of life into our weary bodies. Sem stirred and sat up, his movements tentative and slow.

I gazed at the horizon, aware that the sun, now a source of solace, would soon transform into a merciless furnace. My lips, cracked and parched beyond measure, twisted into a bitter smile. "Let's go," I croaked.

After a night and half a day of silence, my voice felt foreign, and as I spoke, my upper lip split open, sending a trickle of blood into my mouth. I licked it instinctively, the metallic taste mingling with the sting of the wound.

Sem pointed at me and managed to say, "Look at you!" before his own lips followed suit, staining his mouth with blood.

I quickly gestured for him to follow and took his arm, leading us forward. The day had barely begun, and already

Sem was stumbling, his strength waning with each step. As the sun climbed higher, I found myself half-dragging him.

Ignoring the searing pain in my lips, I shouted, "Sem, you have to find your strength. Look, there's smoke ahead; there might be a car!"

Each time I offered this glimmer of hope, Sem would look at me, his eyes clouded with despair. I sighed inwardly. To think that less than a day and a night in the desert could break a man. It was a testament to the fragility of humanity. As we advanced in technology and material comforts, we grew weaker, more reliant on conveniences that had dulled our survival instincts.

Sem, a man of intellect and expertise, was now reduced to fragility. In a world where even a short distance required the aid of transportation, here he was, struggling for his life, as fragile as glass.

My words of encouragement seemed to fall on deaf ears, and his responses grew increasingly muted. Anxiety gnawed at me. I couldn't let Sem perish here—not just because he was my only link to the temple's secrets but because his death would weigh heavily on my conscience. After all, it was my actions that had led us here.

I stopped and hoisted Sem onto my back, his body limp and lifeless. The added weight made each step a trial, but I pressed on, clinging to the hope of a miracle. Yet, hope felt like the cruelest of deceptions, painting illusions of salvation without delivering.

Time seemed to stretch endlessly under the sun's relentless glare. I glanced at Sem on my shoulder, his eyes fluttering between open and closed, his expression caught in a strange, indescribable flux.

I inhaled the dry, scorching air, feeling as if I had swallowed fire. I paused, despite my curses against hope, and looked to the sky, praying for rain.

Instead, I spotted a shadow overhead—not a vulture but something mechanical, accompanied by the unmistakable sound of an engine.

A helicopter!

Disbelief turned to elation as the helicopter drew closer. I patted Sem, urging him to look up. As the chopper hovered above us, a faint smile crept onto his lips, a flicker of life returning at the prospect of rescue.

"Helicopter!" Sem croaked, his voice barely a whisper, as he began to struggle in a sudden surge of energy. His unexpected movement caused both of us to tumble onto the sand.

The helicopter circled above us, its descent slow and deliberate. My heart leaped at the sight of this potential salvation, but caution tethered my hope. The helicopter bore no markings, no insignia—a silent enigma against the sky.

Despite the instinct to rejoice, I remained wary. An unmarked aircraft was a puzzle, one that could spell danger as easily as rescue.

"Stay quiet," I whispered to Sem, my voice firm. "That helicopter might not be here to save us."

Yet my words were redundant. Sem, drained of strength, could do little more than breathe.

We lay still, our bodies painted in the golden hues of the swirling sandstorm created by the helicopter's descent. Fifteen meters away, the machine finally touched down. I held Sem in place, suppressing his urge to rise. If they intended to help, they'd find us regardless; if not, invisibility was our ally.

Through squinted eyes, I watched as the helicopter's door opened. Two figures emerged—a pilot and a gaunt, sharp-featured Arab, the latter wielding a pistol.

Relief flooded through me for having chosen caution over haste.

Sem, sensing the shift in the atmosphere, wisely stilled his movements beside me. We both lay silent, our breaths shallow.

The Arab approached, each step measured, until he paused mere feet from us. The ominous click of a safety being disengaged echoed in the desert air.

In that heartbeat, time stretched, and I felt my blood turn to ice.

If the Arab decided to fire, we were defenseless. Yet, if he drew closer, I was prepared to launch myself at him, a desperate bid for survival.

But instead of shooting, he nudged me with his foot, then turned back to the helicopter. "He's dead. The boss can rest assured," he called out, his voice carrying over the hum of the idling rotors.

In a swift, decisive move, I grabbed the Arab's calf and yanked him back, interrupting his advance. As he toppled backward, I rose, seizing the opportunity to snatch his pistol from his grasp.

With the Arab subdued beneath my knee, his face buried in the yellow sand, I turned my attention to the helicopter. My aim was true as I fired at the pilot, the gunshot ringing out in the desert silence. Metal clanged as the pilot's weapon slipped from his grasp, his hand now slick with blood.

The pilot, a white man, hesitated at the threshold of the helicopter, his hands raised in surrender. Blood dripped from his injured hand as he finally stepped down, conceding to my authority. The Arab, defiant despite his position, glared at me with burning eyes.

Seizing the moment, I pulled Sem to his feet and brandished the gun, my voice commanding, "Get down, get down!"

The pilot, a white man, hesitated before reluctantly stepping out of the helicopter. The Arab, his eyes burning with malice, stood defiantly.

In that moment, the odds tipped in our favor. The prospect of survival momentarily dulled our thirst. I fixed them both with a steely gaze. "Your boss must be Lomono," I taunted.

The Arab, fluent in English, snapped back, "I don't know what you're talking about!"

I chuckled darkly. "You don't need to understand me. Just understand this: the desert is now your adversary."

The pilot, desperation tinged with fear, protested, "You can't leave us here. I'm injured!" My lips curled into a sneer. "Call your boss for help."

He yelled, "How are we supposed to do that? Should I yell for him?"

I offered a lifeline, "Tell me who sent you. Maybe I'll consider helping."

The pilot hesitated, on the verge of revealing their orders, when the Arab turned and delivered a punishing blow to his jaw. The ruby ring on his middle finger gleamed malevolently, leaving a bloody streak on the pilot's cheek.

The sight of that blood-red ring ignited something within me. Without a second thought, I squeezed the trigger, and the bullet found its target in the Arab's right leg. He crumpled to the ground with a howl of pain, the sand beneath him darkening with blood.

Chapter 13

A Corridor Full of Spells

The Arab groaned, collapsing onto the sand. Without wasting a second, I lunged toward the white man sprawled nearby, gripping him by the shoulders. "Tell me," I demanded, my voice edged with urgency, "who sent you here? Whose side is Lomono on?"

His mouth quivered, eyes bulging as he struggled to form words. A guttural noise escaped his lips, but it was meaningless. Suddenly, his eyes widened grotesquely, and he slumped lifelessly—poisoned.

The realization struck me as I noticed the eerie crimson of the Arab's ring—a lethal weapon disguised as jewelry. I let the white man's body fall back into the desert, turning my gaze to the Arab.

He sneered, his voice dripping with mockery. "He can't answer your questions, sir!"

Rage flared within me. "No, he can't," I retorted, "but you can."

The Arab's laughter echoed strangely, "Neither can I!"

Before I could react, he ran the ring across his wrist, leaving a crimson streak. His eyes bulged, mirroring the white man's fate, and within thirty seconds, he too was dead, his face twisted in agony.

Two lives snuffed out in under three minutes. Sem stood paralyzed, repeatedly asking, "Who are they? Who are they?"

"Spies," I replied curtly, the word hanging in the air.

I searched their bodies but found no documents—nothing to reveal their true identities. Their deaths, seemingly due to the desert's venomous scorpions, would arouse no suspicion.

After a tense silence, I signaled to Sem. "Let's go."

We boarded the helicopter, my mind racing with unanswered questions. The aircraft, devoid of identifying marks or clues, could belong to anyone—any faction.

I checked the fuel gauge—plenty to get us out of here. "Buckle up," I instructed Sem, firing up the engine. The rotors spun, kicking up a storm of sand that concealed the bodies as we lifted off.

Our destination: the construction site. An hour later, the sight of a massive convoy transporting materials greeted us. Temporary structures offered a haven for the travelers below.

I landed the helicopter near one such building, and we dashed inside a makeshift bar. The cold beer we found there tasted like ambrosia, each sip reviving us.

In fifteen minutes, my strength returned. Sem had secured a small jeep from the transport captain, a man he knew well. The captain had agreed readily, recognizing Sem.

We gathered supplies, and with renewed determination, set off in the jeep.

As dusk settled over the horizon, Sem and I drove out of the desert, greeted by the welcoming sight of green grass. The vibrant hue, often overlooked, now seemed like a soothing balm to our parched souls.

With each mile, the barren landscape transformed into fertile land, and as the sky darkened, the silhouette of the grand temple loomed ahead. Even from a distance, the temple's majesty was undeniable, its towering stone pillars standing like sentinels in the twilight.

The temple lay near the bustling construction site, where the hum of machinery filled the air and lights flickered against the encroaching night. The ambitious project aimed to create a vast artificial lake, transforming the desert into arable land. Yet, beneath its promise lay a poignant truth: this ancient temple, with its millennia of history, would soon be submerged under forty meters of water.

Sem steered the jeep to a halt at the temple's base. By now, the guides and tourists had long departed, leaving the temple shrouded in eerie silence. I leaped from the vehicle and ascended the stone steps, my eyes tracing the fifty stone pillars that lined the entrance. The temple's five doors yawned like the gaping maws of ancient beasts, their depths cloaked in shadow and mystery.

Sem joined me, a powerful flashlight in hand. "Let's explore together," he suggested.

Taking the flashlight, I replied, "I need to do this alone. Just tell me where to find the seven secret sacrificial chambers of the Sopa tribe."

He hesitated, "After everything we've been through, why leave me out now?"

I smiled, placing a reassuring hand on his shoulder. "Return to the construction site. If I'm not back by dawn, alert the authorities. This place, these secrets — they're tangled with international intrigue. I can't risk pulling you into this."

Hurt flickered across his face, but he nodded reluctantly. As he turned to leave, I prompted, "Wait! How do I find the chambers?"

With a sigh, Sem detailed the path: "Enter through the main hall, take the left corridor, and follow the wall. When you see the red stones, turn—there's a courtyard with two wells. Descend the one without a well frame. At the bottom, a long corridor leads to the chambers."

His directions were precise, and I committed them to memory. Just as I was about to proceed, he called out again, "Be careful in the corridor. Yige warned not to look back or around, or you'll face untold disasters."

I chuckled, waving off his concerns, watching as he drove back to the construction site. Then, turning to the temple, I faced the ancient edifice alone.

The night air was thick with anticipation. The temple's darkened corridors awaited, promising secrets guarded by curses as old as time itself. With Sem gone, it was just me and the mysteries that lay within.

A chill settled over me as I ventured deeper into the temple, pondering the ancient curses that supposedly haunted its corridors. It seemed absurd for a modern person to fear such spells, yet the oppressive atmosphere pressed down on my spirit, making it hard to dismiss the possibility of their power.

As I crossed the threshold of the ancient temple, the sounds from the construction site faded away, leaving an eerie silence that enveloped me completely. The quiet was so profound, it was as if the world outside had ceased to exist. The architects of ancient Egypt, unmatched in their skill, had crafted a sanctuary that absorbed sound, creating an unsettling stillness.

I flicked on the flashlight, casting its beam across the empty expanse. The temple had been stripped bare—only the towering stone pillars remained, standing like silent sentinels. Even the stone slabs underfoot had been removed. As I walked, I tried deliberately to make noise, but the peculiar acoustics swallowed my footsteps, leaving me in a soundless void.

A sudden thought struck me: How would I know if someone were following me? I spun around, the flashlight's beam slicing through the darkness, but saw nothing.

The air was thick with a sense of foreboding, and the ancient stone walls seemed to close in around me, echoing the silent warnings of the past.

I knew that Lomono, having sent a helicopter, would be determined to track us down. The likelihood of him being here in the temple loomed large in my mind. He could be anywhere—in the shadows, behind the pillars, or even lurking just out of sight. The thought was unsettling.

Clicking off the flashlight, I stood in the oppressive darkness, allowing my eyes and ears to adjust. The quiet was absolute, as if the temple itself held its breath, waiting. I strained to detect any sound, any hint of movement that might betray another's presence, but the only noise was the distant, muffled thud of my own heartbeat.

Emerging from the main hall, I found myself at a crossroads, three corridors stretching into the shadows before me. Trusting Sem's guidance, I veered into the leftmost passage.

Barely a few steps in, a sharp metallic clang resonated from the middle corridor. The temple's unique architecture absorbed sound in an uncanny way, rendering this noise both muted and mysterious. For it to reach my ears, it must have been significant in volume, a realization that made me instinctively hug the stone wall for cover.

Silence reclaimed the temple, the metallic echo fading into nothingness. I stood motionless for five tension-filled minutes, debating whether to investigate. Prudence prevailed; if antiquities thieves were at work, I had no desire to cross their path.

With caution, I slipped the flashlight into my pocket, allowing only a sliver of light to guide me forward, minimizing the risk of revealing my presence. Seven or eight yards deeper into the temple, another fork appeared. There, among the uniformity of gray stones, a single reddish-brown stone stood out.

Curious, I raised the beam, discovering two cryptic symbols etched into its surface. The ravages of time had worn them to near illegibility, their meanings lost to all but the most knowledgeable scholars.

I turned the corner, pressing onward into the unknown.

The atmosphere was otherworldly, as if I were traversing the boundary between life and death. Death, that final mystery, is a journey with no return. In that moment, shrouded in darkness, I felt as though I glimpsed its enigmatic realm—a void where the living could only imagine its secrets.

In that moment, as I pressed forward, the concept of death became more than abstract—a tangible presence that enveloped me. It was dark and silent, a vast emptiness where the world seemed to vanish, leaving only the cold touch of stone walls as a reminder of reality. I moved on, the flashlight's beam cutting through the oppressive darkness, revealing more forks in the road. Each time, an ochre-red stone marked the path, inscribed with those enigmatic symbols, clearer now as fewer had tread this path.

These symbols were undoubtedly hieroglyphs, cryptic messages from the past. Only the most erudite scholars could hope to decipher their meaning, lost to ordinary eyes.

The temple itself was an architectural marvel, constructed from massive square stones. These red stones were integral, not afterthoughts, suggesting that this intricate design was conceived with them in mind. It struck me then: the temple's very purpose might be to conceal the fabled seven secret sacrificial chambers.

But who were the Sopa people, and why had the Egyptians erected such an imposing structure solely to hide these chambers? These questions swirled in my mind, pushing back the oppressive weight of the temple's silence and the haunting specter of death.

The passage twisted and turned endlessly, a labyrinth that seemed to stretch on forever. Yet, after what felt like an eternity, a glimmer of light beckoned me forward. I emerged into a square courtyard, enclosed on three sides by towering stone walls devoid of any windows. Only the side I had entered from held an iron door, ajar, untouched by time.

The door itself was adorned with intricate patterns, unmistakably a relic of great antiquity and value. Perhaps it had remained because few had ventured this far, sparing it from the fate of the temple's other treasures.

Stepping out of the iron gate, I paused to glance back. The moonlight revealed the relief on the door—a glowing stone encircled by an array of human and animal skeletons—the same motif etched into the brass box. This was unmistakably the right place.

The courtyard, modest in size, housed two wells side by side. One, with a crooked frame, leaned precariously; the other stood bare, without any frame. Ignoring the first, I approached the frameless well, flicking on my flashlight to peer into its depths.

The light revealed only a series of stone ledges along the well's wall, seemingly designed for descent. The well was deep, its bottom hidden beyond the reach of even my powerful flashlight.

I lingered at the edge, contemplating the descent into darkness and the corridor rumored to be laden with ancient spells. A shiver of apprehension coursed through me.

Taking a deep breath, I banished my fears and swung my legs over the edge. As I descended, a peculiar buzzing filled my ears, akin to the hum within a sealed bottle—a testament to the well's depth and airtight nature.

Carefully, I navigated the stone footholds, noting with some relief that they were crafted for human passage. The descent, though daunting, was manageable.

I kept count of my steps, measuring the distance as I delved deeper into the earth. At roughly ten yards down, I paused, intending to illuminate my surroundings with the flashlight.

But then—a metallic clatter echoed from above, distinct even through the persistent buzz in my ears. The deeper I ventured, the louder the sound became, akin to being trapped in a room with malfunctioning air conditioners. Despite its distortion, the noise bore an unmistakable human origin.

I extinguished the flashlight, pressing myself against the well's wall, remaining utterly still. The darkness embraced me, my heart pounding as I waited, acutely aware that I was not alone in this ancient place.

I looked upwards, straining to pierce the darkness above, but saw nothing. I remained still, listening intently for the sound to return, hoping to discern its origin.

Within less than a minute, the noise came again—a chilling combination of metal clashing and a shrill, piercing scream that sent shivers down my spine. Though it lasted only a fraction of a second, the scream left an unsettling impression that lingered long after, gnawing at my nerves.

It was undeniably human, yet so unnaturally terrifying that it seemed beyond mortal capability. In my mind, I rationalized it as a ghostly wail, a feeble attempt to mask the dread that crept over me.

Silence reclaimed the air, and despite my heightened senses, no further sounds emerged. I hesitated, caught between the urge to ascend and investigate or to press on into the depths below.

Ultimately, resolve steeled my nerves, and I resumed my descent.

The flashlight illuminated the well's base, revealing it to be unexpectedly clean. A door stood ajar, leading into a tunnel. I quickly reached the bottom and approached the door.

A cold draft seeped through the door's gap, chilling me to the bone. With a firm push, the door swung open, and I advanced cautiously, flashlight in hand.

The tunnel stretched ahead, about twenty meters long, terminating in another door. I switched off the flashlight, moving forward deliberately, resisting the temptation to glance back or sideways, driven by an unspoken fear of what might be lurking.

Reaching the door, I pushed it open and stepped inside, enveloped by impenetrable darkness. I realized I had entered one of the fabled seven secret sacrificial chambers.

Gently, I closed the door, intending to leave it as I found it. Yet the door clicked shut with an unexpected finality, as an iron hook latched it in place. I turned on my flashlight, confirming the hook's presence. It was a minor concern—I could easily unhook it when the time came to leave.

Turning my attention back to the room, I swept the flashlight across its barren stone walls. There was only one other door leading to an adjacent chamber. Aside from this, the room was empty, save for a statue carved into the left wall—a god with a bull's head and human body, its visage fearsome and grotesque, mirroring the relief I had seen on the brass box.

After examining the first chamber and finding nothing noteworthy, I proceeded to the second stone chamber, pushing open its heavy door. Like the first, it was barren, its left wall adorned with a carved deity — this time, a human body with a serpent's head.

Disappointment gnawed at me. If all the chambers were like this, my journey here would have been for naught. I chastised myself for not pressing Sem for more details. Had I known, I might have reconsidered venturing into this eerie temple, especially given its ominous history—a relic from here had once caused bizarre phenomena, rendering people transparent or invisible.

Undeterred, I moved forward through the sequential chambers. The third, fourth, fifth, and sixth were identical in their stark emptiness, each distinguished only by the statues on their walls. Each statue shared the human body, but their heads were those of various beasts, each more unsettling than the last.

In the sixth chamber, the statue's head was something I couldn't place — a monstrous visage that defied any creature I knew, its form utterly terrifying. Driven by curiosity, I stepped closer, directing my flashlight to examine it more closely.

As the beam crossed the statue's features, the eyes of this strange, tiger-like monster suddenly glimmered with an eerie light.

Chapter 14

Bloodshed in the Sacrifice Chamber

The jolt of fear made me step back, nearly dropping my flashlight. My nerves were frayed, and in that tense moment, the irrational thought crossed my mind: Had I somehow angered the statue, triggering an ancient curse?

I stood there, heart pounding, waiting for something—anything—to happen. But the statue remained inert, its eyes dark. Gathering my courage, I approached once more, flashlight steady, and illuminated the statue's face again.

This time, I was braced for whatever might come. The eyes glinted under the flashlight's beam, dazzling yet lifeless. Curiosity piqued, I moved closer, examining them with newfound clarity. I gasped, my breath catching in my throat.

Could it be true? The statue's eyes were not mere carvings but roughly hewn diamonds, each as large as an egg. Their size rivaled even the famed diamond on the British crown jewels.

Years of lacquer had dulled their brilliance, but time had worn it away in places, allowing the flashlight to reveal their hidden splendor.

I reached out, attempting to pry one loose, but they were set deep, immovable. Recalling the other statues, I realized their eyes also protruded. Could they, too, be diamonds of similar magnitude?

The value of these twelve massive diamonds was beyond imagination. It seemed unlikely Yige knew of this secret; if he did, he would need only one "eye" to live in unimaginable luxury, never needing to sell the brass box to Sem for a mere sixty Egyptian pounds.

Reluctantly, I left the diamonds untouched, driven by a greater purpose. I turned my attention to the seventh stone chamber.

The door resisted, requiring considerable effort to budge. As it finally swung open, the familiar metallic clanging rang out again.

This was the third time I'd heard it since entering the temple. This time, the sound was distinct—metal striking metal, as if someone were hammering away with intent.

A sudden realization struck me. I recalled the door to the first chamber, which I'd inadvertently latched. Whoever was trying to enter would find it difficult and time-consuming to open from the outside.

I was certain now that someone had descended to the well's depths. Their goal was not the oppressive darkness, but the seven stone chambers themselves.

My pulse quickened. Whoever they were, they were closing in, and I was not alone in this ancient, secret-laden place.

I wasn't sure who the intruder was—it might have been Professor Lomono, but I'd managed to stay one step ahead. Deciding to ignore the noise and focus on the task at hand, I moved into the seventh stone chamber, pressing my back against the door to close it quietly.

Switching on the flashlight, I focused its beam on the door, noticing an iron hook similar to the others. I quickly latched it, securing the door before turning to survey the chamber.

This chamber was unlike the others. Dominating the space was a stone altar, upon which rested seven masks. Each mask was disturbingly lifelike, complete with hair and painted in a reddish-brown hue, unmistakably reminiscent of Native American features. The mask in the center bore a striking resemblance to Yige, both in spirit and form.

In front of the altar stood a solitary stone pillar, its surface bare. I surmised it might once have displayed the brass box.

Instead of statues, the walls were covered with hieroglyphs. Though I couldn't decipher them, I was certain they held the key to unraveling the mysteries of the chamber. Determined to capture their essence, I pulled out a small notebook and began painstakingly copying the cryptic symbols.

The task proved laborious, and after half an hour, I had managed only a partial transcription. Just then, the sound of approaching footsteps echoed ominously through the corridor.

I froze, pressing my ear to the door. The footsteps halted briefly in the sixth chamber before approaching the door separating us.

With the intruder mere inches away, I backed up, positioning myself behind the door. When it rattled against the hook, I knew it wouldn't hold against a determined effort.

Quickly, I switched off the flashlight and stowed my notebook. The door hook wouldn't delay a determined adversary for long, and I needed a plan.

The door shook persistently, and soon, a barrage of gunfire erupted, the muzzle flashes illuminating the chamber. With a crash, the door was forced open.

Holding my breath, I remained hidden behind the door. I heard someone stride into the room, dragging something heavy.

Edging into position, I peered into the chamber just as the intruder illuminated it with a flashlight. The figure was unmistakably Professor Lomono. In that moment, I understood the origin of the harrowing scream I had heard earlier.

Lomono's left hand gripped Yige, whose face was a ruin of torn flesh, evidence of brutal torture. Yige's eyes were barely open, a testament to his suffering.

Lomono's light swung around, and I quickly retreated. He seemed unaware of my presence, his focus on the seven masks.

Recognizing the opportunity, I sprang from my hiding place, leaping forward with the precision of a predator. My palm struck the back of Lomono's head with force and precision, catching him off guard. He crumpled to the ground with a groan, rolling away from the altar.

Ensuring he was unconscious, I turned my attention to Yige. His eyes fluttered open, and he struggled to speak, "Mr. Morris, it's you. Let me guide you and reveal the origins of these seven sacrificial chambers."

His words, though faint, were filled with promise. I had stumbled upon a saga woven through time, and now, standing in this sacred chamber, the path to understanding lay before me.

Of course, I was eager to learn the origins of these seven sacrificial chambers, yet how could I press Yige, whose lips were torn and whose every word brought fresh pain? His bloodied state made it impossible for him to recount the tale.

Gently, I cradled his head on my knees, whispering, "Yige, you're hurt. Save your strength; I'll try to help you." But Yige shook his head, his voice barely a whisper, "I...I am ok...the wild donkey, he...he struck me...I..."

His face twisted into a mask of helplessness, and a thought struck me. "Yige, do you know what those words on the stone mean?"

He shook his head weakly, "These are the ancient words of our...tribe...I...don't understand them."

Determined to get Yige to safety, I helped him to his feet. "If you don't know, that's okay. Let's get out of here..."

My plan was to escort him out of these ominous chambers and return to deal with Lomono. But I made a grave error, one that haunts me to this day.

I had assumed my strike rendered Lomono insensate for longer than it did. But his resilience was formidable. As I supported Yige and took a step, Lomono's voice cut through the silence.

"Ash Morris, raise your hands!" His voice was dry, yet commanding.

A cold wave washed over me as I recalled the gunfire when he breached the door. I had foolishly overlooked retrieving his weapon after incapacitating him—and now he was armed behind me.

Faced with no alternative, I raised my hands, inadvertently letting Yige slip from my grasp. He staggered, and before I could stabilize him, tragedy struck.

Gunshots exploded behind me, and Yige's body jerked violently, propelled forward by the force of the bullets. He crumpled just outside the door, lifeless. I squeezed my eyes shut, unable to bear the sight of his ravaged form.

I braced for my own end.

Yet, Lomono held his fire. As the echoes faded, his grim voice followed, "Did you see that?"

I remained silent. Of course, I had seen it. An innocent life extinguished in a moment of brutality. If the Sopa people ever existed, their last descendant had perished in this ancient chamber.

The weight of Yige's loss hung heavy, and I knew that his death had only deepened the mysteries surrounding these chambers—a saga I was now irrevocably entangled in.

Lomono's laughter was unsettling, a strange, mocking sound. "Ash Morris, what have you found?" he taunted.

I steadied myself, trying to project calm. "Nothing much," I replied, "just copying some hieroglyphics from the stone tablet."

"Really?" Lomono's skepticism was palpable.

I forced a nonchalant shrug, though the tension in my muscles must have made it look awkward. "Go ahead, search me. You've got the upper hand here."

His response was a chilling series of sneers. I heard his footsteps as he moved around the chamber, no doubt scrutinizing every detail while keeping his gun trained on me.

The question nagged at me: why hadn't he already pulled the trigger? If he hadn't done so immediately, did that mean I still had a sliver of a chance?

Despite the stiffness in my limbs, my mind raced. Yet, no clear escape plan materialized in the oppressive atmosphere.

After what felt like an eternity, Lomono broke the silence. "Mr. Morris, I can't believe you think you still have a chance to beat us."

His use of "us" puzzled me. "Unless your bullet pierces my heart right now, the word 'failure' isn't in my vocabulary."

I heard him approaching, felt his hand on my shoulder. Instinct screamed at me to grab him, but he was quick, retreating before I could act. "Your spirit is admirable," he mused. "Join us."

His offer caught me off guard. This was why I was still breathing—the possibility of recruitment. Buying time, I asked, "Who exactly are you?"

Lomono chuckled. "Braque and I. Together, with you, we'd be an unstoppable trio."

I had suspected Braque, the infamous assassin, operated independently of any global espionage network, his elusiveness a constant thorn for international security agencies. Lomono and Braque were indeed formidable.

I replied coolly, "You must think highly of me. Yet, your friend Braque has threatened my life."

"On the contrary," Lomono assured, "he sees your potential and hopes you'll join us."

I needed to play along, searching for any leverage. "And what's in it for me?"

Lomono laughed, "Managing Braque's operations nets us over six million pounds annually, tax-free. We're stretched thin, turning down lucrative opportunities. With you, our profits could skyrocket."

I nodded slowly, "I see. So, one cold-blooded Braque isn't enough—you want a cold-blooded Ash Morris, too?"

"You could say so, you have those conditions," Lomono replied, his voice tinged with greed.

I suppressed my anger, a sudden realization dawning on me. Lomono's insatiable greed could be my advantage. I sneered, "Do you really think hundreds of thousands a year would sway me?"

He looked taken aback. "Young man, what do you mean?" he asked, a hint of confusion in his voice. "Why do you think I'm here?" I retorted.

"Is it not to find a way to reverse invisibility?" Lomono ventured, his voice cautious.

I continued my mocking tone. "Maybe there's a way to make people 'invisible and visible' at will here, but you're welcome to that pursuit. It doesn't interest me."

He pressed further, a stern edge to his voice. "What do you mean?"

I fell silent, letting the tension build.

"If you don't speak, I won't be polite," Lomono warned. I feigned a reluctant sigh. "Fine, but I want a share."

He sneered, "Why not half?"

"Half is too much," I countered swiftly. "Just 10% would be enough for me to build another pyramid."

His sudden shout startled me. "Ash, what did you find?" he exclaimed, slipping into German in his agitation.

The revelation struck me — Lomono was German, possibly Braque too. People often revert to their native language under stress.

"Why don't you take a look yourself? It's hard to describe. Check the statue's eyes," I suggested.

Lomono rushed out, barely sparing Yige's fallen form a glance. As he moved, I seized the moment, stepping forward. Yet, he quickly whirled, shouting, "Don't move, hands up!"

His flashlight swept over the statue's eyes, and the diamonds blazed brilliantly. He seemed entranced, his expression almost possessed. His own eyes mirrored the statue's, wide and unblinking. He muttered to himself, words lost in the air, his body trembling with a mix of awe and greed.

As his focus remained riveted on the diamonds, I lowered my hands, unnoticed. The urge to act surged within me, but the risk was too great. Instead, I quietly lifted Yige's body, mustering all my strength before hurling it toward Lomono.

Though distracted, Lomono's instincts were razor-sharp, and he reacted with astonishing speed.

As Yige's body hurtled through the air, Lomono instinctively turned, firing his pistol in a blaze of sparks. I had already hit the ground, and the bullets likely thudded into Yige's lifeless form. The weight of Yige's body crashed into Lomono, and in the chaos, his flashlight shattered against the stone wall, plunging the chamber into total darkness.

In that instant, darkness became an ally, stripping Lomono of his clear advantage. Silence enveloped us both, an oppressive blanket that neither dared disturb.

Though Lomono's pistol was a threat, the pitch-black surroundings leveled the playing field. Neither of us moved, each waiting for the other to make a revealing mistake. I remained silent, my breath shallow, clutching a small knife, ready to strike if Lomono betrayed his position.

But he revealed nothing. The room was so silent that even the smallest noise would have echoed like a thunderclap. Listening intently was futile; the quiet was absolute. It was a battle of endurance, a test of who would falter first.

I lay prone, unmoving, my senses heightened. Lomono could be anywhere—perhaps mere feet away—but without sound or sight, distance was unknowable.

Time stretched, an endless void. Then, a subtle shift in the air—a movement? It was a feeling, an intuition that prickled at my forehead, that sixth sense that alerts you to an unseen presence. It was like the sensation of a finger approaching your face when your eyes are closed, a faint itch foretelling proximity.

My mind raced to identify the intruder. It couldn't be Lomono; he would have been stealthy, but this presence was different, more primal. Nor could it be a giant, whose approach would be perceptible in other ways.

What creature thrives in such darkness, moving with silent grace? The answer struck me like a bolt: a snake.

Panic surged through me, and I felt the heat rising in my body, a dangerous signal to the approaching serpent. I knew that staying calm was crucial, for snakes are attuned to warmth and motion. Yet, despite my awareness, fear gripped me, my body tensing involuntarily.

The proximity of the snake was almost palpable, and I struggled to maintain composure, fully aware that the desert's venomous inhabitants could be deadly. Sweat beaded on my brow, the tingling sensation intensifying as if the snake was mere inches away.

In a moment of desperation, I acted on instinct, rolling to the side with a scream.

The decision proved fortuitous. Gunfire erupted, Lomono emptying his clip where I had just been. A spray of shattered bricks pelted me, but I was unharmed.

The flash of gunfire illuminated the chamber in brief, staccato bursts, providing a fleeting glimpse of Lomono's position. Scientists say the human eye retains an image for one fifteenth of a second, and that was all I needed. As the last shot rang out, I seized my knife, its blade gleaming momentarily in the dying light.

In that fractional moment, I launched the knife toward Lomono. A strangled shout echoed as the blade found its mark, followed by the clatter of his pistol hitting the ground.

I knew my knife had struck true, slicing into Lomono's right hand, incapacitating him before he could retaliate. I seized the moment, charging forward and slamming into his body with all my might, sending him crashing into the wall. The sickening crack of bone told me I'd used enough force to ensure he wouldn't be getting up soon.

With adrenaline coursing through me, I lunged at him again, lifting his limp form and delivering two powerful punches. I didn't stop until his body went slack, no longer resisting. Only then did I pause, lighting a small flame to assess the situation.

Quickly, I retrieved his gun and found his flashlight. A minor adjustment brought it back to life, casting light on the room — and revealing the massive cobra poised ominously nearby. The sight was terrifying, but I steadied myself and fired three decisive shots. Each bullet struck true, and the snake's body thrashed briefly before falling still.

Turning back to Lomono, I was taken aback to realize my final blows had been unnecessary. His skull had fractured in the fall, his lifeless eyes staring blankly. My punches had landed on a corpse. Despite the grim scene, I felt a somber satisfaction. Yige had been avenged.

Kneeling by Lomono's body, I searched his pockets, discovering another pistol. A shiver ran through me at the thought of how close I'd come to death if he had been able to draw it earlier. The margin between survival and peril had been razor-thin.

Securing the second gun at my waist, I rifled through his jacket, finding a thick notebook with a crocodile leather cover, clearly of importance. Inside was a letter addressed to a hotel in Cairo, meant for Lomono, penned in Braque's distinctive handwriting.

Pocketing the notebook and letter, I returned to the seventh chamber, determined to finish transcribing the mysterious hieroglyphs. The task was painstaking, consuming much of my time, and when I finally emerged from the chambers and traversed the passageway to the well's base, daylight had already broken.

I recalled my agreement with Sem: if I didn't return by dawn, he would come looking for me at the construction site. Though I hadn't fully unraveled the enigma behind the object of transparent light or discovered whether those affected by it could recover, I had gathered potential clues.

The hieroglyphs I copied might hold the answers, perhaps detailing everything I sought to learn. For now, my priority was to meet Sem and rest, reflecting on the night's harrowing events and preparing for whatever revelations lay ahead.

I climbed out of the well and made my way along the trail, exiting the temple just in time to see Sem approaching in the jeep. Ahead of him was a large truck, and I wondered briefly if he'd alerted the authorities. But as the jeep pulled up to the stone steps and Sem waved, I realized the truck carried engineers, not police.

I hurried down the steps and climbed into the jeep, feeling the weight of exhaustion. "I need a good rest," I told Sem.

As he started the engine, Sem mentioned, "The pilot was bribed. Lomono and Yige have arrived at the construction site!"

I sighed, "I know. I've seen them. They're both dead." Sem was so startled that the jeep swerved dangerously. We were lucky to be in the open wilderness—such a maneuver in the city could have been disastrous.

Once on the main road, Sem asked, "Dead? How did they die?"

I rubbed my forehead, answering, "Yige was killed by Lomono. I avenged him."

Sem sighed, "Ash, you killed a math genius!" I shook my head, correcting him, "No, I killed a dangerous criminal genius."

Sem persisted, "But he was also a math genius!"

"While he may possess a solid grasp of mathematics," I conceded, "but his expertise is not significantly beyond that of a typical university professor."

Sem argued back, "That's nonsense. Everyone knows Lomono was the most qualified for the Nobel Prize, as soon as his new work was published."

"If he's such a genius, why hasn't his work been published yet?" I retorted coldly.

"A genius mathematical work takes time. Do you think everyone can write thousands of words in an hour like you?" Sem challenged, his voice growing heated.

Feeling my own temper rising, I snapped, "Are you personally attacking me, Sem? I didn't kill Professor Lomono!"

Sem insisted, "No, I've checked. Professor Lomono was visiting Egypt. You killed him."

I shrugged, asking, "Where is Professor Lomono from, then?"

"He was Ukrainian," Sem explained. "He left Russia after 1917, lived in Germany, and went to Britain during World War II. After the war, he returned to Germany but only stayed for half a year before moving to the East."

I chuckled, "You know his history well. "

Sem sighed, "Even though he nearly killed me in the desert, I'm still his admirer."

I patted his shoulder, saying, "I believe the real Professor Lomono was replaced by a German spy after the war. The man I encountered was that spy, and I dealt with him."

Sem seemed reluctant to accept this, shaking his head as I spoke. I continued, "I'll notify the international police. I have Lomono's notebook—it's all in German."

"He lived in Germany for a long time, so naturally, he'd write in German," Sem replied.

Taking out the notebook, I opened it to a random page and began reading. I hadn't examined it since finding it, but as I skimmed the lines, I was stunned to discover it was a diary. It didn't record daily events, just the significant ones.

Chapter 15

The Mystery of Hieroglyphics

As I flipped through the pages of the notebook, a particular entry caught my eye: "I received 200,000 US dollars from xxx. The price of killing a person is not low, especially for xxx, a stinky pig. How much is his life worth? Braque will do it well."

The first name was a prominent figure often mentioned in the media. The second individual was deceased, undoubtedly a victim of Braque's ruthless efficiency. This was a clear case of political assassination, and if such information were to be leaked, it could have devastating repercussions for the country involved.

The realization of what I held in my hands made my palms sweat. This notebook was a veritable ledger of post-World War II political assassinations—a document that countless individuals would covet and kill for.

If I were the type to engage in blackmail, this notebook would be a gold mine. But I wasn't, and its existence was more a curse than a blessing. It was a dangerous artifact that could bring disaster upon me.

I closed the notebook and sat in silence, grappling with the gravity of its contents. Sem's erratic driving mirrored my turbulent thoughts as I wrestled with the decision of what to do. Ultimately, I resolved to destroy the notebook. Its contents were too vile, too revealing of the darkest facets of human ambition and deceitful power plays cloaked in respectability.

Politicians who outwardly garnered respect and admiration were implicated in these pages, their public personas mere facades hiding a web of corruption and murder. They had ascended to power through any means necessary, including hiring assassins like Braque.

The passing landscape went unnoticed as I remained lost in thought, only snapping back to reality upon hearing the cacophony of machinery. We had reached the construction site, bypassing the office to arrive at the engineer's dormitory—a simple, mobile structure that Sem occupied due to his status. It was modest outside, but well-equipped within.

Sem led me inside, observing me silently before admitting, "Ash, maybe I was wrong. You know how impulsive I am. Don't hold it against me, alright?"

I offered a reassuring smile, patting his shoulder. "Go handle your work. I need some rest."

With a sheepish grin, Sem left for the office. As soon as he was gone, I took swift action, dousing the notebook with gasoline over a porcelain plate and setting it alight. I watched as the pages turned to ash, eradicating the damning evidence of human malice.

However, I didn't destroy Braque's letter. Sitting down, I unfolded it and began to read. Halfway through, I couldn't suppress a laugh.

When Jack and I discovered that the cold-blooded Braque had become invisible, our initial reaction was one of sheer panic. Braque was already a significant threat, and invisibility would amplify his danger exponentially, making him a virtually unstoppable force.

Yet, as I read Braque's letter to Lomono, I realized our fears were misplaced. The letter revealed that Lomono's mission in Egypt was parallel to mine. While I sought a way to restore visibility to Liam and Nora, Lomono sought the same for Braque. His ambitions might have even extended toward mastering the ability to appear and disappear at will.

With Lomono gone, his ambitions would remain unfulfilled. But what about my own goals? Could I succeed where Lomono could not? At that moment, uncertainty clouded my thoughts.

The letter from Braque, or "Hess" as he addressed Lomono, confirmed my suspicions about Lomono's true identity. Hess was a common German name, affirming that Lomono was a German imposter, not the real Professor Lomono.

Braque's letter continued:

"Hess:

Return the money handed over by xxx. I cannot complete this task. It seemed simple at first. Our target ignored all warnings and left his country, giving us an opportunity, yet I couldn't get near him.

You might wonder, haven't I become invisible? Why can't I complete the mission? Hess, consider this: I can't carry a gun! The moment I arm myself, the gun is visible while I remain unseen. Imagine the chaos that would cause! And I can't simply approach and strangle the target. This is it, Hess, our venture is at an end!"

"I went to the airport and was very close to my target, but I didn't act. I was terrified of being discovered. For years, a gun was like an extension of my body, as natural as my own limbs. But now, my body betrays the gun. My body is invisible, but the gun remains visible. If only the gun could disappear too, how powerful that would be.

I can't even wear clothes. Though people can't see me, I feel exposed—Hess, you wouldn't understand. Imagine being the only one naked in a world where everyone else is clothed. Have you ever felt that way?"

(I chuckled at this part, imagining poor, invisible Braque navigating life unclothed.)

"I hope you find a solution soon. I want to be seen again, to be ordinary. I'm tired of hiding indoors. Once, I went to the movies, and someone sat on me. When I pushed him off, his expression was unforgettable. Since then, I've never dared to see a movie again."

"I'm not usually so verbose, Hess, but I'm scared! Braque."

The letter revealed Braque's transformation from a fearless killer into a man haunted by his own invisibility. His once unshakeable confidence was replaced by fear and isolation—a fitting punishment for someone of his past deeds.

After reading, I fell into a deep sleep on Sem's bed, comforted by the thought that Braque's own condition was justice in itself.

I awoke not of my own accord but to the sound of distant explosions, a series of rumbles that seemed far from the construction site. Dusk was settling, and engineers were returning to the dormitory, unfazed by the noise, as if it were a routine occurrence.

Curious and concerned, I stepped outside and saw smoke and flames rising from the northwest—the direction from which I'd come. Just as I was about to inquire further, Sem approached.

I asked him urgently, "Sem, what's going on? Is there an arsenal over there?"

He shrugged nonchalantly, "Of course not!"

"Then what's exploding over there?" I pressed.

Sem answered, "It's that big temple!"

I stood there, momentarily stunned, as the memory of the construction vehicle I had seen earlier that morning surged back. It had been loaded with boxes of high explosives, but in my haste, I hadn't given it a second thought.

"Why?" I asked, my voice tinged with urgency. "Why demolish the temple?"

Sem replied, "Once our project is complete, the temple will be submerged. The unique structure of the temple's roof could cause a vortex, disrupting water flow. So, we decided it was best to demolish it. You've been inside— why lament its loss?"

A part of me wanted to scream about the world's largest diamonds hidden beneath the temple's shadowed depths, treasures that could fund the entire water project and more. But what was the point now? The temple was gone, its secrets buried beneath rubble and water forever.

Sem eyed me curiously. "What are you thinking about?"

I managed a bitter smile. "Nothing. I just want to get back to Cairo. Is there a plane available?"

"Yes," Sem nodded, "the very one we flew in on." His words surprised me. "With the same pilot?"

He shook his head. "The pilots were bribed by Lomono. Who knows what they were paid? They resigned as soon as we landed. The plane is grounded, waiting for a new pilot from Cairo."

I considered my options. "Maybe I could fly it myself."

Sem brightened. "That would be amazing. Two of our senior staff are desperate to return to Cairo."

"Alright," I agreed. "Make the arrangements."

An hour later, Sem returned with the news that everything was set. He advised against flying at night, but I was too eager to wait. At the makeshift airstrip, my passengers eyed me warily, their anxiety palpable.

Recalling what the American pilot had said on our journey here, I quipped, "Pray to God."

Their faces blanched as they boarded. One asked nervously, "Isn't there a co-pilot?"

Ignoring their question, I climbed into the cockpit of the old plane. I knew the controls; the challenge was the unfamiliar route and the darkness of night. But constant communication with Cairo would guide me.

The flight went smoothly, and when we touched down in Cairo, the passengers were still visibly shaken.

Once at my hotel, I tried to rest until dawn. But "rest" meant poring over the hieroglyphs I had meticulously traced from the stone walls of the temple's seventh secret room. Despite hours of effort, the meaning eluded me.

As the first light of day crept over the city, I watched the streets fill with hurried pedestrians. Reaching out to a local university, I discovered Professor Gedina, an expert in ancient scripts. His secretary arranged an appointment, offering a glimmer of hope that the puzzle might be solved.

At 10 a.m., I found myself stepping into the cluttered yet fascinating office of Professor Gedina. An Englishman by birth, Gedina had spent so many years in Egypt that his skin had taken on the sun-kissed hue of the locals. His allegiance to Egypt was profound—an unusual trait for a Westerner.

As I entered, he was immersed in a sea of ancient texts, preparing lecture notes with the assistance of two diligent secretaries who captured his every word—fruits of his specialized research. I stood by quietly, respecting his process, until after several minutes, he finally acknowledged me, adjusting his glasses to peer over the tomes. "Young man," he began, "I hear you require my assistance?"

I nodded eagerly. "Yes, Professor." He gestured to the mountains of books surrounding him. "As you can see, I'm quite occupied. Please, state your business."

I quickly retrieved the sheet of hieroglyphs from my bag and handed it to him. "I discovered these inscriptions in an ancient temple. They seem to pertain to something highly mysterious, and I'm at a loss to decipher them. I hoped you might read them."

Gedina's initial curiosity turned to ire as he scanned the page. He looked at me, waving the paper in frustration. "Young man, what is the meaning of this?"

Taken aback, I feared I'd presented the wrong document. Yet, as he brandished the paper, I confirmed it was indeed the hieroglyphs I had meticulously copied. Perplexed by his anger, I could only listen.

"Do you assume I'm fluent in every ancient script from every corner of the globe?" he demanded. "Why not present me with ancient Chinese oracle bones while you're at it?"

Once his outburst subsided, I calmly pointed to the paper. "Professor, these inscriptions were genuinely copied from an Egyptian temple."

His anger gave way to a moment of contemplation. He scrutinized the paper more closely. "Where exactly is this temple located?"

"It was adjacent to Egypt's largest water conservancy project," I began, hesitating as I recalled the morning's explosive events. "But... the temple has since been demolished."

His expression darkened further as he hurled the paper back at me. "Young man, waste your own time if you must, but don't waste mine!"

"Do you not believe me?" I implored.

Settling back into his chair, he sighed. "I can't. The Great Temple was among Egypt's most enigmatic. Before its fate was sealed, a team of esteemed scholars and I documented it extensively. We photographed every conceivable corner, preserving its essence in film—"

He paused, deep in thought. "But none of us encountered these inscriptions. Your fabrication is quite elaborate."

I stifled my frustration, surprised by his obstinacy. Clearing my throat, I ventured, "Professor, have you ever heard of the 'Sopa' people?"

He answered swiftly, "No. The ancient Egyptian tribes are numerous and intricate, especially those in the desert. But I'm certain there is no record of a Sopa tribe—or, none has been discovered—"

His voice trailed off, a flicker of recognition crossing his features. Adjusting his glasses, he muttered to himself, "Soppa? Sopa?"

In that moment, I sensed a glimmer of hope. Perhaps the key to unraveling the mystery lay within the professor's newfound curiosity.

Professor Gedina muttered the name "Soppa" several times before instructing his secretary, "Julie, fetch the 'Ancient Egyptian Overseas Transportation Data Collection' from the library."

Eager for answers, I pressed, "Professor, what have you found?"

Adjusting his glasses, Professor Gedina replied, "I recall reading about the 'Soppa' people. Once the book arrives, I'll show you the mention of them. However, if memory serves, it was a brief reference."

Intrigued, I asked, "You mentioned earlier that this temple is the most mysterious in Egypt. Why is that?"

No longer seeing me as a nuisance, the professor pondered for a moment before explaining, "Our research suggests this temple was constructed during Egypt's golden age — a time when many grand temples were erected, each dedicated to well-known gods of the era. This temple, however, is an anomaly."

I leaned in, "Which god was it dedicated to?"

Professor Gedina shook his head, baffled. "Oddly, the temple worshipped an 'invisible god,' a deity unrecorded in Egyptian history. Such a colossal structure could only have been commissioned by a Pharaoh."

He scratched his head in bewilderment. "This is perplexing. Pharaohs typically saw themselves as the embodiment of the gods worshipped by their people. They wouldn't sanction the worship of another god. Yet, here we have a temple built for an unseen deity."

The mention of an "invisible god" sparked a theory in my mind—a wild, yet plausible idea.

"Professor," I ventured, "could it be that these 'invisible gods' were actually invisible people, prompting the Egyptians to construct a temple in their honor?"

The professor stared at me, clearly questioning my sanity.

But I felt a certainty in my hypothesis: these "invisible gods" were indeed invisible people. The pieces of the puzzle began to align.

After the Inca Empire's collapse, about seven individuals carried the brass box containing the mineral— capable of emitting a light that rendered them invisible. They traversed the globe in search of a cure.

I speculated they eventually reached Egypt. Their invisibility would have astonished the Egyptians, inspiring the construction of such a grand temple. I also surmised that Yige might be their descendant, which meant they must have discovered a means of restoration in Egypt.

The hieroglyphs I had transcribed likely held the key to this story, yet even Professor Gedina couldn't decipher them.

I took a deep breath and asked, "Professor, are you aware of the seven secret sacrificial rooms within the temple, specifically designed for the Sopa people?"

Professor Gedina chuckled, "I've heard tales, certainly. A madman named Yige used to regale anyone who'd listen with his story, claiming there was an exquisitely crafted box he'd sell for 200 pounds."

His words left me with a profound sense of melancholy. Poor Yige—his truth dismissed as madness. When no one believed him, he reduced the price to 50 pounds, eventually finding a customer in Sem.

I smiled bitterly. "So, you don't believe him either."

Professor Gedina shook his head, repeating, "Mad, crazy!"

I couldn't tell if his disdain was directed at Yige or me. Just then, his secretary returned with three hefty volumes. Professor Gedina grabbed one, flipping through its pages until he found what he was looking for. "Look here," he said, pointing.

I leaned in to see an image of a fragmented stone, etched with ancient Egyptian characters. Though I couldn't decipher them, the caption below translated the inscription to read, "The Sopa people brought the invisible..."

Of course, the sentence was incomplete, the stone itself fractured. The book's annotation explained that in 1843, a caravan of Arab merchants had stumbled upon a solitary pyramid in the desert. An Englishman in their party had dislodged the stone and brought it to Cairo, only to succumb to a fever soon after—his demise attributed to an ancient curse for defiling the pyramid. The pyramid itself faded from memory until the 20th-century archaeologists reignited interest. Expeditions were launched, guided by the Englishman's detailed diary, but the desert sands had swallowed the pyramid whole. The stone's inscription, however, persisted, hinting at the "Sopa people" who had once journeyed to Egypt.

The tome, dedicated to ancient Egyptian interactions with other cultures, noted that at least one "Sopa tribe" had indeed visited. Yet, the tribe's identity remained elusive, their legacy obscured by time. The book's author expressed hope that rediscovering the pyramid might shed light on this mystery. Remarkably, Professor Gedina had recalled these scant details from memory, a testament to his scholarly prowess.

Closing the book, I said, "I've learned quite a bit."

I held up my paper again. "Professor, are you certain this isn't ancient Egyptian?"

"Quite certain," he replied curtly.

Clinging to a thread of hope, I asked, "Do you have any idea where this script might originate?"

Professor Gedina fixed me with a gaze. "Do you expect someone who specializes in ancient Egyptian texts to identify every obscure hieroglyph?"

Defeated, I forced a smile. "Thank you, Professor. I'll be on my way."

With a dismissive wave, Gedina returned to his work. I left his office, lingering outside the door before shuffling down the corridor, head bowed.

I had hoped Professor Gedina could unlock the secrets of the hieroglyphs. Instead, I left with more questions than answers. Yet, I also gained an unexpected lead—a hidden pyramid tied to the Sopa people. The inscription "The Sopa people brought the invisible" likely completed to "brought the invisible god," reinforcing my earlier theories.

But what good was this revelation? Days had passed with Liam and Nora awaiting my return on that isolated isle, their hopes pinned on my success. What had I achieved so far?

Lost in thought, I wandered into the sunlight, its warmth coaxing me to lift my gaze. What was my next move?

Deciphering the hieroglyphs was imperative, but who could assist me?

Standing at the corridor's end, watching students cross the campus, I felt adrift—an unfamiliar sensation after years of seamless adventures. Now, it seemed, I was on the brink of a significant setback. I sighed deeply, grappling with the weight of uncertainty.

Chapter 16

The Lost Pyramid

Though I had pieced together the origin of the enigmatic mineral capable of emitting "transparent light," its significance eluded me. My goal wasn't to unravel why the mighty Inca Empire vanished but to discover how to reverse the effects of the "transparent light" on those exposed to it.

While my journey seemed promising initially, deciphering those ancient hieroglyphs proved to be a formidable challenge, halting my progress entirely.

Leaving the university, I carried the weight of frustration with each step.

Over the next three days, modern transportation became my ally as I traversed Egypt, visiting renowned ancient temples. I sought out the monks residing there, hoping one might recognize the hieroglyphs.

I knew that the monks in these temples were well-versed in ancient Egyptian scripts, their knowledge rivaling even that of Professor Gedina.

In each temple, I was welcomed with courtesy. Even the eldest monks took the time to meet with me.

Yet, the responses were unanimous: "We do not recognize this script. It might not be of ancient Egyptian origin."

After three days of fruitless searching, disappointment settled over me. I confined myself to my room, determined to uncover some clue hidden within the hieroglyphs.

But the more I scrutinized them, the more they seemed to taunt me. Those strange symbols danced before my eyes like mischievous spirits.

With a heavy sigh, I rose, realizing I hadn't eaten all day. The setting sun cast Cairo in an even more mysterious light.

I rang for the waiter to order dinner. Moments after he left, a knock sounded at the door once more.

I glanced up, bemused. "I don't recall summoning you again."

The waiter smiled. "Shet, sir. Call me Shet." My patience waning, I replied, "What do you want? Out with it."

Shet maintained his smile. "I want nothing, sir, but you might want help. You seem troubled."

I jumped to my feet. Shet stepped back. "You haven't left your room today, sir. That suggests you're in quite the bind. While I can't solve others' problems, I can certainly point them toward a solution."

I waved dismissively. "I didn't come to Cairo for belly dancing."

Shet remained undeterred. He folded his hands, adopting a thoughtful expression. "Ah, but sir, Egypt doesn't only boast belly dancing; it is an ancient and mysterious land."

His words struck a chord. "What mysteries does Cairo hold, then?"

Shet rubbed his hands together eagerly. "Many, indeed. The older, the better, you say?"

I nodded. "Precisely."

Shet's eyes gleamed. "In a place tourists would never find without a guide, there's an astrologer who claims to see past and future—"

I cut him off with a wave. "Spare me. Locals don't visit such places. Only tourists fall for that."

Shet blushed, sheepish. He rattled off a few more "mysteries," none more than tourist traps.

I shooed him away repeatedly, but he lingered. Then, suddenly, he paused, hand to his forehead. "No! You mustn't be searching for the lost pyramid!"

His words caught me off guard. "Lost pyramid? What do you mean?"

In that moment, curiosity piqued, I realized that Shet might hold the key to the next step in my quest.

Shet spread his hands wide, his expression a mix of intrigue and caution. "An entire pyramid lost to the sands of the desert. In all of Egypt, only one person knows the full tale. Would you care to hear this mystery?"

My curiosity piqued instantly. "Where can I hear this story?"

Shet hesitated theatrically, shaking his head. "Ah, I shouldn't have mentioned it, sir. Best to forget it."

His reluctance was an obvious ploy, a bid to make the tale seem more valuable. I slipped a five-Egyptian pound note from my pocket. "Tell me."

To my surprise, Shet's face flushed with indignation. "Sir, do you think I'm just after money?"

I met his gaze, puzzled. "Aren't you?"

Shet's expression turned plaintive. "Why do people assume I'm only in it for the money? I merely wish for foreigners to find Egypt engaging."

His sincerity caught me off guard, and I quickly apologized. "Shet, I'm sorry. I misjudged you."

He waved it off. "Forget what I said, sir. Over the past five years, I've led five curious tourists to hear the tale of the missing pyramid. Each one ventured into the desert afterward, never to return. It's said the story compels them to seek the pyramid. I've vowed not to mention it again to anyone."

Hearing Shet mention the "missing pyramid in the desert" triggered a memory of Professor Gedina's account of the "Sopa tribe." That record spoke of a pyramid swallowed by the sands.

The pyramid's disappearance wasn't mystical—it was the desert's relentless shifts, concealing it beneath drifts of sand. It could be buried hundreds of feet deep, or perhaps its peak lay just beneath the surface. This must be the very pyramid linked to the Sopa tribe.

A glimmer of hope ignited within me. "Shet, where is the person who tells these stories? Please, I must know!"

Shet, visibly concerned, implored, "Sir, I beg you. Don't follow the path of those before you and vanish into the desert. Promise me you won't."

I placed a reassuring hand on his shoulder. "Shet, forgive me, but I can't make that promise. If the story aligns with what I seek, I must go to the desert."

Shet sighed, a mix of resignation and bewilderment in his voice. "I don't understand why people risk everything for such pursuits. Life is the most precious thing."

I brushed aside his concerns. "Find someone to take me there, quickly."

Shet's eyes widened. "But, sir, the dinner you ordered—"

"Bring it up and have it here yourself," I instructed. "I have more pressing matters to attend to."

Shet swallowed hard, seemingly relieved. "Thank you, thank you. We have a saying: a pile of gold is not as valuable as a pile of delicious food. I'll find someone to guide you there!"

With surprising agility for his size, he dashed off and soon returned with a slight, wiry Egyptian boy in tow. The boy lingered hesitantly at the doorway. "This is my nephew, Sally," Shet explained. "He'll lead you."

I approached Sally, offering a reassuring pat on the shoulder. "Alright, let's get going."

As I prepared to leave, Shet called after me, "Sir, would you mind if my wife joins me for the dinner you so kindly provided?"

I chuckled, "Of course, enjoy it together!"

Shet beamed, eyes crinkling with gratitude. Sally and I stepped out into the encroaching twilight. He was quiet, focused, guiding us through Cairo's labyrinthine streets as night descended. The bustling cityscape of hotels and nightclubs faded away, replaced by the simplicity of unlit streets and shadowed alleys.

Sally navigated confidently, intuitively selecting paths at each fork. After about half an hour, hunger gnawed at me, and we stumbled upon a row of food stalls. I bought two sizable rolls of flatbread, the vendor slathering them with a mysterious dark sauce whose aroma was both fresh and spicy.

I handed one to Sally, who accepted it without hesitation, eating as we walked. The sauce was delicious, though to this day, its name and ingredients remain a delightful mystery.

Once we finished our meals, Sally gestured toward a dim alleyway. Peering ahead, I saw towering, ancient buildings flanking it, the narrow passage exuding a musty odor.

I motioned to Sally, confirming if this was our destination. He simply nodded, "Yes," in his basic English.

Following Sally into the alley, I felt the weight of history and mystery pressing in. If any foreigner had ventured here before, I would be the sixth. The five who preceded me had vanished into the desert, their journey commencing with this foreboding corridor. The alley seemed like the throat of a mythical beast, ready to consume and erase any trace of its visitors.

Counting each step, I marked forty-two before we reached the alley's end where Sally turned right. I followed.

As we rounded the corner, a faint glow emerged. Before us stood a small, nondescript house, devoid of windows or conventional doors, just a door-shaped gap.

Peering through this opening, I noticed an elderly man bent over a table, engrossed in sorting glass bottles and tin cans—likely salvaged from the refuse of the city. I shook my head at the sight, but Sally pressed forward, and I trailed behind.

We entered through the makeshift doorway, the old man still examining a bottle under an oil lamp, as if expecting a genie to emerge from its depths.

Sally called to him, and the old man looked up, addressing me in unexpectedly fluent English, "Sir, what do you seek?"

Stepping closer, I realized there was nowhere to sit but a single, rickety stool occupied by the old man himself. "I've heard you know the tale of a pyramid that vanished mysteriously in the desert," I said.

The old man sat up, his stool wobbling precariously. "Do you wish to hear it?" he asked.

I nodded, resolute. "That's precisely why I've come to you."

The old man's face creased into an almost mischievous smile as he asked, "Might I request a small reward, sir?" I replied, "Of course. How much are you asking for?"

Leaning in conspiratorially, he said, "Would one pound suffice, sir?" I could almost feel the anticipation radiating from him. For someone living so modestly, a single pound was indeed a significant sum. I didn't want to make him uncomfortable, so I paced a few steps, pretending to consider. "How can I be sure your story will satisfy me?"

The old man rubbed his hands eagerly. "Sir, you'll be more than satisfied. Everyone who has heard it leaves content. Though I'm not versed in English or those peculiar symbols, I know that anyone seeking secrets will find what they need here."

I pondered this for a moment. "So, the story you offer isn't merely spoken by you. Instead, you have something to show me, a record of sorts, correct?"

He nodded enthusiastically. "Yes, precisely."

I handed him an Egyptian pound and gave a few coins to Sally, who bowed in gratitude and departed. The old man inspected the note under the lamp's flickering light, folding it carefully before tucking it away.

"Sir, you may examine it as long as you wish," he said, stepping aside. Yet, he produced nothing for me to look at, and for a moment, I suspected this might be a foolish ruse. But then the old man gestured to the large stone serving as his table, directing my gaze to one side. There, etched into the stone, were words—ancient, mysterious, and waiting to be deciphered.

My heart raced as I lifted the oil lamp closer to the stone, revealing ancient Egyptian hieroglyphs that were indecipherable to me. The stone was missing a corner, and

I immediately recognized it as the same piece referenced in the books — the one engraved with "The Sopa people brought the invisible."

The realization hit me like a bolt: the British explorer who found the desert pyramid had not merely chipped off a corner but had taken an entire section. This very stone lay before me now, strangely buried in this squalid setting, while its fragment was revered and displayed in a museum.

Initially, I considered copying the hieroglyphs to seek Professor Gedina's expertise, but then I noticed English inscriptions beneath them. The words were shallow, as if carved in haste, and time had eroded some, requiring educated guesses to fill in the gaps.

As I read the English text, an overwhelming sense of awe and urgency swept over me. It became clear why those five tourists had ventured into the desert after visiting this place. Indeed, as Shet had warned, the story's allure was irresistible, compelling anyone who learned of it to pursue further, despite knowing the desert's perils.

I pieced together the narrative, noting that the English had been derived from the hieroglyphs:

"The Sopa people brought invisible gods, astonishing the court. There exist other deities beyond the true God. Pharaoh decreed utmost secrecy. The Sopa hailed from a distant land, where a boundless light emerged from the earth, rendering their tribe into invisible gods. Unhappy with their plight, they sought a means for mortals to perceive them. Failing globally, they succeeded in great Egypt. They thrived here, uniting god and man, affirming Pharaoh as a divine incarnation. The Sopa interred their leader with the secret of invisibility, wishing their progeny to avoid becoming invisible gods again."

My translation might lack the eloquence of the original text, but it conveyed the essence. The English, albeit worn, captured the essence of the ancient hieroglyphs.

The secret of invisibility lay within that pyramid! The Sopa, originating from South America's plains and rendered invisible by the translucent light, found restoration in Egypt. They chose not to return to their homeland but to remain, establishing a lineage that continued to the present-day Yige.

It's no wonder the pyramid has escaped the attention of archaeologists and remains absent from historical records. The individual entombed within is not an Egyptian pharaoh but the leader of the Sopa tribe, originating from the distant Inca Empire of South America. This connection, spanning thousands of miles, resolves the mystery of the pyramid's obscurity.

I can only speculate on the events of millennia past, but it seems likely that the Egyptian pharaoh of the time exploited the Sopa people's invisibility to reinforce his doctrine of the divine nature of rulers, thereby consolidating his power. Surely, the pharaoh reaped substantial benefits from this association, prompting him to erect a temple for the Sopa people and a pyramid for their deceased leader.

The secrecy surrounding these events ensured their absence from historical records until now. Yet, the stone remains, a testament to the reality of invisibility—not a mere fantasy, but a tangible possibility.

The idea that invisibility existed so long ago, and that there were methods to render the invisible visible, is astonishing. It implies that one could master the "magic of invisibility," appearing and disappearing at will, simply by locating and entering that pyramid.

The allure of such power is undeniable. Imagine the possibilities unlocked by invisibility — the ability to accomplish tasks otherwise inconceivable. Even without Liam and Nora, the words on this stone alone would compel me to venture into the desert to uncover the lost pyramid.

I also envision the British explorer, eager to revisit the pyramid after deciphering the hieroglyphs, only to succumb to fever. Had he survived, and had the pyramid remained unentombed by sand, humanity might have discovered the secrets of invisibility two centuries ago, rather than today.

A strange thought crossed my mind: how different might history have been if invisibility had become commonplace? While it's impossible to predict all changes, one certainty emerges — tyranny would have been eradicated.

Who would dare to be a tyrant when, among millions, anyone could eliminate them using the power of invisibility? The prospect of the people possessing such power would deter any ruler from tyranny, compelling them to govern benevolently.

I stood before the stone for a long time, contemplating. The old man interrupted my reverie. "Are you satisfied?" he asked, a sly smile playing on his lips, as if amused by my fascination.

I nodded. "Yes, I'm satisfied." His expression suggested he saw me as naïve.

"You know the engravings and their meaning, don't you?" I pressed.

"Someone explained it to me," he admitted.

"And do you believe it?" I inquired.

He spread his hands. "Sir, I trust a penny in my hand more than thousands in the bank. Do you think this is possible?"

He shrugged, and I mirrored the gesture. I wanted to tell him: It is possible. There exists a mysterious mineral whose light renders bodies invisible, and an unknown method to restore visibility. The world is full of wonders yet to be fully understood.

Silence lingered between us, heavy with unspoken truths. I refrained from sharing my revelations with the old man; the tale was too intricate, too unbelievable for most. As he'd noted, the world clung to tangible certainties, like a penny in hand, over distant promises of wealth.

I turned away, exiting through the door-like opening and maneuvering through the dim alleyway, head bowed in contemplation. Upon emerging into the light, I found Sally patiently waiting. "Sir," he called, a familiar anchor pulling me back to reality.

With a nod, I signaled Sally to lead me back to the hotel. My mind churned with thoughts, the world around me fading until his voice brought me back to the present, standing at the hotel's entrance.

Inside, the electric clock's ticking marked the passage of time—two hours, lost to my journey and musings. Surely, Shet and his wife had concluded their meal by now. I ascended to my room, where Shet greeted me with effusive gratitude, his words a blur of appreciation.

Gently, I ushered him from the room, closing the door behind him. Solitude enveloped me as I reached for the phone, dialing a connection across the distance.

First, I contacted Wilson. He recounted his visits to the island, each time departing after delivering supplies, never glimpsing a soul. I instructed him to leave a message on his next visit, assuring them I had found a way and urging patience.

Wilson hesitated, questions unasked, as I severed the connection. Pacing the room, I considered the letter I asked him to leave for Liam and Nora. It proclaimed I had uncovered a path to their restoration—a statement rooted not in comfort, but in truth.

The cryptic inscriptions on the monumental stone had illuminated my understanding, relegating the strange symbols I'd copied from the temple's secret chamber to secondary importance. The key to reversing invisibility lay within the buried pyramid—clear and tantalizingly close.

Yet, the path to success remained treacherous and uncertain. The pyramid languished beneath desert sands, its location a mystery that had already claimed five lives.

That night, rest eluded me as I paced the room, thoughts racing with possibilities and peril, until exhaustion finally claimed me near midnight.

The next morning dawned bright and filled with purpose. I made my way to Cairo's largest library, scouring through volumes on ancient Egypt's foreign exchanges. In the dusty appendix of a British chronicle, I meticulously noted the coordinates of the elusive pyramid. Armed with this revelation, I acquired a treasure trove of maps, desert literature, and essential gear, including a robust vehicle and trailer capable of conquering the harsh desert landscape.

To bolster my expedition, I placed an ad in the newspaper, seeking a first-rate desert guide. The ad was explicit—I aimed to uncover a lost pyramid buried in the sands. Despite the allure, three days passed in silence, and by the fourth evening, I pondered venturing out alone. Just then, Shet interrupted my thoughts, announcing an applicant's arrival.

I leapt from my seat, instructing, "Please invite him in."

Shet hesitated, his concern evident. For days, he had cautioned against my desert quest. But I dismissed his worries with a wave. "Enough, bring the applicant in!"

Moments later, Shet returned with a man in tow.

I scrutinized the applicant, caught off guard. I had envisioned a desert guide as a robust adventurer, brimming with vitality. Yet, before me stood a slender figure, accentuated by Shet's bulk. His attire was modest, but his eyes held a steely resolve that piqued my interest, compelling me to hear him out.

As I assessed him, he returned my gaze, unflinching.

I rose to greet him. "You're here to apply as a guide? What's your name?"

He advanced with a measured grace, incongruous with his humble appearance. Not an Arab, I noted. He squared his shoulders, announcing, "Romy. You may call me Viscount Romy, though titles mean little to me."

His English, tinged with a French accent, surprised me. After days of unanswered ads, a French nobleman had come forward to guide me through the desert—an unlikely pairing.

The French and the desert seemed disparate, yet I concealed my skepticism with a polite smile. "Mr. Romy, I believe you may have misunderstood the nature of this endeavor."

Romy remained unfazed, his silence speaking volumes. From his pocket, he produced a folded, yellowed paper. "Sir, do you read German?" he inquired.

Momentarily taken aback, I replied, "A bit, though I doubt it's necessary for desert travel."

His question hung between us, a puzzle within a puzzle. What secrets did this enigmatic Frenchman hold, and how did they intertwine with my quest for the lost pyramid? The answers lay ahead, veiled in the desert sands.

Chapter 17

"A Grain of Sand in the Desert"

Romy extended the paper towards me, his eyes unwavering. "Please, take a look," he urged.

Curiosity piqued, I accepted the yellowed document. What could be so significant about an old piece of paper? I unfolded it cautiously, revealing a photograph of a youthful, wiry figure, exuding an undeniable energy.

Despite the passage of time, the resolute expression on the photographed face mirrored that of the man standing before me. I realized instantly that this was Romy in his younger days.

It was a wanted notice. The signature at the bottom belonged to none other than German General Rommel. The notice declared a hefty reward for Romy, identified as the leader of the Allied Intelligence Working Group operating in the desert under the alias "A Grain of Sand in the Desert."

The nickname was as unique as it was telling. A grain of sand—an entity so seamlessly integrated into the desert's vastness, much like Romy himself, who had become one with the harsh landscape. Compared to Rommel's "Desert Fox," Romy's moniker suggested an elemental connection to the sands.

Having absorbed the contents of the notice, I regarded Romy with newfound respect. "If Rommel deemed you worthy of such a bounty, then you're surely qualified to guide anyone through the desert."

Romy extended his hand, reclaiming the paper. "May I have it back?"

I returned the document, unable to resist asking, "Might I inquire—"

He cut me off with a dismissive wave. "You're wondering how someone of my caliber could end up here, correct?"

I nodded, slightly abashed.

In a tone as cold as the desert night, Romy replied, "I'm here to apply as a guide, not to share my life's story."

I shrugged it off. "I'm only interested in a competent guide, not one who dwells on the past."

He studied me closely. "So, I'm to be your employee?"

"Ten Egyptian pounds per day," I offered. "All equipment provided. Does that suit you?"

His hand extended again. "That's more than I anticipated, but I require three days' pay in advance."

Without hesitation, I agreed. Romy struck me as a man burdened by unseen challenges, yet he didn't exude the deceit of a charlatan. Lying wasn't tattooed on one's forehead, but I was willing to take the chance. Trust was paramount; in the desert, honesty and reliance on one another were vital for survival. I counted the thirty pounds, placing them in his grasp.

He accepted the money with a firm grip, his eyes locking onto mine. "I'll return in an hour to finalize our preparations." His departure was swift, and I maintained my composure, refusing to entertain doubts of his return.

As I waited, Shet attempted conversation several times, but I dismissed him, focused on the task ahead. True to his word, Romy returned before the hour elapsed, a renewed vigor in his step. He sat down immediately. "Let's examine your preparations."

Proudly, I displayed the supplies and provisions I'd amassed, detailing the acquisition of a vehicle capable of traversing the desert without the need for constant refueling.

To my surprise, Romy erupted into laughter, a sound unexpected and infectious.

Romy's laughter echoed through the room, a stark contrast to the serious mission ahead. "Cars that don't need water, canned supplies, sunscreen—do you think we're off on a joyride through the desert to Las Vegas? Whatever you're planning in the desert, it's not a quick day trip, is it?"

I nodded, resolute. "Of course not. I'm searching for a lost pyramid."

His reaction was immediate—shock etched across his face as he stepped back.

I continued, feigning ignorance of his surprise. "This pyramid was reportedly discovered by a British explorer in the 18th century, but now lies buried beneath the sands."

As I spoke, I noticed the color drain from Romy's face, leaving him as pale as the desert moon.

"Why?" I asked. "Are you thinking of backing out of our agreement?" Romy murmured, "Five... five of the best desert guides vanished searching for that cursed pyramid."

I managed a wry smile. "If you're afraid of becoming the sixth, there's no obligation to join this quest. The advance is yours to keep."

A glimmer of nobility returned to his features. "No, I'll go."

I assured him, "Romy, I would never compel you."

He replied with quiet dignity, "No one can compel me, sir."

We shook hands, solidifying our pact. "My name is Ash Morris. Call me Ash. Formalities aren't necessary between us."

His grip was firm as he responded, "I've heard of you, Ash. If it's you, perhaps I can find the courage to face this."

I clapped his shoulder, "And you've given me renewed courage."

Romy didn't delve into the reasons behind my quest for the pyramid. Instead, he offered practical advice. "Your preparations won't suffice. We'll need to be ready for twenty days or more in the desert. First, twenty camels, not a car."

I respected his expertise—after all, he was "a grain of sand in the desert." I had no grounds to dispute his judgment.

He elaborated, "Camels are our lifeline. They signal dangers and opportunities—when to halt for a whirlwind, when an oasis is near, when scorpions threaten, and they carry food without refrigeration requirements."

I jotted down in my notebook: twenty camels.

He paced thoughtfully around the room. "We'll also need a mineral deposit detector. I can modify it to respond to high concentrations of quartz, feldspar, and mica."

I nodded, grateful for Romy's expertise. His presence felt like a stroke of luck. Clearly, he was well-versed in the intricacies of desert survival and the unique challenges of our mission. His plan to modify the detector for sensitivity to quartz, feldspar, and mica was a crucial step, as the pyramid's granite construction comprised these minerals.

Pacing again, Romy continued, "Sixteen watertight leather bags, each capable of storing twenty gallons of water."

I couldn't help but interject, "That much water?"

He paused, his tone somber. "The desert is unforgiving. If we get lost, a single mouthful of water could mean the difference between life and death."

I nodded, acknowledging the harsh reality, and resumed jotting down his instructions.

"Eight pairs of thick rubber-soled boots, four bags of flour, twenty pounds of salt, twenty bottles of wine—" he continued, listing essential supplies.

I dutifully recorded each item, realizing that my initial preparations were woefully inadequate. Romy's list was extensive, and only a fraction of what I had gathered was suitable. When he finally paused, I asked, "Is there anything else?"

He shook his head. "That's all."

I smiled, curious about his past. "When you worked in the desert as an intelligence operative, did you carry so much equipment?"

His eyes flared with intensity. "Back then, it was for anti-fascism. But now?"

I met his gaze, unwavering. "Now, it's to uncover the pyramid and perhaps discover the secret of invisibility."

Romy's eyes widened in disbelief. "What?" he exclaimed.

I explained, "The pyramid holds a mystery—a way to become invisible. That's why I'm determined to find it."

Romy shouted:"What?"

For a moment, we stood in silence, the gravity of my words hanging between us. Romy's skepticism was palpable, yet beneath it, I sensed a flicker of intrigue. He was a man who had faced the unknown before, and perhaps the allure of unraveling a new mystery was enough to spur him on this unconventional journey.

I repeated, "Invisibility."

Romy paused, absorbing the weight of my words. "Alright," he finally said, "whatever you're seeking, I'm just your guide."

I smiled, relieved. "Let's split the preparations. Think we can be ready in two days?"

"Yes, two days should suffice," Romy agreed.

I handed him some money, and we both set to work, gathering supplies and transporting them to our departure point. By the end of the second day, our provisions were secured on the backs of twenty camels.

On the third morning, we mounted our camels, setting forth into the vast desert. Equipped with a compass for navigation, Romy diligently studied the directions recorded by the British explorer.

An hour later, we were deep in the desert. Initially, the familiar sight of people and pyramids lingered, but by afternoon, it was just us and the endless expanse of sand.

Throughout our journey, Romy remained contemplative, his gaze fixed on the horizon. At dusk, he finally broke his silence. "I've been here before," he remarked.

Excitement surged within me. "You've been there?"

He nodded. "Yes, it's a remarkable place."

I was puzzled. "Remarkable? The desert looks the same everywhere. What's so special about it?"

Romy explained, "To most, the desert seems uniform. But for those of us who have spent years here, each part is distinct. You can't tell one grain of sand from another, nor one dune from the next, but I can."

Intrigued, I pressed on. "So, what's special about the pyramid's location?"

He pondered for a moment. "It's hard to describe. The sand there is different—" He paused, excitement lighting his eyes. "Of course, it was shaped by a whirlwind."

I looked at him, curious. Romy elaborated, "A whirlwind can transport millions of tons of sand from miles away, layering the desert with unique grains. That's why the sand there is different."

Hope swelled within me. "So there might be a pyramid buried under all that sand?"

"It's possible," Romy conceded. "But finding it is another matter."

I persisted, "Then why did those who searched before us disappear?"

Romy fell silent, suddenly urging his camel forward. I followed, pressing him, "Romy, do you know why they vanished?"

His avoidance was telling.

I pressed Romy again, hoping for an explanation. "You're so familiar with the desert—can't you tell me what to expect?"

He remained silent for a long moment, then finally said, "What I can share is this: don't ask me anymore. When we're near our destination, no matter how strange things may seem, don't be surprised."

His words only deepened the enigma surrounding our journey, wrapping it in even thicker layers of mystery.

"But what strange things might we encounter?" I asked urgently.

"Don't ask me anymore," Romy repeated. "Perhaps we'll arrive without incident, and there will be nothing to fear."

I couldn't help but smile wryly. "Romy, do you think I'm on the verge of a nervous breakdown?"

"Of course not," he replied, "but the desert is unlike any other place—the sky, ocean, and land belong to the three-dimensional spaces we know, while the desert is akin to a fourth dimension, one beyond our understanding. In the desert, reality bends, and the improbable becomes possible."

I had to agree with him. The desert's monotony and dry air could indeed distort perceptions, creating illusions so vivid they seemed real. I remembered a fellow desert traveler who had sworn he'd seen "headless people" in Australia's vast desert. He insisted he'd seen them himself—a testament to the desert's tricks on the mind.

I didn't argue further. We continued our trek through the silent desert, speaking little. For days, we journeyed deeper into its vast and mysterious heart, each step carrying us closer to the unknown.

The relentless sun and arid air were oppressive. I found myself nostalgically longing for the humidity of the air , pouring water over my head to stave off the heat. Though my hair dried quickly, the fleeting relief was welcome.

Initially, I thought we carried an excess of water, but soon realized even a pondful wouldn't suffice. In the desert, hydration wasn't just a physical need — it was a psychological lifeline.

By the fifth day's dusk, according to Romy's records, we had reached the vicinity of the pyramid noted by the British. He checked the battery and activated the modified detector, which hummed to life.

The detector's pointer remained stubbornly at zero. Romy explained, "If this pointer moves, we might have found mica—or the pyramid itself."

I scanned the horizon. The desert stretched flat and wide, the setting sun casting a golden glow over the sands. If anything stood tall, it would be visible even without a telescope. But there was nothing.

Romy shouted commands, halting the camel train. "Are we camping here tonight?" I asked.

"Yes," he nodded. "Where are the weapons we packed? We should have them ready."

Surprised, I queried, "Do you expect trouble?"

"Possibly," he replied, his tone noncommittal. "Better to be prepared."

Following his lead, I set up camp and kept an eye on him as he adjusted the detector and guided the camel to carry it forward. By the time I finished preparing our meal, he still hadn't returned, though I could still make out his figure in the fading light.

Through my telescope, I noticed something unusual. The camel stood motionless, the detector still balanced on its back as before. But Romy was close by, his body inverted—hands pressed into the sand and feet pointing toward the sky.

My heart skipped a beat. What could he possibly be doing? It was as if the desert had swallowed him whole, and he was reaching out to grasp its secrets from a different perspective. The sight was surreal, and a chill ran down my spine. What had we truly ventured into, in this realm where reality wove seamlessly with the unknown?

The strange scene with Romy had left me bewildered, questioning my own senses. Was the desert playing tricks on me, or was there a rational explanation for his bizarre posture? As dusk deepened and the desert transformed under the moon's silvery glow, I tried to dismiss my unease.

When I looked through the telescope again, Romy was leading the camel back to camp, appearing perfectly normal. Whatever had happened out there, he showed no sign of it now. I decided not to mention what I had seen. If Romy wanted to keep it to himself, I would respect that.

As we settled down for dinner, Romy casually mentioned our plans for the next day. "I should go further in the morning. We can't rely on the Englishman's notes entirely; he might have been mistaken about the pyramid's location."

"Of course," I agreed. "But the pyramid can't be too far from where he recorded."

Romy nodded, finishing his coffee. "Did you find the guns?"

"Yes," I replied. "We each have a pistol and a rifle."

To my surprise, Romy shook his head. "No, I have two pistols and two rifles. You don't."

I was taken aback but tried to remain composed. As he deftly secured the firearms, I realized he was intent on keeping them to himself. "Why don't I have a weapon, Romy?" I inquired, my voice steady despite my growing concern.

He fastened the pistols to his belt. "Get some sleep after dinner. I'll take the watch."

I insisted, "We should take turns."

But his expression was unyielding. "I'll be on duty. No shifts."

His resolve was unsettling, yet I decided against pressing the issue. With all the guns in his possession, provoking him could be dangerous if his mental state was indeed fraying. Instead, I shrugged off my apprehension, retreated to the tent, and settled in, removing my cumbersome boots.

Lying there, I couldn't shake the feeling that the desert was testing us, pushing at the edges of our sanity. Romy's earlier words about the desert being another dimension echoed in my mind. Whatever lay ahead, I hoped we'd both emerge unscathed, the mysteries of the sands unraveling before us without further incident.

I lay quietly in the tent, observing Romy through the small opening. His movements were deliberate and composed, not at all like someone whose mind was unraveling. He methodically extinguished the fire, disposed of the leftovers, gathered the camels together, and then settled down beside one, rifles within easy reach.

Content that he had no immediate intention of harm, I closed my eyes. Though my initial plan was to rest without sleeping, the exhaustion of our journey soon overcame me, and I drifted into a deep slumber.

I was jolted awake by the unmistakable sound of a rifle being cocked. Instinctively, I turned toward the sound and saw Romy poised atop the camel, his rifle trained forward.

Curious and concerned, I followed his line of sight but saw nothing out of the ordinary. Just as I was about to step out of the tent, my attention was drawn to the slow, deliberate movement of three small sand dunes.

The dunes, each only about half a foot high, crept toward our camp like shadows in the night. It became evident that beneath the sand, three figures were advancing, inching forward in a prone position. I was taken aback—why hadn't Romy fired?

Choosing caution, I remained in the tent, watching as Romy performed an unexpected maneuver. He tossed a red branch into the sand, landing it directly in the path of the leading figure.

In an instant, three figures emerged from the sand as if conjured by magic. Their appearance was striking—skin dark and rough, torsos bare, and lower bodies clad only in ragged cloth. Each held a peculiar weapon that resembled a blowgun.

What happened next was even more bewildering. Romy, instead of confronting them, threw his rifle to the ground.

I was stunned. This was not the reaction I expected from Romy, whom I had believed to be resourceful and fearless. His apparent surrender puzzled me. The trio, whom I presumed to be desert-dwelling Arabs, had managed to invoke such a reaction from Romy.

Questions swirled in my mind. Who were these men, and why did Romy seem so deferential to them? What was the significance of the red branch, and why had Romy discarded his weapon so readily? The night held its breath, cloaked in the mysteries of the desert and the secrets of its inhabitants.

Realizing Romy wasn't afraid but rather aligned with the three mysterious figures changed everything. As he approached them with open arms, the three mirrored his gesture, their movements synchronized and devoid of hostility. This display of camaraderie only deepened my unease, suggesting a shared purpose or understanding between them.

The desert held tribes known for both their hospitality and ferocity, and I couldn't discern which path these three might tread. Romy's clandestine communication with them piqued my curiosity. His actions were shrouded in secrecy, yet I sensed no immediate threat.

I opted for silence, observing as Romy engaged the trio in conversation. He spoke in a dialect of Arabic unfamiliar to me, his words a murmur in the desert night. The three Arabs listened intently, responding with silence. Whatever Romy sought from them, their initial response was a collective shake of their heads—a refusal.

Desperation etched Romy's features as he gestured toward our camels and rifles, offering them in French: "For you, all these are for you!"

The three exchanged glances before the central figure responded, again in the elusive dialect. Romy's impatience grew, evident in his interruptions. Despite the language barrier, his urgency was clear.

Abruptly, the trio turned and began walking, with Romy retrieving his rifle and following. They were leaving, their destination unknown, as was the nature of their alliance with Romy.

I knew one thing for certain: I had to follow them. Despite the lack of cover in the desert, the method the Arabs used to approach—crawling beneath the sand— provided a stealthy solution. My training in martial arts had honed my ability to control my breathing and movements, giving me an edge.

Leaving the tent, I lay flat against the sand, crawling forward. To my advantage, the desert's soft surface enveloped me, allowing a natural concealment as I progressed. Keeping my head above the sand, I was able to track their direction, ensuring I remained on their trail.

The pursuit felt surreal, the vast desert a silent witness to our covert passage. Each movement brought me closer to unraveling the connection between Romy and these desert dwellers, and the true nature of our quest. Whatever lay ahead, I was determined to uncover the secrets hidden beneath the sands.

The pursuit continued as Romy and the three Arabs pressed on, eventually veering westward. Following them through the sand was grueling, each advance a test of endurance. Yet, I persevered, driven by curiosity and the need to uncover their intent.

As they journeyed east, the landscape shifted, revealing jagged cliffs silhouetted against the moonlit sky. Even from a distance, the cliffs loomed ominously, their sharp edges resembling a row of cold, gleaming blades.

Their path led directly to these cliffs, and I maintained my pursuit, keeping a cautious distance of about ten steps. As we neared the cliffs, my nerves heightened. The purpose behind their journey was becoming clearer, but I still needed to maintain discretion.

Knowing their destination allowed me to pause. I no longer needed to crawl with my head raised, which risked exposure. Instead, I buried myself in the sand, lifting my head only intermittently to track their progress.

Each time I glanced up, they continued toward the cliffs, the silhouette of danger drawing ever closer. But then, unexpectedly, they vanished.

One moment they were there, a mere ten steps ahead, and the next—gone. The desert stretched out before me, empty and flat, as if they had never existed. I scanned the area frantically. Left, right—nothing. The four of them had disappeared, leaving no trace.

They couldn't have reached the cliffs in such a short time, and there were no visible hiding places. It was as if they'd become invisible, evaporated into the night air. But how? Even if they had somehow turned invisible, where were their clothes? How had they vanished so completely?

I grappled with the inexplicable. Had the desert's illusions finally ensnared me, casting shadows where none existed? Were Romy and the Arabs mere figments of my imagination, conjured by the desert's tricks?

Desperately, I fought to keep my thoughts rational, considering all scenarios. Was there a hidden path or entrance I had overlooked? Had they descended into a concealed cavern or passageway?

Determined to solve the mystery, I inched forward, cautiously advancing toward the cliffs. There had to be an explanation, a tangible reason for their disappearance. The answer lay hidden in the sands, and I was determined to find it.

I was sure they had headed for the cliffs, and I wondered if they had buried themselves in the sand as a tactic—perhaps they sensed they were being followed. But after waiting twenty minutes without any indication of movement, my theory seemed flawed.

Reluctantly, I considered the unsettling thought that perhaps they were mere illusions, phantoms crafted by the desert's whims. Yet, the effort I'd spent tracking them felt too substantial to dismiss so easily.

As I stood to dust off the sand, a sudden "chi chi" sound pierced the air. Instinct kicked in, and I dropped to the ground, rolling aside just as several arrows embedded themselves where I'd been standing moments before.

I peered toward the cliffs, catching a fleeting glimpse of a figure before more arrows rained down. Quick reflexes saved me again as I rolled out of harm's way. The arrows were too precise and powerful to be fired from a hand-held bow—perhaps an ancient mechanism lay hidden in the cliffs.

With no cover in the barren desert, running seemed futile. The archer's range was likely vast, and retreating might only increase my vulnerability. I pressed myself deeper into the sand, minimizing my profile.

The barrage continued, but my new position seemed to thwart the archer's aim. Then, the eerie wail of a horn echoed from the cliffs, reminiscent of a hyena's call. I glanced up, spotting the glint of Arab scimitars and several figures silhouetted against the rock face.

The cliffs likely housed a tribe, perhaps the same one Romy had encountered. I questioned my next move — should I attempt to pass through, or retreat? As I deliberated, the unexpected happened.

The sand in front of me shifted, and an Arab rose from beneath the surface, his presence startling me. He brandished a scimitar, but I reacted swiftly. Lunging toward him, I veered at the last moment, maneuvering behind him and locking his head and neck in a tight grip.

He struggled, but I held firm, compelling him to drop his weapon. The scimitar fell with a dull thud, and I maintained my hold, aware that this was a precarious situation. I needed information, and this man might hold the answers to the mysteries I sought. The desert's secrets were close, and I was determined to uncover them, no matter the risks involved.

Chapter 18

The Best Arab Knifeman

As I leaned over to retrieve the scimitar, I was met with an astonishing sight—a tunnel, its entrance hidden beneath the sand where the Arab had emerged. The existence of such a passage in the desert was beyond belief, a concealed artery in the expanse of sand.

With the scimitar poised at the Arab's neck, I prepared to interrogate him. But before I could speak, two more Arabs surfaced from the tunnel, blowpipes aimed steadily at me. Their emergence was swiftly followed by a dozen more, until I found myself encircled by fifteen Arabs, their expressions a mask of hostility.

In that moment, I was at a loss. Holding one man hostage offered little protection against the poised blowpipes surrounding me. There was no cover, no strategic advantage, just the oppressive density of adversaries.

Tension filled the air, a standoff crackling with potential violence. Then, cutting through the silence, Romy's voice rang out.

"Ash, don't hurt anyone! Put down the knife!" he urged, his voice carrying urgency and authority. Before I could decide, Romy appeared, leaping from the tunnel, commanding the scene in Arabic with a raised hand. The men around me lowered their weapons.

Following suit, I relinquished the Arab and dropped the scimitar. Romy hurried over, his expression a mix of relief and panic. "Why are you here? God, why are you here?" he exclaimed.

I matched his urgency with my own question, "Why are you here?"

Before he could respond, another figure emerged from the tunnel. Instantly, all the Arabs fell to their knees in deference. The newcomer was clearly their leader, his presence commanding respect.

He was distinctive, adorned in a cape embroidered with gold thread, a stark contrast to the shirtless or simply clad men around him. The scabbard of his scimitar, inlaid with gems, declared his status and authority.

The tense standoff shifted as the chief's presence commanded respect from his followers, who knelt silently. Romy urged me to bow, saying, "Ash, bow quickly, he is the chief."

I couldn't help but scoff at the notion. "Why should I bow to him?" I replied defiantly.

The chief, with an air of superiority, approached me. His voice, confident and fluent in French, demanded, "Salute!"

I met his gaze, my tone icy. "Courtesy is a two-way street. If you don't salute me, why should I salute you?"

His hand moved to the hilt of his knife, anger flashing across his face. Romy intervened, pleading with the chief, "Your Excellency, he's my best friend!"

The chief's anger didn't wane. "Your best friend refuses to show respect," he retorted.

Romy glanced at me, hoping for a change of heart, but I remained resolute, unwilling to yield to intimidation.

The chief's raised arm signaled a potential attack, prompting the Arabs to rise, their eyes fixed on me with fierce intent. I stood my ground, brandishing the scimitar across my chest, ready to defend myself.

Romy's voice cut through the tension. "Ash, can you really take on so many alone?"

I replied with a smirk, "Romy, you don't understand."

Romy turned to the chief, appealing to his sense of fairness. "This is too unfair. Aren't Arabs known for their fairness?"

The chief hesitated, his arm lowering at Romy's words. He considered for a moment before proposing a duel. "I can let him fight with Yupdo to decide his fate."

The color drained from Romy's face. "Sir Chief, this is still unfair. You, the greatest among all Arab nations with a blade, and Yupdo, your most renowned knifeman—this is not fair."

Romy's efforts to secure fair treatment for me indicated his goodwill, and I realized my own actions might have complicated matters.

Romy spread his hands in a gesture of helplessness, his eyes meeting mine with a mixture of frustration and concern. I offered a reassuring smile, my voice steady. "I believe the chief is being fair. Besides, I'm intrigued to meet this legendary knifeman—the finest among the Arabs."

The chief chuckled, his hand landing on Romy's shoulder with a hearty slap. "Friend Romy, do you still think I'm unjust?"

Romy sighed deeply, resignation etched into his features. "Ash, you've turned everything upside down."

I gave a small, apologetic shrug. "Romy, what choice do I have now? Is showing weakness even an option?" His voice rose with a note of urgency. "You can't show weakness, but you're risking a duel with Yupdo simply because you refused to bow. Do you even know who he is? His sword moves with the swiftness of lightning, his agility unmatched. By the time you notice his hand move, the sands are already soaked with your blood."

I maintained my calm demeanor. "Romy, perhaps there's something out there even swifter than lightning, more agile than a mongoose."

Romy clapped his hands together, exasperation giving way to incredulity. "Is that something you? Before Youpdo earned his reputation as the tribe's greatest knifeman, I witnessed him leap forward and dispatch two German soldiers before they could even draw their weapons!"

With sincerity, I replied, "Thank you, Romy, for your concern. Yet, I'd rather face Yupdo than bow to him."

With a sigh, Romy accepted my decision. The chieftain led the way into the cave, followed by several others, with Romy and me trailing behind. As we entered, the mystery of their sudden disappearance became clear — they'd simply entered the tunnel.

Yet, questions lingered in my mind. The tunnel was built of massive stone blocks, ancient and enduring. "Where does this tunnel lead?" I asked Romy.

"To an ancient city," he answered, his voice carrying a hint of nostalgia. "A city long forgotten by history."

I paused in awe. "Is the city within these cliffs?"

"Yes," Romy confirmed. "The structures are camouflaged with local stone, invisible from above. The

Germans flew countless reconnaissance missions but never found it. That's why it remained hidden."

"So, this was your base?" I inquired.

Romy nodded. "Yes, one of them. During the war, I saved Chief Feisha from German soldiers, and he granted me access to the city. I'm the only outsider allowed here."

I laughed, "Now there are two, and I'm one of them."

Romy gave a wry smile, "I mean, I'm the only one who can enter and leave this ancient city unharmed."

A burst of laughter escaped me, catching the attention of the Arabs ahead. Chief Feisha turned, his gaze piercing through the dim light of the tunnel. "Romy, do you believe Yupdo will surely finish me off?"

Before Romy could respond, Chief Feisha's voice boomed through the passage. "No one escapes once Yupdo sets his sights on them."

I smirked, "Chief, surely you won't hesitate to unleash Yupdo on me unless you fear your boasts might crumble against reality."

Romy's expression paled, and though the darkness obscured Feisha's face, his heavy steps forward betrayed his fury. I understood what I'd invited—a duel with the finest Arab swordsman, a dance of blades where skill met destiny. It was a rare moment in an era overshadowed by modern warfare, offering a chance to embrace the ancient art of combat.

Romy sighed repeatedly, while I, undeterred, pursued my curiosity. "When was this ancient city built, Romy?"

"I'm no archaeologist," he replied, "but the pyramid you seek is linked to it."

This revelation thrilled me. "How do you know?"

"In that city, there's a statue called the 'Invisible God'— mostly destroyed. Aren't you searching for invisibility secrets in the pyramid?"

His words confirmed my hopes. This city could have housed the Sopa people, transported here by an Egyptian pharaoh. They likely abandoned the harsh desert for the Nile, leaving the city forgotten and untouched by history.

"Why didn't you tell me sooner?" I chided.

"I wasn't sure if they still lived here. Egypt's seen immense change. It's absurd that the tribe remains loyal to a deposed king. The government searches for them, clueless to their whereabouts."

"Then why did you do a handstand on the sand?" I pressed.

Romy shot me a look. "So you were watching me? You don't trust me?"

"Please, Romy," I hurriedly reassured, "it just seemed strange."

He shrugged. "This Arab tribe is the desert's pride. Skilled in blades, archery, and sand crawling. I knew if they were still here, they'd notice us and send scouts."

"But why the upside-down stance?" I asked.

"Don't you see? Standing makes it hard to spot movement in the sand. Upside down, my eyes are closer to the ground, making it easier to detect shifting dunes."

I chuckled, "Why not just lie flat?"

"I couldn't hide that way. Lying on the ground would seem suspicious, like I was concealing myself, and they'd see me as a threat."

I nodded, "You didn't want me on watch in case I provoked them?"

Romy sighed, "Yet you still managed to offend them, and it was Chief Feisha himself!"

As we walked through the tunnel, I pondered aloud, "Romy, if I manage to defeat Youpdu, what do you think they'll do to me?" Romy shook his head, dismissing the notion. "It's impossible," he said. I pressed on, "I said 'if.' Humor me."

Romy sighed, "Many in their tribe have tried to best Yupdo, but all have fallen to his blade. The tribe leader has forbidden further challenges. Yupdo is the spiritual pillar of this community. If you were to defeat him, can you imagine your standing among them?"

I nodded, imagining the possibilities. "Perhaps Chief Feisha would salute me instead."

"It's possible, if you can win," Romy conceded.

Just then, we emerged from the tunnel into blinding light as a massive stone door swung open. We climbed a series of stone steps to reach a stone square. The sight before me was astonishing—a hidden ancient city nestled within the cliffs, its stone structures exuding a timeless, legendary aura.

Despite the grandeur of the stone architecture, the tribe's poverty was palpable. The camels were emaciated, their clothes threadbare, yet there was a vitality in their eyes, a resilience that defied their circumstances.

Chief Feisha raised his hand, commanding attention. "This outsider will face our hero, Yupdo!" he announced.

His proclamation spread like wildfire, and within moments, the entire city buzzed with the news. Feisha turned to me, extending an invitation. "Anyone who challenges Yupdo is my guest. Please, join me at my residence."

I quipped with a wry smile, "Feels a bit like a condemned man's last meal, doesn't it?"

Feisha glared, his expression stern, and led the way. Romy nudged me, resigned. "Come on, enjoy your pre-execution meal."

I couldn't suppress my excitement. The prospect of dueling Yupdo was thrilling. While I didn't underestimate him, I relished the challenge. The parallels between Arab and ancient Oriental martial arts fascinated me, and I longed to test my skills against a worthy opponent.

We followed Feisha through the city, its vastness and stone architecture reminiscent of the Arabian Nights. Yet reality was stark—the true rulers here were poverty and disease, starkly contrasting the opulence of those fabled splendor.

Wherever we went, people gathered, their spirits unbowed by hardship. Even the children, thin and ragged, jeered playfully, their strange sounds echoing like a challenge.

We soon arrived at Chief Feisha's residence—a temple. Its walls bore intricate carvings, their preservation remarkable. The reliefs of animal-headed, human-bodied figures mirrored those in the seven secret sacrificial chambers.

I thought of the diamonds set in the eyes of those statues. If I defeated Yupdo, I might reveal this secret to Chief Feisha, persuading him to offer it to the Egyptian government. This could be the key to ending their nomadic existence, for despite their strength, remaining in this ancient city meant inevitable decline.

The chief's residence was spartan—an old military blanket draped over a large stone. Yet when Feisha settled there, he exuded the majesty of a king on a gilded throne.

I surveyed the surroundings, and Feisha remarked, "Simple, isn't it?"

I shrugged, maintaining my composure. "I believe you have the potential to improve the lives of your people, but it seems you're choosing not to, Chief Feisha."

Feisha's pride flared. "Of course, my people need me."

"But it seems you don't truly value them," I countered.

Feisha's face flushed with anger, and those around him turned tense. Romy warned, "Ash, you should watch your words."

I spread my arms wide. "I've been cautious, can't you see? Chief Feisha is keeping his people in poverty and hardship!"

Feisha let out a furious roar, drawing his scimitar and charging at me with the ferocity of a tiger. I retreated, step by step, evading his swift and relentless strikes.

"Fight back, coward, fight back!" Feisha bellowed, halting his assault.

I met his gaze coolly. "Where is Yupdo? I want to face the best knifeman."

I had spoken deliberately, hoping to provoke Feisha into realizing his limitations. The world had moved on from the days of Arab conquest. He was not a leader of a great empire, but a chief in a hidden city, clinging to outdated ideals. If he could let go, there might be hope for him and his people.

My words struck a chord, and Feisha's confidence wavered, his face paling. His scimitar paused mid-swing. "Do you wish to meet Yupdo now?"

I smiled. "Has my last meal been canceled? Then please, summon Yupdo."

Feisha barked orders to an Arab nearby, who promptly dashed off. Silence fell over the temple, save for Feisha's disdainful sneers. Ten minutes later, the messenger returned, breathless and excited. Behind him strode Yupdo—the only other Arab wearing a shirt besides Feisha and the women.

Feisha's demeanor shifted instantly, his arms outstretched in welcome. Yupdo reciprocated, and they embraced, patting each other's shoulders in a gesture of respect.

Romy leaned in, whispering, "That's Yupdo."

I observed Yupdo carefully. He stood tall, a good half-head above me, with unusually long arms. A scimitar hung at his waist, its gem-encrusted scabbard a stark contrast to his worn clothing. Yet, his proud and noble bearing surpassed even the opulence of his weapon. His eyes, sharp as an eagle's, locked onto mine.

As I studied him, Feisha spoke animatedly with Yupdo, undoubtedly discussing me. Yupdo's gaze remained fixed on mine. After a tense half-minute, he bypassed Feisha and approached me.

I straightened, meeting his steady gaze. In halting French, he stated, "You want to compete with me, yes?"

I nodded. "Yes."

Yupdo continued, "I never underestimate my opponents, but I ensure their defeat is honorable."

In that split second, Yupdo's arm flicked, and the air sang with the sharp "clang" of metal. A brilliant flash of light sliced through my vision, followed by a sudden chill atop my head. Then, just as swiftly, the sound echoed again, and Yupdo resumed his poised stance before me, as if nothing had occurred.

The entire sequence unfolded in less than a heartbeat.

Romy's voice broke the stunned silence, tinged with disbelief. "Ash, oh, Ash!"

I turned, bewildered, "What? Romy, what's going on?"

Laughter erupted around us, a chorus of amusement, with only Romy and Yupdo remaining solemn.

Romy gazed at me with a mix of sadness and disbelief. "Touch your head, Ash."

The sensation was sudden and chilling. Yupdo's blade had barely grazed me, but my head felt disturbingly cold. Something was off. My hand instinctively shot up to touch my scalp.

My fingers froze mid-motion as they encountered the alien smoothness. A large swath of hair had vanished. The spot felt as though it had been meticulously shaved with a razor, its surface unnaturally smooth.

As my hand slowly traced the damage, I discovered the cut was not a random bald patch. It was a precise strip, two fingers wide, spanning from my left ear to the right. Not a single hair remained in its path.

Although no mirror was at hand, I imagined the grotesque mask my face must have become. Chief Feisha's laughter filled the room, tears streaming down his cheeks in uncontrolled mirth.

In that moment, Romy's descriptions of Yupdo's prowess crystallized in my mind. His waist knife, with its razor-sharp edge, had sheared my hair effortlessly, sparing my scalp. What sort of mastery was this? A fraction more force and my ear would have been severed. Yet, he wielded his blade with surgical precision. Such control, such... power.

Even armed with a pistol, I would have been defenseless. Yupdo's strike was too swift, too unexpected. Drawing my weapon in time would have been a futile endeavor.

Finally, after what felt like an eternity, I withdrew my trembling hand.

As the laughter subsided, I finally lowered my hand, the weight of the encounter settling in. Yupdo's prowess was a testament to both the art and the danger of ancient martial traditions, a humbling reminder of the skills honed far from the modern world's gaze.

Yupdo smirked, "I don't think you dare challenge my swordsmanship again, right?"

Without waiting for a response, he turned and began walking toward Chief Feisha. I let him take two steps before calling out, "Yupdo, hold on a moment." He halted, and I spoke slowly, "You seem quite confident. I haven't given my answer yet."

Yupdo spun around, and the Arab who had been laughing loudly was suddenly silent, mouth agape.

Ignoring their reactions, I addressed Yupdo, "Just now, I witnessed what might be the fastest sword technique in the world, but that doesn't mean I've abandoned the idea of competing with you."

As I spoke, I advanced toward him with deliberate calm. Concealing my intentions, I kept the scimitar behind my back and continued, "I admire the speed of your blade, but that doesn't mean you have scared me!"

At the end of my sentence, my scimitar quivered in my hand. Although I wielded an Arabian scimitar, I employed an ancient Chinese sword technique. The blade carved a perfect circle in the air, its tip landing precisely at Yupdo's chest. Before anyone could grasp what had happened, I had already withdrawn the knife and stepped back.

The temple fell into an uneasy silence, broken only by Yupdo's laughter. He glanced down, observing a perfect, round hole a foot in diameter cut into the fabric of his chest garment. The fallen cloth at his feet prompted another bout of laughter. "Sure, you can challenge me. Yes, you are indeed qualified for that!"

Chief Feisha's eyes widened in disbelief as he exchanged words with Yupdo.

Romy approached me, ""Feisha is asking Yupdo if he believes he can absolutely win, and Yupdo said no."

I quickly asked, "Then, what might their next plan be?"

Romy reassured me, "Don't worry, they are proud, but not mean." I nodded, "That's good." Romy stared at me for a moment, but said nothing.

In the ancient city, strange horn sounds echoed and faint, noisy voices filled the air. Chief Feisha's expression was no longer as proud as when Yupdo had cut off my hair. He turned to me coldly, "The competition is about to begin." With that, I strode out.

As I exited the temple, Yupdo rushed over, walking beside me. Neither of us spoke; he didn't even glance at me. We marched forward with a shared seriousness.

I stole a few glances at him, and my own expression grew grave.

I was challenging the honor of their nation. The gravity of the situation left no room for laughter.

The weight of the moment pressed down on me as I walked alongside Yupdo, the path lined with solemn faces, young and old alike.

This was more than a duel; it was a challenge to the very honor of their nation. The gravity of it all made laughter impossible, even if I had the urge.

As we reached the stone platform, the haunting melody of the horns ceased abruptly, leaving a profound silence in its wake. The open space around us was teeming with people; it felt as though the entire tribe had gathered to witness our confrontation. Yet, despite the crowd, an eerie stillness enveloped us.

Dawn's first light cast a gray hue over the ancient city, its rich history and proud people lending an air of mystique to the scene. I stood there, grappling with emotions that were impossible to articulate.

Chief Feisha approached us with measured steps, his presence commanding respect. "You have the right to choose a good knife," he offered, breaking the silence.

I glanced at the scimitar in my hand, its weight familiar and reassuring. "Thank you, I think this one is very good," I replied, appreciating the balance of the weapon.

"Then, raise your weapon horizontally," Chief Feisha instructed.

I complied, lifting my scimitar to meet Yupdo's in a horizontal stance. The tips of our blades touched, intertwining to form a strange "S" shape—an emblem of the dance of steel that was about to commence.

As Chief Feisha stepped back, my heart pounded with anticipation. I expected the command to begin the contest at any moment, and the tension was almost unbearable. The world seemed to hold its breath, waiting for the inevitable clash.

Chapter 19

Life and Death Duel

The tension in the air was palpable as Chief Feisha's voice cut through the silence, delivering news that sent a shockwave through me. "It's getting light, the almighty sun is about to rise, and you two can start the contest when the first ray of sunlight shines into the ancient city. May the true God Allah protect you!" His words echoed in my mind.

The contest would begin with the first light of dawn—a moment I couldn't predict, but one that Yupdo, a native of this ancient city, would anticipate with ease. The thought unnerved me. A half-second advantage could mean the difference between life and death, and Yupdo's blade was swift.

I glanced at Romy, whose face was ashen, reflecting the gravity of the impending duel. Yet, in that moment, clarity struck me. I devised a strategy, focusing intently on Yupdo, not on his face, but on his chest, where a circle cut in his clothing revealed his bare skin — a funny vulnerability amidst his stoic facade.

As I fixed my gaze, unease crept into his eyes, betraying his discomfort. The crowd, a sea of expectant faces, bore witness to his exposed state. His scimitar began to tremble ever so slightly, the pressure of countless eyes weighing heavily upon him.

While my shorn hair was a testament to Yupdo's prowess, it was my status as an outsider that spared me from ridicule. Yupdo, however, was not afforded such leniency. His pride was on the line, and I could see the anger brewing within him.

This was my aim—to provoke him, for anger in battle often led to misjudgment. I stood poised, awaiting his move, knowing that in his fury, he might falter.

The sky lightened incrementally, the sun a mere promise on the horizon. Despite Yupdo's growing rage, the memory of his blade's precision left me wary. I held my breath, every muscle taut with anticipation, as I awaited the first rays of sunlight to seal our fates.

In that fleeting moment, I caught a glimpse of Yupdo's face, a mask of long-suppressed tension about to explode into action. It was the telltale sign—the first ray of sunlight was about to pierce the ancient city's horizon. Instinctively, I lowered my body just as Yupdo's scimitar, catching the sun's first light, sliced through the air toward my shoulder like a bolt of lightning.

I had already braced myself to retreat, but despite my swift movement, his blade still managed to graze my sleeve. As I fell back, Yupdo pressed forward with an agility that surpassed my expectations, his knife skills far more refined than I had anticipated.

For the next five minutes, I danced on the edge of mortality. The air around me was filled with the silver streaks of his blade, each swing a near-miss that felt like the wrath of the heavens themselves. It was as if the universe had decided my time was up and sent down a storm of lightning to claim me.

I twisted and turned, leaping and rolling in a desperate bid to evade each lethal arc. Yet the relentless assault left its mark—my body bore many bloodstains, and my clothes hung in tatters.

Then, I seized the moment to counterattack.

Our scimitars clashed, the metallic clang resonating with a thrilling intensity that held the crowd in breathless anticipation.

Gradually, I sensed a change in Yupdo; his breath came in heavier gasps, and the precision of his strikes began to falter. Five minutes into my counteroffensive, his advantage waned, and in his haste to secure victory, missteps crept in.

I swung my blade in a wide arc toward his waist, and he ducked, almost squatting to evade the blow. My scimitar whizzed past his head by mere inches.

In that moment, Yupdo made a critical error. Instead of retreating to reassess, he lunged forward, stabbing upward with his scimitar in a bold attempt to end the duel decisively.

It was a move that could have spelled my end, yet it was the opportunity I had been waiting for. As he committed to the strike, I launched myself over him, soaring past his head to land deftly behind him.

Yupdo had put all his force into that thrust, expecting it to conclude our battle. As I leaped, his blade sliced through empty air, his momentum unchecked, causing him to stumble forward, off balance, and vulnerable.

I had anticipated this exact moment. As I landed behind Yupdo, my elbow swiftly retracted, driving the handle of my knife into his back with precision. He let out a primal howl, the sound echoing like a wounded beast, as he stumbled forward.

Yet, Yupdo's skills were not to be underestimated. Even as he faltered, he spun around with remarkable speed, launching a backhanded stab in my direction. But I was already a step ahead. My blade met his hand with a decisive strike, forcing his fingers to release their grip. His scimitar began its descent, severed from his control before it could complete its arc.

In a fluid motion, I withdrew my hand, allowing my knife to clash against his with a resonant "clang." In that instant, I released my grip, letting both blades clatter to the ground in unison.

To the onlookers, our exchange appeared as a synchronized dance, our scimitars seemingly flung aside by mutual force. But Yupdo knew the truth. He stood motionless, his face a canvas of disbelief and frustration.

Seizing the moment, I shouted, "Romy, look! I've held my own against this master Arab knifeman!"

Yupdo's body trembled slightly, his eyes locking onto mine with a mixture of confusion and incredulity. I offered him a smile, extending a gesture of camaraderie amidst the chaos. "Perhaps the true God Allah desires for two great knifemen to coexist in this world. So when our blades clashed, they both found their place on the ground."

In that moment, I extended not just a challenge, but a recognition of mutual respect—a testament to the skill and spirit that had brought us to this defining confrontation.

Yupdo stretched out his arms, his lips quivering, unable to find words for a long moment. The tremor in his voice spoke volumes, and I knew he had grasped my intentions. With a smile, I watched as he finally whispered,

"Allah!" It was a powerful invocation, a recognition of the moment's significance.

In an instant, he closed the distance between us, enveloping me in a bear hug with his powerful arms. I returned the embrace, our camaraderie expressed in the solid thud of hands on backs. Around us, the crowd erupted into a cacophony of thunderous cheers, their voices echoing with such force that any patrol within thirty miles could surely pinpoint this hidden city's location.

As we parted, Yupdo handed me his scimitar, and I reciprocated, exchanging weapons as a gesture of mutual respect. Though our duel had lasted less than half an hour, the sun had risen fully, casting its light over every forgotten corner of the ancient city.

The people around us were jubilant, their cries reaching a fever pitch. Yet, as Chief Feisha approached, the noise hushed into an expectant silence. Standing before us, he paused, then made a gesture that caught me by surprise—a salute.

In an ironic twist of fate, I found myself bowing in return to the man whose authority I had once defied. As I rose, Chief Feisha placed a hand on my shoulder and spoke softly, "Actually, you didn't have to return the greeting." I laughed, asking, "Do you think I am impolite?"

Chief Feisha, a swordsman of note himself, had seen through the guise of our duel. He knew I had emerged victorious.

His salute was more than a gesture; it was an acknowledgment of my skill and our shared respect. As the tribe's leader, he saluted me before his people, a testament to the nobility of their character. Had he been less honorable, he might have ordered my downfall. But his choice to honor our duel spoke volumes about the integrity of his nation.

Romy rushed to my side, and we embraced. Chief Feisha, holding both Yupdo and me, led us forward, and the crowd's cheers rose anew. In the temple, as the echoes of celebration lingered, Chief Feisha sat with us. We were served earthen wine, its quality humble, yet presented in exquisite ancient Egyptian vessels. As I drank the harsh brew, Chief Feisha asked, "You are not here to travel, so what is it for?"

Wiping the wine from my lips, I replied, "We are here to find a lost pyramid."

At this, Chief Feisha's hand trembled, spilling his drink.

Startled, I asked, "What's wrong?"

He quickly responded, "Nothing. Where is the pyramid you are talking about?" His reaction betrayed a flicker of recognition, hinting at secrets buried beneath the sands, waiting to be uncovered.

I could sense that Chief Feisha was withholding something. I met his gaze, unflinching. "It's near here. Can you tell me where the pyramid I'm searching for is?"

His reaction was telling; his hands shook, spilling wine from his glass once more. He laughed—a hollow, forced sound meant to mask his unease. "This is interesting. I don't know what pyramid there is near here," he claimed.

Initially, I had my doubts about Chief Feisha's knowledge of the pyramid's location. After all, it had vanished beneath the sands for countless years. But his awkward denial only confirmed my suspicions—he knew more than he let on.

My eyes locked onto his, but he quickly averted his gaze.

Just as I was about to press further, Romy interjected with a sigh, "Friend Feisha, you have changed."

Chief Feisha's face flushed crimson. "Romy, what do you mean by this?"

Romy remained composed. "You know it yourself, friend."

Emotion flickered across Feisha's face as he stood abruptly. "Romy, should I reveal what I know, risking the fate of our entire tribe? Tell me."

Romy replied calmly, "You can say that you can't reveal it, instead of pretending ignorance."

Feisha exhaled deeply, turning to me with a pained expression. "Alright, I'll admit it. I know where the pyramid is, but I can't tell you, despite my respect for you."

Feigning indifference, I smiled, though inwardly I was elated. This was a breakthrough, a clue I couldn't ignore. "Can you tell me why?"

Chief Feisha replied, "This pyramid is vital to our tribe's safety. We can't allow outsiders to disrupt it."

I nearly exploded with frustration. His reasoning was steeped in superstition—illogical, yet deeply rooted.

Maintaining a facade of understanding, I said, "So, when you say 'no outsiders are allowed to invade,' you mean the pyramid is somewhere accessible to outsiders?"

Chief Feisha met my eyes, his resolve unwavering. "That's all I can say. I have nothing else to add."

Rising from my seat, I challenged him, "It seems your guardian isn't providing for your people, as you're impoverished and struggling to survive in this ancient city."

Though anger flashed in his eyes, he couldn't refute the truth. "At least the Egyptian government's army hasn't found us, allowing us to endure," he retorted.

Pushing further, I suggested, "Have you considered negotiating with the government?"

Feisha sighed, leaving Romy to explain, "There's no way. The current government received false intelligence that the deposed king holds valuable treasures. They're pursuing him not for political reasons—everyone knows he won't return."

This revelation aligned perfectly with my own plans. Eagerly, I proposed, "I have a way for you to meet the Egyptian government's demands, so you and your people can leave this ancient city behind!"

Feisha's eyes remained fixed on me, searching for any hint of deception. Romy, however, shook his head skeptically. "Ash, you can't possibly manage this. The Egyptian government demands treasures of immense value."

I nodded, assured. "I understand. I can offer a clue about the treasure, and Chief Feisha can present this to the Egyptian government. In exchange, they could gain their freedom."

Feisha's disbelief lingered, but I pressed on. "The treasure consists of twelve unrefined, hand-cut diamonds, each weighing about 300 carats."

Romy staggered in shock. "You're dreaming! This is a dream!" Feisha questioned, "Why not claim them for yourself?"

I shrugged. "We all crave wealth, but beyond a certain point, what difference does it make? I may not have millions, but I have what I need. To me, those diamonds are merely reflective stones."

Chief Feisha murmured, "Such a treasure could indeed liberate my people."

I explained further, "Beneath the ruins of a temple lies the treasure. You need only prove its existence to the government."

Feisha considered this. "Yes, that would allow us to settle by an oasis, rather than relying on deep, muddy wells."

I smiled gently. "Friend Feisha, do you trust me?"

Feisha laughed heartily. "Friend Ash, why would I doubt you? Once you return from the pyramid, I will accompany you to Cairo."

Joy surged through me, though I maintained my composure. I asked casually, "Isn't the pyramid buried under the sand?"

Feisha nodded. "Yes, otherwise it would have been discovered long ago. However, this city and the pyramid are connected by a tunnel leading to its heart."

I leaned in, intrigued. "Really?"

Feisha confirmed, "I've walked partway through the tunnel. Ancient inscriptions suggest it leads to a pyramid. Don't underestimate me; I'm not just a tribal chief but also a scholar of ancient Egyptian history."

I chuckled. "Old friend, I never doubted your knowledge."

Feisha continued, "I turned back last time, but with more people, we can reach the pyramid's interior."

I cautioned, "Entering a pyramid is dangerous. Ancient spells and trapped air could be deadly. Why risk it, Feisha?"

Feisha countered, "If I don't, who will guide you?"

Chapter 20

❧

Exploring the Pyramid

By this point, the three of us—myself, Romy, and Chief Feisha—had formed a bond that transcended mere acquaintance. We called each other "old friends," a testament to the camaraderie that had blossomed amidst these ancient sands.

Romy, ever practical, rose to arrange logistics, requesting two Arabs from Chief Feisha to retrieve essential supplies from our camp. Meanwhile, I stayed behind in the temple, engrossed in conversation with Feisha.

Knowing Feisha's expertise in ancient Egyptian history, my curiosity was piqued. "When was this ancient city built?" I inquired.

Feisha pondered for a moment. "According to my research, it was established shortly after the fall of the Asilia Empire."

I nodded, though the timeline meant little to me. My true interest lay in the purpose behind the city's construction. I asked him directly.

With a wry smile, Feisha replied, "My friend, I can recount endless facts about ancient Egypt, even recite Antony's orations, yet you ask about the one thing I do not know?"

I couldn't help but grin at the irony. "What are your thoughts on the 'invisible god'?" I ventured.

Feisha's expression grew thoughtful. "That is not a deity of Egypt, which puzzles me. What do you think?"

I shared my theory, a tale of a distant tribe rendered invisible, seeking a cure for their plight. "They traveled far, reaching Egypt, where they found what they sought. The secret of invisibility lies within the pyramid we're about to explore."

Feisha chuckled, raising a hand in mock surrender. "Old friend, your imagination outshines the brightest diamond. Truly, you have no need for wealth."

I returned his smile, leaving my story unfinished. To explain fully would require delving into the history of the brass box—a tale for another time.

Our conversation meandered through other topics until Romy returned, carrying a bundle of essential tools: a flashlight, rope with a grappling hook, an oxygen cylinder, and a set of chisels for breaching any barriers we might encounter.

"Everything's ready," I announced. "Where is the entrance to the tunnel?"

I asked again, "Okay, where is the entrance to the tunnel?"

Feisha, with the oxygen cylinder securely on his back, grabbed a powerful flashlight and an infrared viewer for our descent into darkness, ensuring we wouldn't be lost even if the light failed us.

Romy and I trailed behind Feisha as he led the way to the temple's rear. We arrived at a small courtyard where two wells stood side by side—one with a wooden frame, the other bare.

I pointed decisively to the frameless well. "Don't ask how I know, but I'm certain. The tunnel entrance is in the well on the left."

Feisha turned to me with a bemused look. "You seem to have all the answers, don't you?"

I chuckled, understanding his curiosity. The architect who designed this ancient city and temple had a distinctive style, and the similarities in the tunnel entrances were unmistakable to a trained eye.

Feisha entered the well first, carefully lowering himself into its depths. I followed closely, feeling the cool stone walls against my hands, while Romy brought up the rear, ensuring our path was secure.

Reaching the well's bottom, our flashlights pierced the darkness. Feisha cautioned us to conserve power, so I switched mine off, and Romy took the lead. The corridor, hewn from massive stones, bore testament to the extraordinary engineering of ancient Egyptians, their ingenuity echoing through time.

Though not matching the grandeur of the Great Pyramid, this corridor was a marvel in its own right. Its length was daunting, and as we traversed its confines for forty minutes, anticipation grew with each step. Finally, the flashlight beam revealed a round, gilded door, its brilliance both captivating and foreboding.

The door, reminiscent of a submarine hatch, was just large enough for a person to crawl through. The sight prompted me to reignite my flashlight. Feisha advised us to don our oxygen masks before proceeding, a necessary precaution against potential toxic gases within the pyramid.

With masks in place, Feisha and Romy strained against the golden door. The passage's narrowness confined me to the rear, watching as they gradually forced it open. As the door yielded, an eerie sound emanated from within — neither laughter nor tears, but an unsettling mix of both.

The sound chilled me to the bone, conjuring images of ancient mummies welcoming us with their ghastly serenade. Even Feisha, a scholar and authority, was visibly shaken, retreating to the corridor's wall, his body trembling.

Yet, as the initial shock subsided, logic prevailed. The sound was the result of air exchange — a natural phenomenon as fresh air met the stagnant air of the pyramid. I quickly scrawled a message on the wall: "This is the sound of air convection. We don't need to panic."

Feisha, gathering his composure, nodded in understanding. Romy illuminated the passage beyond the door with his flashlight, revealing another corridor. This one, however, required us to crawl, our movements cumbersome under the weight of the oxygen cylinders.

The confined space was challenging, allowing no room to turn. Twenty feet in, we encountered another golden door, adorned with a bull-headed humanoid figure. Despite its size, the statue exuded an intimidating presence, its eyes seeming to follow our every move.

We understood the significance of this moment. We had reached the heart of the pyramid, a sacred and mysterious place buried beneath the shifting sands. The weight of history pressed upon us as we prepared to unlock the secrets hidden within this ancient chamber.

In the heart of a lost pyramid, the strangeness of our situation was both thrilling and terrifying.

Romy pushed the small round door with determination, crawling forward before suddenly vanishing from sight. His body tilted downward, and with a thud, he fell. Chief Feisha and I exchanged a glance of concern, the sound indicating a drop of about three meters—not far, but enough to cause worry.

Feisha quickly attempted to reach out, but was just a moment too late. We both listened intently, relief washing over us as we heard the familiar rhythm of Morse code from below. Romy was communicating: "I hurt my ankle. Be careful when you come down." Feisha responded in kind, tapping out, "We know."

With the oxygen masks covering our mouths, Morse code was our most effective means of communication. Carefully, Feisha crawled forward and descended, followed by my own cautious approach. Prepared for the drop, we landed without injury, despite the cumbersome oxygen cylinders strapped to our backs.

Once grounded, we immediately checked on Romy. Thankfully, his ankle injury was minor, allowing him to walk with assistance. As I helped him up, I swept my flashlight around to illuminate our surroundings. We found ourselves in a stone chamber, starkly empty save for a massive stone coffin at its center. At the far end, a stone door hinted at further mysteries beyond.

Romy knocked on the stone coffin, asking silently, "What do you think?" I nodded, replying, "Let's open it. The secret we seek might be inside."

Armed with chisels and hammers, we set to work, chipping away at the coffin's seal. The cover, nearly as large as the coffin itself, eventually yielded to our efforts, sliding aside with a resounding rumble. Our anticipation was met with a bitter twist of fate—a bronze coffin lay nestled within.

We had hoped to uncover the secrets hidden within the stone coffin, only to be faced with another barrier. Undeterred, I examined the bronze coffin and felt a surge of excitement upon discovering it was secured with bolts. Unlike the stone, these could be easily removed.

Working together, we extracted the bolts one by one and heaved the bronze lid aside. Our flashlights revealed a chilling sight—a mummy, lying undisturbed for centuries.

The mummy lay there, meticulously wrapped, indistinguishable from any other, and the room offered no further clues. With a shrug, I gestured toward the door. It was clear we needed to press on, deeper into the pyramid's mysteries.

Romy pointed to the oxygen gauge, and my heart sank. We had already consumed half of our supply. Feisha quickly communicated via Morse code, "I will withdraw and bring more oxygen cylinders. You continue forward." His departure left Romy and me to forge ahead.

We approached the stone door, pushing it open with combined effort to reveal another chamber. Inside, an iron table stood, its design reminiscent of crafts made from natural tree roots. On this peculiar table rested a brass box, the room otherwise barren.

As I picked up the box, its weight was reassuring. A shake elicited a soft "boo" from within, confirming contents inside. The craftsmanship was identical to the brass box Sem had given me, raising the stakes of our discovery. Was it the key to reversing the curse of invisibility, or did it harbor the very mineral that could doom us to transparency?

If it held the solution, our quest was complete. But if it contained the hazardous mineral, exposure in this chamber meant inevitable transformation for Romy and me. The gravity of the decision weighed heavily as I stood in contemplation.

Romy, sensing my hesitation, urged me to explain. I conveyed the situation through code, revealing the true peril of our find. Understanding the risk, Romy responded with resolve: "If we are destined to become invisible, let's face it. Open the box."

With determination, I wielded the chisel and hammer, working at the box's seam. The hinge gave way under the pressure, and I opened the lid, stepping back instinctively. My heart raced, the anticipation electric.

The contents of the box revealed a mineral unlike anything I had ever encountered. It was about the size of four fists and emitted a mesmerizing array of multicolored lights. These weren't just the standard colors of the rainbow; they blended and morphed into dozens of hues, each more vibrant than the last. It was a spectacle both beautiful and bewildering.

Staring at the mineral, a thought crept into my mind: Was this the infamous "transparent light" that could render someone invisible? Panic flickered as I considered the possibility. I quickly examined myself, checking my hands and arms, reassured to find them still solid and visible. Romy, too, remained unchanged, though equally entranced by the mineral's display.

Was this not the light that transformed people? Or had we not been exposed long enough for the effects to take hold?

For a moment, I was paralyzed by these questions, fixated on finding an answer rather than acting. Precious minutes slipped by before the realization struck—I needed to close the box. If the transformation required more time, shutting the lid might prevent it.

With urgency, I snapped the lid shut, breaking the mineral's captivating spell. Romy tapped out, "My God, what is this?"

I responded, "That is transparent light."

He questioned, "Why didn't the two of us become transparent?"

I smiled wryly as I typed, "I don't understand either. That mineral, with its strange, colorful light, seemed like it must be 'transparent light'—wait—"

In that moment, a realization struck me. Recalling what Liam and Nora had described, I remembered they had seen a blinding white light, not a spectrum of colors like this. My fingers danced over the keys with renewed energy, "Transparent light is a strong white light, not colorful. What we found must be 'anti-transparent light.' We've achieved our goal."

Romy knocked out a message, "Then let's take the box and retreat; the oxygen is running out." I nodded, securing the brass box under my arm, and we began our careful retreat through the corridor.

As we neared the exit, Feisha and his team appeared, ready with additional supplies. We sealed the small round door to the pyramid's heart and removed our oxygen masks.

"Why did you withdraw?" Feisha inquired.

Romy answered, "We found what we were looking for."

Feisha asked, "No need to go further into the pyramid?"

"I don't believe we need to," I replied.

Feisha grinned, "I have good news too. I've contacted our representative in Cairo via transmitter. He agrees that your proposal could indeed free our tribe, and he's already in talks with the government."

I shook his hand warmly. "Congratulations on your progress."

With that, we navigated the corridor and emerged from the well. Though Feisha wished for us to stay longer in the ancient city, I was eager to return to Cairo. Liam and Nora were surely waiting anxiously on that isolated island.

We bid farewell to Chief Feisha and made our way back to camp. Romy reclined in the tent, admitting, "Ash, when you fought with Yupdo, I was truly scared."

I chuckled, "Believe me, I was scared too."

Romy regarded me with admiration. "You seem capable of anything."

"Don't say that," I replied hastily. "I'm no more than a fortunate adventurer, not omnipotent."

"But now you possess the secret to invisibility," Romy pointed out. "Isn't that something?"

"I don't wish to be invisible," I confessed. "I know someone who, after becoming invisible, found no joy in life."

Romy laughed, and I continued earnestly, "I just want to help those two young people who became invisible. By exposing them to the mineral's colorful light, they can return to normal. This adventure of mine, it seems, has been worthwhile."

Chapter 21

Becoming Invisible

As I spoke, my hand absently rested on the lid of the brass box, which was positioned directly before me. Sitting cross-legged on the ground, I finished my sentence and lifted my hand. The broken hinge allowed the lid to shift slightly, creating a narrow gap between the lid and the box.

In that instant, a blinding white light burst forth from the gap, so intense it was as if a searing white fireball had ignited within our tent. Romy leapt up, startled, and the overwhelming brightness momentarily blinded me.

A wave of inexplicable terror washed over me, my body trembling uncontrollably. I heard Romy's frantic shout, "Oh my God! My hand!"

Instinctively, I looked at my own hands and cried out in disbelief. Before my eyes, the flesh and muscles of my hands vanished, leaving only skeletal remains. The transformation was rapid and shocking, leaving no time to process what was happening.

Amidst this chaos, I heard a sound—a cry. I turned to see Romy, or rather, his skeletal form, hands raised to his face. The muscles on his head and face had disappeared, leaving me unable to discern his expression, though the sound of his voice suggested he was crying.

Compelled by a desperate need to understand, I touched my own face. The muscles were there, but invisible to my eyes, a realization that heightened my panic to unprecedented levels.

In the following minutes, panic consumed me. My mind spun as I grappled with the reality of our situation. Then, with a surge of determination, I lunged forward and slammed the lid of the brass box shut.

The tent, once filled with brilliant white light, plunged into darkness. I panted heavily, the urge to cry out loud stifled by a sense of despair. It felt as though I had regressed to childhood fears, trapped in a nightmarish void.

I recalled the description of the transparent fish from the "Original Color Tropical Fish Atlas": an overwhelming sense of self-fear. As a newly invisible person, I understood that fear intimately, a terror that gripped every nerve and cell in my body, more profound than any fear of judgment or persecution.

Despite our strength, Romy and I were reduced to tears and gasps, struggling to process the transformation. It was a long time before I could quell the paralyzing fear, allowing a semblance of calm to return.

At that moment, Romy stopped crying, though his voice was still shaky. "Ash, what is going on?" he asked, desperation lacing his words. I took a deep breath, trying to steady myself. "I don't know, Romy, but we have become transparent people."

Romy pressed on, "Why did it change? You mentioned the box emitted 'anti-transparent light.' Why did it suddenly become transparent light?"

I gave a bitter smile, shaking my head. The sight of a skull shaking atop a spine is surely unsettling. "I don't know why," I admitted.

"What should we do?" Romy asked, his voice filled with urgency. "I only know that if we keep exposing ourselves to this light, we might become fully invisible, which might be better than this half-state," I replied, though without conviction.

Romy was quick to reject the idea. "No!" he exclaimed, horrified by the thought.

The irony wasn't lost on me. In my quest to help Liam and Nora regain their visibility, I had unwittingly become what I sought to cure—a transparent person myself.

Dejected, I sat there while Romy pleaded, "Think of a way. I don't want to be a transparent monster or an invisible person. Let me be an ordinary person, even if it means being a drunkard or a wanderer in Cairo!"

I had no comforting words for him. I shared his sentiment—I would rather be a beggar scratching at scabs on the street than live as a transparent being, unable to see my own skin.

After some time, I asked, "Do you remember the center of the pyramid?" Romy replied, "What about it?"

"Why did the mineral emit colorful light there but changed to bright white here?" I wondered aloud.

Romy shrugged, "Who knows? Maybe a witch cast a spell."

Suddenly, a thought struck me. "Romy, don't lose hope. The transparent people who arrived in Egypt millennia ago did find a way to return to their original form here. There must be something in Egypt that can emit 'anti-transparent light.'"

"You said you found it!" Romy reminded me.

Resolutely, I placed my hand on the box's lid and opened it once more. The blinding white light filled the tent, prompting Romy to shout, "What are you doing?"

I quickly surveyed the box's contents before closing it again. The mineral was unchanged, yet its light had transformed from colorful to white. What caused this shift?

Confused, I sat there, avoiding looking at Romy huddled in the corner. We were trapped in our helplessness, waiting without knowing what for.

My mind was a chaotic whirl, a vortex of thoughts spinning too fast to grasp. Then, amidst the confusion, a realization dawned on me.

In the pyramid, we wore oxygen masks. I had tried to use a lighter, which failed due to the lack of oxygen. The Egyptians knew how to preserve mummies by expelling air from the pyramid, creating near-vacuum conditions over the centuries. Radioactive substances can emit different types of radiation in varying environments.

This insight was like a beacon in the darkness. Perhaps the environment within the pyramid altered the properties of the mineral's light. My heart surged with hope, convinced we had found a clue to reverse our predicament.

The realization struck me like lightning—the mineral in the brass box was identical to the one that had turned Liam, Nora, and Braque into transparent people. This mineral, brought by the wandering Inca Empire group, emitted transparent light in normal air, a blazing white light. But when isolated in the near-vacuum environment of a pyramid, it emitted the colorful, anti-transparent light.

I stood up abruptly, excitement coursing through me, confident in my deduction. This explained why the Sopa tribe wanderers found restoration in Egypt. Without modern vacuum technology, they had stumbled into the pyramids, discovering the mineral's transformative light by accident.

"Romy, I've found the real translucent light!" I exclaimed.

Romy, skeptical, shook his head, his skeletal form oddly comical despite the gravity of the situation. "You've found it once," he retorted.

"This time it's real," I insisted, "The mineral emits colorful light inside the pyramid but white light here in the tent. Do you know why?"

"God knows why!" Romy replied, exasperated.

"It's not God," I said, "It's because there's no air inside the pyramid. Remember, I couldn't light my lighter?"

"So what?" Romy's voice was still filled with despair.

"We need to go back inside the pyramid!" I declared, standing with determination. Romy laughed, a strange, unsettling sound, his skeletal jaw clattering.

"What are you laughing at?" I demanded.

"Are we going like this? We won't even reach the ancient city before we're seen as monsters and attacked!" Romy pointed out.

His words, though grim, had merit. As transparent people, we carried an overwhelming sense of self-fear. Despite the absurdity of our state, Romy's concern was valid.

After a moment of contemplation, I clapped my hands with a plan. "We can expose ourselves to more transparent light, making even our skeletons invisible. Then we can travel unseen to the pyramid."

"But what about the box?" Romy pointed out. "If we take it, people will see a floating box!"

"You're right," I admitted with a bitter smile. "But we can't avoid risk altogether."

Romy, suddenly exasperated, shouted, "I followed you into this, and look where it got me!" In his frustration, he lunged at me.

I never anticipated Romy's sudden, desperate actions. His hands grasped for my throat, driven by the panic and disorientation of becoming a transparent man. I didn't blame him; the transformation had unnerved us both. But I had to break free. As we struggled, my hand brushed against the box. The lid opened, and once again, the tent was flooded with intense white light.

Romy let out a strange scream, leaping back in fear. I watched as his head faded away, vanishing like a shadow. Looking down at myself, I saw my hands disappear, followed swiftly by my arms. My vision blurred, reducing everything to a hazy white blur.

I was now truly invisible, yet the reality was far from empowering. Instead of feeling liberated, I was overwhelmed by a profound sense of loss, akin to someone waking from surgery to find a limb missing. I felt disconnected, questioning my own humanity.

I glanced at Romy, but saw only floating clothes—a shirt and pants without a wearer. The light penetrated my eyes, reducing my vision to practically nothing. It felt like being enveloped in the densest fog.

Fumbling in the dimness, I managed to close the lid of the box, dimming the light. My vision improved slightly, but it was still far from normal. In our near-blind state, it was impossible to think of executing any plan.

I couldn't help but think of Braque, who had managed to navigate and function as an invisible man. His presence at my home and Major Jack's office was nothing short of remarkable, given the visual impairment he must have faced.

Romy's sobs reached me, his voice trembling with fear. "Where am I? Where am I?"

"You're still here, Romy," I reassured him, "You're an invisible man."

"No," he cried out, "I'm not invisible. I'm dead. I'm just a soul. That's why I can't see myself."

His words, though distressing, brought a wry smile to my lips. "If you're just a soul, you should see your body lying here. Where is it?"

"I can't see anything," he lamented.

"Not even a shadow?" I asked, waving my shirt in front of him.

"I see a vague shadow," he admitted. "Ash, will we be like this forever?"

"Of course not," I assured him. "Once we get back inside the pyramid, we'll return to normal."

"But how do we get there?" Romy's voice was desperate. "We can't see anything."

I paced, grappling with our predicament, when my foot collided with something. Unable to discern what it was through my impaired vision, I bent down to investigate. My hand closed around a small, lightweight device—the infrared observer. I had brought it into the pyramid before, though it remained unused.

The device was a marvel of modern technology, employed by the police force for night patrols. It had the capability to pierce through the darkness using infrared, revealing everything unseen by others. As I recognized it, a spark of hope ignited within me.

With our vision reduced to nearly nothing due to our transparent eyes, the prospect of using the infrared observer was a glimmer of hope. Infrared is a form of "invisible light," and I wondered if it could help us see and navigate.

I quickly grabbed the infrared observer, which resembled a small motion picture camera, and placed it before my eyes. Instantly, a dark red hue filled my vision, and to my amazement, I saw Romy—not just his clothes, but his entire body. His bones were visible, encased in a faint red outline, as if someone had delicately traced them with a light red pen. It was an extraordinary sight.

Moving the observer's lens, the desert outside appeared in the same dark red tone. While not as clear as normal vision, it was enough to allow movement.

"Romy, don't lose hope," I urged, handing him the observer. "Try using this."

There was silence as Romy adjusted to the device. After about ten minutes, he finally spoke, awestruck. "It's incredible! It's like discovering a whole new world through a microscope."

"We can use this to sneak into the pyramid without being detected by the locals," I suggested.

"But what about the viewer and the copper box?" Romy wondered aloud.

"If we encounter anyone, we can set them down," I replied. "And we should travel at night for added safety." Romy seemed buoyed by the plan. "And yes, we'll have to go naked."

"To be truly invisible, that's necessary," I confirmed.

Romy sighed with a hint of humor, "Being invisible is surprisingly uncomfortable. I bet 'Atom Flying Man' and

'Superman' aren't as cozy as they seem. Being a regular person is the best."

I chuckled, "That's quite in line with Oriental philosophy."

We shared a smile, though his was tinged with bitterness. We opened some canned food and brewed coffee, trying to lift our spirits. I reassured Romy repeatedly that once we reached the pyramid, we could reverse our condition, and gradually, his mood lightened.

As we sat together, invisible to the world but not to each other, Romy shared stories from World War II and Egyptian legends. Those tales kept us occupied through the day, as sleep eluded us. Despite our predicament, the camaraderie between us was a comfort, and the hope of returning to normal kept us going.

As night fell, Romy and I prepared for our journey. With the infrared viewer in my hand and Romy carefully cradling the brass box, we shed our clothes, becoming true invisible men. Anyone who might have seen us would surely weave tales of floating objects gliding through the desert—an eerie addition to local legends.

Daylight or darkness made no difference to us; the infrared viewer was our guide through the night. With its aid, we navigated the landscape until we reached the secret entrance to the ancient city.

This entrance, only operable from within, required a signal. Romy jumped up and down, creating a series of "bang bang" sounds, then quickly retreated to conceal the viewer and box under the sand.

Moments later, an Arab emerged from the entrance, his expression puzzled as he scanned the open surroundings. There was nowhere for anyone to hide, and yet the source of the noise had vanished.

Seizing the moment, I darted forward, delivering a precise strike to the cartilage at the base of his neck, rendering him unconscious. I imagined he'd awaken convinced it had all been a dream.

With the Arab incapacitated, I retrieved the viewer and, together with Romy, carried him inside the corridor. We left him there, secured the entrance, and hurried deeper into the ancient city.

The silence of the night enveloped us as we moved swiftly. Reaching the wells, undetected, brought a sigh of relief. Descending the well would lead us to the secret passage, a path to the pyramid's interior where no one would disturb us.

One by one, we descended and advanced through the passage. Romy's tension eased with each step, the fear of discovery diminishing as we remained unseen. In that moment, I comprehended why Liam and Nora chose the solace of their secluded island, retreating from a world they had grown estranged from.

Reaching the first round door, I cautiously pushed it open, only to be greeted by a rush of stale air that forced me to retreat, coughing violently. Had anyone seen me, they'd have noted a look of grave concern on my face.

"Ash, what's wrong?" Romy shouted in panic, his voice echoing in the dim passageway.

I struggled to catch my breath, coughing uncontrollably before managing to speak. "Romy, we overlooked something crucial."

Desperation tinged Romy's voice. "What did we forget?"

I instinctively pointed toward the round door, a futile gesture as Romy couldn't see me. "The air inside—"

He interrupted, "Isn't it supposed to be a vacuum? We can just hold our breath for a minute."

I shook my head, then stopped, remembering he couldn't see that either. "It's not a vacuum. There's air, but it's toxic. We wouldn't last five seconds in there."

Panic gripped Romy, his footsteps a frantic rhythm as he paced. "Then what do we do? What do we do?"

"Calm down, Romy," I urged, trying to inject some calm into the chaos. "The solution is simple. We need to retrieve the oxygen cylinders."

He sounded on the verge of despair. "Oxygen cylinders? They'll see them floating in the air!"

His spirit teetered on the brink of collapse, and I knew I had to act fast. "Wait here for me. I'll go back. If I can, I'll bring two cylinders. If not, one will have to do."

"Hurry," Romy pleaded, his voice barely above a whisper.

Before leaving, I warned, "Whatever you do, don't open that door without an oxygen cylinder. It would be suicide."

He acknowledged my warning, and I set off, gripping the infrared viewer tightly as I retraced our steps. Emerging from the well, I scanned the area, relieved to find it deserted. I sprinted forward, my heart pounding with urgency.

Reaching the secret corridor, I found the Arab man still sprawled unconscious where we left him. The task ahead was daunting, but I had no choice. Lives depended on it.

If only we had thought to bring the oxygen cylinders initially, everything would have gone smoothly. Now, I had no choice but to make another run back to our camp.

As I dashed through the desert, I couldn't shake the worry that the Arab guard might awaken during my absence. What would happen if he did? I had no way of knowing. To buy more time, I delivered another blow to the back of his head, ensuring he remained unconscious a bit longer.

Once outside, I sprinted through the desert, my speed rivaling that of a racing camel. Thankfully, the camp was deserted when I arrived, allowing me to grab two oxygen cylinders without incident.

I raced back towards the ancient city, but despite my speed, dawn was breaking by the time I neared the tunnel entrance.

Entering the corridor, I noted the Arab was still unconscious, but footsteps echoed down the passageway. An icy fear gripped me. For a moment, I was paralyzed, uncertain of my next move. Then, clarity returned — I needed to leave the Arab where he was.

Hurrying forward, I glanced through the infrared viewer and spotted two figures approaching. I quickly set the oxygen cylinders and viewer down, pressing myself against the stone wall, my body trembling inexplicably.

I prayed the two Arabs wouldn't notice the items on the ground. They walked past, engrossed in conversation, oblivious to my presence. As soon as they were a safe distance away, I retrieved the cylinders and viewer, advancing further down the corridor. I glanced back to see them tending to the unconscious guard, but I pressed on, urgency propelling me forward.

Bursting from the tunnel, I found myself in the ancient city, where the first light of dawn revealed early risers on its stone-paved streets.

An old woman balancing a plate on her head caught sight of me—or rather, the sight of the floating infrared viewer and oxygen cylinders approaching her. Her eyes widened in terror, and she stood frozen, unsure whether to flee or scream.

Luck was on my side as I slipped past her. But ahead, more people were appearing. I quickly ducked into a corner, setting the equipment down to avoid drawing further attention.

Anxiety gnawed at me. Romy was still inside the pyramid, possibly growing impatient or worried. What if he did something reckless while waiting for me?

I hoped the people would pass by quickly, but the old woman had run over to a group of men, shouting animatedly. Though I couldn't understand her words, I imagined she was recounting the bizarre sight of floating objects. Her gestures grew frantic as she pointed at the oxygen cylinder I'd left on the ground.

The men gathered in front of me. One bent down, reaching out to tap the cylinder. I could have easily reached out and pinched his nose, but he had no idea an invisible man crouched there before him.

Despite being invisible, I instinctively squatted lower. It was a bizarre reflex, driven by the awareness of my nakedness, even though nobody could see me.

The man flicked the cylinder, then picked up the infrared viewer. My instinct was to knock them down and continue on my way. But I knew that would only draw more attention, making it even harder to escape unnoticed.

I held my ground, listening as the man suddenly laughed and said something to his companions. They all joined in, laughing dismissively while the old woman protested, her cheeks flushed with indignation.

Clearly, they didn't believe her story. The men eventually wandered off, leaving the old woman muttering to herself before she too departed.

Relieved, I grabbed the oxygen cylinders and the viewer, darting forward with renewed urgency.

The city was just waking up, and few people were about, allowing me to reach the two wells without further incident.

I quickly descended into the well, but as soon as I reached the bottom, a sense of unease washed over me. Something was wrong.

Despite my near-zero vision, I could distinguish between light and dark. Now, at the bottom of the well, the tunnel ahead was ablaze with light, akin to a searchlight at its end. I paused, bewildered, raising the infrared viewer to my eyes. Through its lens, the scene crystallized, revealing the unmistakable glow of "transparent light."

Heart pounding, I dashed forward, calling out, "Romy! Romy!" My voice echoed back, unanswered.

Dread tightened around me as I sprinted down the tunnel, the air growing thick and heavy. Breathing was still manageable, so the oxygen cylinders remained unused.

Reaching the tunnel's end, I stood before the small round door, the source of the blinding light. Within it lay Romy, his upper body inside, legs splayed outside. He was no longer invisible, yet far from normal. His bones were starkly visible, but his muscles hadn't reappeared. I pulled him out, his body limp and cool to the touch. He was gone.

I squatted beside him, numb with shock, time slipping away unnoticed. My mind was a whirl of confusion until a realization slowly dawned.

The brass box lay inside the round door, its mineral contents scattered outside. It was clear now — Romy, desperate to reclaim his form, had underestimated the perilous air. Believing he could endure it by holding his breath, he had opened the door and crawled inside after I'd left, eager to reach the brass box.

Impatience had been his undoing. He opened the box prematurely, before fully entering the chamber. In that instant, the mineral emitted "anti-transparent light," revealing his bones. But with the door ajar, the air mingled, transforming the light to "transparent," preventing his full restoration.

The toxic air had claimed Romy's life, leaving me with a chilling revelation: in death, exposure to transparent light no longer rendered one invisible.

I sat there, grappling with the weight of this knowledge, and the loss of my friend. The path ahead was clear, but heavy with the cost of what we had already endured. Romy's fate was a stark reminder of our quest's perilous nature—and the imperative to proceed with utmost care.

Chapter 22

The Eternal Mystery

I gently returned the mineral to its box, sealing it with a quiet finality. The weight of the oxygen cylinder on my back was reassuring, a lifeline as I maneuvered Romy's lifeless form through the small, round door. Crawling alongside him, a sorrowful resolve washed over me.

Our acquaintance was brief, yet Romy had profoundly impacted my journey. Without his guidance, the hidden pyramid might have remained a myth. His untimely demise left a void, a companion lost to a fate as cryptic as the pyramid itself.

Romy's fears had always run deeper than most, shadows of some psychological anomaly I never understood. His transformation into a transparent specter mirrored his inner turmoil, and now, in death, he remained a mystery. I couldn't risk his body being discovered. It had to remain within the pyramid's secrets, unseen by the world.

Carefully, I pushed through the second door, entering the stone chamber that housed the sarcophagus. With a steadying breath, I placed Romy within the stone confines, sealing it as if locking away a part of myself.

The brass box beckoned, its secrets tantalizingly close. Yet, as I opened it, my heart plunged into an abyss of dread. For a fleeting moment, the absence of the vibrant "anti-transparent light" threatened to unravel all I believed. My theory, my path back to normalcy, teetered on the brink of collapse.

But then, like dawn breaking over a shadowed land, colors burst forth in a symphony of light. The chamber transformed into a kaleidoscope, a realm of wonder. Where despair had been, now surged an elation so raw, I couldn't contain it. In those radiant hues, I saw my bones, my flesh, and with them, a resurgence of confidence. I was alive, reborn.

I embraced the "anti-transparent light," allowing it to saturate every fiber of my being until I was whole once more. With a finality, I closed the box, plunging the chamber into darkness. I cradled the brass box and prepared to leave.

Yet, as I took a step, reality struck. Daylight awaited outside, and I was starkly unprepared to face it. The absurdity of my situation elicited a laugh, echoing against the ancient stones. My joy was boundless, for I was ordinary once more.

Invisibility had been a fantasy, a youthful dream of freedom. Reality, however, had proven it a curse. Having lived as a phantom, I vowed never to return to that shadowed existence.

I couldn't simply walk into the light. Darkness had to be my ally once more. With limited oxygen, I waited in the corridor, anticipation a tangible presence as the day stretched on.

At last, night descended. I emerged, cautious under the cover of shadows. Voices from the ancient city lingered, but patience was my guide. Only when the world slumbered did I climb out, bending low, the walls my silent accomplices in this clandestine escape.

Fortunately, the path remained deserted as I made my way through the dim tunnel. My footsteps were as quiet as whispers, each one calculated, until I reached the tunnel's exit. There, a guard stood oblivious, and with a swift, decisive move, I knocked him out. The open desert stretched before me, and I bolted across it like a startled groundhog, racing back to the safety of the camp.

The moment I reached the camp, I scrambled into my clothes, my skin slick with sweat, evidence of the adrenaline-fueled journey. Though the water we carried was enough for a refreshing bath, I couldn't bring myself to strip down again. I needed the comfort of those clothes, a shield against the memories of my recent ordeal.

As I lay in the tent, exhaustion tugged at my limbs, but thoughts of Romy churned within me. His impatience had driven him into the pyramid too soon, sealing his fate before the oxygen cylinder could arrive. The weight of his loss pressed heavily on my heart.

After a brief rest, I carefully placed the brass box into a large leather bag, securing it with meticulous care. The thought of exposing the mineral to the air, risking another invisible existence, was too much for my frayed nerves to bear.

I shed all unnecessary weight, keeping only four camels for the journey back to Cairo. The return trip was uneventful, a stark contrast to the perilous adventure I had endured.

Upon my arrival at the hotel, Shet, the portly waiter, regarded me with wide eyes, as if confronting a specter from the past.

My stay in Cairo was fleeting, and soon I was airborne once more. The moment the plane touched down, I reached out to Wilson. His voice crackled through the line, recounting a visit to the deserted island just days before. Liam and Nora had been anxiously awaiting my return, eager for any news, good or ill.

Their urgency was palpable, and I understood it all too well. Having experienced the haunting isolation of invisibility, I shared their desperation.

Without delay, I contacted Major Jack, requesting his assistance in discreetly transporting the mineral through customs. A public display of its power could unleash chaos beyond imagination. Major Jack, head of the secret working group, wielded the authority needed to bypass such scrutiny and readily agreed to help.

I also arranged for an employee to station a yacht at the nearest airport dock, while my car awaited me at another dock closer to home. With everything in motion, I wandered the airport, anticipation mingling with a lingering tension.

When I reached the dock, the yacht was already waiting, a sleek silhouette against the fading light. I boarded quickly, the sea chart spread before me, its familiar lines guiding my way. The location of the deserted island was etched into my memory, so I set course without hesitation.

By the time I reached the island, the sky had surrendered to dusk, painting the horizon in hues of orange and purple.

I called out for Liam and Nora, my voice slicing through the tranquil evening as I made my way towards their camp.

As I approached the tents, Liam's voice emerged from within, tinged with a tremor. "Mr. Morris, are you back?" The underlying anxiety was palpable, a sentiment I deeply understood, having once been trapped in the same invisible purgatory.

Before they could voice their fears, I spoke. "I have found a way to restore you both."

Silence hung in the air, heavy and expectant, until both Liam and Nora responded in unison, "Really? You're not lying to us, are you?"

I assured them, "Of course not. I was once transparent and invisible myself, but now I am fully restored. You too can regain your physical presence."

Liam whispered a prayer of gratitude, "Thank God. Please, restore us now." But I had to temper their eagerness. "Not yet," I cautioned.

Their anxiety flared again. "Why? What's stopping us?" they pressed. I reassured them, "There are no obstacles. The mineral, when exposed to normal air, emits a transparent light. But under a vacuum, it produces an anti-transparent light."

Liam's voice held a note of concern. "That mineral is no longer with us."

I reassured them, "It's okay. I managed to secure a small piece of the mineral in Egypt. First, let's head back to my place. Once I've set up a vacuum chamber, you can enter with oxygen cylinders. The translucent light will restore you completely."

Nora asked, "Should we go with you now?"

"Yes," I replied. "Get dressed, put on hats, and cover your faces with cloth. I'll guide you to the shore. A car will be waiting to take you directly to my house where you'll be safe and unseen."

They hesitated briefly before agreeing, "Okay, please wait a moment." When they emerged from the tent, they wore clothes but no hats or face coverings, a sight that felt oddly disconcerting.

I maintained a calm demeanor and turned to lead the way. "Come with me."

Together, we made our way to the yacht, then onto the speedboat. By the time we reached the mainland, it was midnight. Liam and Nora had donned hats and scarves, their faces concealed. I assisted them onto the shore where my car awaited.

We drove in silence to my home, where I settled them into my bedroom. After a long, hot shower, I reclined in the study's armchair, contemplating the challenge of finding a vacuum chamber. Several large factories might have what I needed.

I called a trusted friend, waking him from sleep, yet he bore no grudge and promised to investigate immediately.

Hanging up, I settled in for a brief nap. With the situation nearing resolution, my mind craved rest. I closed my eyes, but just as slumber approached, the phone jarred me awake.

Startled, I reached for the phone, impressed by my friend's promptness. "Hello," I answered eagerly. "Do you have any results?"

Silence greeted me. Unease prickled my senses. "Who is it?" I inquired, waiting for a response that never came. "If you don't speak, I'm going to hang up."

There was no response the first time, so I hung up. But barely half a minute had passed when the phone rang again. This time, as soon as I picked up, a voice came through, eager and almost desperate. "It's me, it was me just now!"

The voice had an unmistakable German accent, and I couldn't help but feel a mix of irritation and amusement. "I'm sorry, you've dialed the wrong number," I replied, feigning ignorance.

"No, Mr. Morris, it's me!" insisted the voice.

I paused, a flicker of recognition crossing my mind before I straightened in my chair. "Are you Braque?"

The relief in his voice was palpable. "Yes, I am Braque."

The sky outside was tinged with dawn's first light, and I couldn't resist a sardonic smile. "Good morning, Mr. Braque. What can I do for you at this hour?"

Braque's breathing was heavy, betraying his agitation. This was the same man who once moved with the cold efficiency of a killer. Now, reduced to an invisible shadow, his predicament was almost laughable. The memory of my own invisible days surfaced, and I couldn't suppress a chuckle.

"Have you seen Lomono since you returned from Egypt?" Braque asked, his voice tinged with a hint of desperation.

The idea of restoring Braque, a cold-blooded individual, to visibility was far from my mind. For someone like him, even a death sentence seemed lenient. Letting him remain an invisible man, tormented by his inner fears, was a fitting punishment.

I replied coolly, "I'm sorry, I haven't seen him."

Braque's urgency leaked through. "I don't mean to trouble you. I merely want to know the reason for your trip to Egypt."

Feigning innocence, I answered, "Oh, I went to check out a water conservancy project at a friend's behest. It's quite an impressive endeavor, and my friend is one of its designers."

His voice fell, laced with disappointment. "So that's it, I—I—"

Feigning concern, I asked, "Are you feeling unwell?"

He hesitated, the silence stretching before he finally spoke. "Mr. Morris, I'd like to meet you. Can I?"

I chuckled softly, responding to Braque's request with a touch of irony. "Meet? Mr. Braque, isn't there a flaw in your plan? You can see me, but I might not be able to see you, correct?"

Braque's voice was tinged with embarrassment. "Please, don't be like that. Haven't you always shown mercy to those who concede defeat?"

I replied, my tone icy. "The question is: do you admit your failure?"

With a heavy sigh, Braque conceded, "How could I not?"

I mused aloud, "I fail to see the purpose of our meeting."

"I need your help," he admitted, a hint of desperation creeping into his voice.

I sidestepped his plea. "What help could I possibly offer you? You nearly cost me my life several times. Frankly, you're my enemy. Isn't it a bit degrading to now ask for my assistance?"

Silence hung heavy on the line. Just as I considered ending the call, a gunshot rang out on his end.

Stunned, I shouted, "Braque! Braque!" But the line remained silent. Though I hadn't witnessed it, I knew he had taken his own life.

I disconnected, my mind reeling, and quickly informed the police of my suspicions through another call. I left them to piece together the mystery, choosing to remain anonymous.

The morning light streamed through the window as I pondered the unfolding events. If I had known Braque would take such drastic measures, I might have tempered my words.

I wondered how the police would handle Braque's remains. Was he still an invisible corpse even in death?

These questions lingered, unanswered. The police kept the matter shrouded in secrecy, refusing to acknowledge my call or divulge any details. It seemed that Braque's final act would remain as enigmatic as the man himself, leaving me to grapple with the implications of a world where transparency and invisibility could govern a person's fate.

The entire situation was wrapped in layers of mystery, and despite my connections within the police force, the official classification of the incident as top secret left me with more questions than answers.

The deaths of Romy and Braque weighed heavily on my mind, yet my focus remained on Liam and Nora, still trapped in their invisible state.

I reassured myself that it was only a matter of time. Once the mineral emitted its "anti-transparent light" in the vacuum chamber, their plight would be over, and the world would move past the strange phenomena of invisible people. However, the thought of the larger piece of this mineral in Braque's possession haunted me — had he destroyed it, or was it hidden somewhere, waiting to be discovered by another?

These thoughts swirled in my mind as I drifted into a fitful sleep, my consciousness a tangled web of uncertainty and hope. Despite the chaos in my head, a sense of calm prevailed, believing the ordeal was nearing its end.

I would never have predicted the unexpected turn of events that followed. That twist left a mark of regret that lingers even now. Allow me to recount those events. I awoke in the afternoon to the shrill ring of the phone, shaking me from slumber.

Liam and Nora were in my study, still wrapped in their mummy-like attire, scarves concealing their identities. Answering the phone, I heard Major Jack's voice. He asked about the luggage that couldn't pass through customs. I instructed him to send it directly to my residence and stressed the importance of keeping it sealed.

Major Jack agreed, and I took the opportunity to mention Braque's situation. His reaction was one of disbelief, as if hearing a tall tale, and he promptly ended the call.

Turning to Liam and Nora, I reassured them, "You don't have to stay like that. I've grown accustomed to it and don't find it alarming anymore."

Liam responded with a bitter laugh, "It's better for us this way. Even if you're not afraid, we remain anxious."

Understanding their apprehension, I recounted my Egyptian journey, detailing how I discovered the mineral's dual nature. Their tension eased considerably as they absorbed the story.

Just then, my friend called back. "Ash," he started, "there's a vacuum chamber at a precision instrument manufacturing plant."

"That's excellent," I replied. "But will they permit me to use it?"

"Yes," he confirmed. "But it's quite small, much smaller than the secret room you requested."

I leaned in eagerly. "How small is it?"

"Three cubic meters," he replied. "It's designed for storing precision instruments."

Elated, I instructed, "That's sufficient. Please arrange two oxygen cylinders and meet me at the factory entrance to escort me inside." He agreed, and we ended the call.

The doorbell's chime announced the arrival of the copper box. A reminder of its potent contents, I dared not open it, lest I risk becoming invisible once more. Instead, I secured it carefully before joining Liam and Nora in the car.

In twenty brisk minutes, we arrived at the factory gates. My friend stood waiting, accompanied by a man with the demeanor of an engineer. Despite my reassurances, Liam and Nora hesitated, anxiety keeping them car-bound. "No one knows your secret," I reminded them gently. "People might be curious about your attire, but that's all."

With a resigned sigh, they emerged, only to retreat hastily when my friend approached a bit too eagerly. I met him halfway, patting his shoulder with a grin. "Is everything set?" I asked.

"All ready," he confirmed, lowering his voice conspiratorially. "But who are they? Dressed like that, they look like they've come from Saturn!"

I chuckled, nudging him playfully. "Nothing of the sort. Let's keep things simple. Just lead us to the vacuum chamber, no need for any fuss."

My friend's light-heartedness was infectious, and I found myself laughing along with him. As our laughter subsided, Liam and Nora rejoined us, and I guided them forward, each arm linked with theirs. Technician , our guide within the factory, was introduced, and after a brief exchange, my friend departed with a promise to reconvene later.

We navigated through the factory, arriving at a modern building where an elevator whisked us to the third floor. A door opened to a spacious control room filled with intricate equipment. "This is the control room," Technician Davis explained. "I'm in charge here. The oxygen cylinders are ready. Who will be using them?"

I nodded toward Liam and Nora. "They'll be conducting an experiment in the vacuum chamber."

Technician Davis nodded, eyeing them with professional curiosity. "The chamber can accommodate two."

He unlocked a door that resembled a colossal safe, revealing the vacuum chamber within. I retrieved the oxygen cylinders, handing one to Liam and the other to Nora.

I leaned closer to them, speaking softly. "Once inside, put on your oxygen masks. When the chamber reaches a vacuum, I'll signal you to open the brass box. Once you're visible, knock, and we'll refill the chamber with air. Remember to close the box afterward. I'll ensure the mineral is destroyed to prevent further harm."

They listened intently, their nods conveying trust and anticipation. I passed the brass box to Nora, noticing her hands trembled slightly—not from fear, but from the thrill of impending liberation. "Don't worry," I assured them. "No more accidents."

Yet, their reply carried a shadow of doubt. "I hope so," they murmured, voices tinged with unease.

I sensed their apprehension but chose silence, confident in the imminence of their transformation.

One after the other, they entered the chamber. Davis sealed the door and began his work at the control panel. "When the pointer hits 'zero'," he explained, "the chamber will be fully vacuumed."

I watched the meter intently as the needle crept toward zero, a process that took an excruciating five minutes. Once it reached its mark, I knocked on the copper door of the vacuum chamber multiple times, sure that Liam and Nora could hear the signal.

Patiently, I waited by the door, anticipating the moment they would knock back to confirm their successful restoration. I lit a cigarette, the smoke curling lazily as my mind remained calm and hopeful.

But as the minutes passed, and I found myself on my third cigarette without any response, unease began to gnaw at me. I glanced at Davis, whose expression mirrored my growing concern. "Their oxygen should be nearly depleted by now. Could something have gone wrong?" he mused, a note of worry in his voice.

My voice wavered as I responded, "Something wrong? What kind of accident could have happened?"

Davis shrugged, perplexed. "I don't know. What exactly did they do in there?"

His question hit me hard. How could I succinctly explain the extraordinary circumstances surrounding Liam and Nora's experiment? Realizing the urgency, I urged, "If their oxygen is low, we need to open the chamber quickly."

Davis resumed his work at the control panel. After a tense few minutes, he instructed, "You can open the door now. Turn the handle to the left, fully, then pull it open."

As I approached the door, a knock resonated from within. Relief washed over us both; they were alive, responding at last. I eagerly turned the handle, pulling the door open.

"Long time no see, both of you," I called out as the door swung wide.

Stepping back with the door, I couldn't immediately see into the chamber. Davis, however, looked in first, his expression shifting to one of shock, as if struck by an unseen force.

Alarmed, I asked, "What's wrong?"

He pointed into the chamber, his mouth agape, words failing him.

Realizing I couldn't afford to wait, I moved around the door to peer inside.

What I saw left me speechless. Inside the chamber lay Liam and Nora's clothing, cast aside. The brass box was open, but the mysterious mineral sat inert, a dull gray-white in hue, devoid of any light or luster.

My heart sank as I processed the scene. The mineral had failed, or perhaps something else had gone awry, leaving only questions in its wake.

Liam and Nora were gone, leaving only their clothes strewn on the chamber floor!

For a moment, I stood frozen, grappling with the sudden, confounding reality. What had transpired in those crucial moments?

Davis, overwhelmed by the shock, let out a scream and dashed for the door. "Davis, please come back!" I called, but he was too rattled to respond. In his haste, he stumbled heavily at the threshold, rising to meet my gaze with a face drained of color.

A sudden thought flashed through my mind, a sliver of hope or perhaps desperation, urging me to act. "Close the door, close the door!" I shouted, realizing too late that my words were cryptic to Davis, who remained bewildered.

I dashed to the door myself, slamming it shut with a resounding "bang." But clarity struck just as quickly; my actions seemed irrational, so I reopened it, finding Davis still standing there, paralyzed by fear.

"Mr. Davis," I asked urgently, "did you feel anyone pass by you?" His expression was one of near hysteria, unable to provide an answer as he echoed my question back to me, bewildered.

With a sigh, I pulled him back into the room and closed the door. His scream pierced the air again. I acted on instinct, delivering a firm slap to his face to jolt him from his panic. "Don't scream!" I commanded.

Davis gasped for breath, and I faced him squarely. "Something unusual happened here, didn't it?"

He nodded, his voice trembling, "Too—too unusual."

I asked, "What exactly is unusual? Can you explain it to me?"

Davis cast a nervous glance at the vacuum chamber, his expression growing more fearful. The chamber's door stood open, revealing only two oxygen cylinders, a set of men's and women's clothing, the brass box, and the gray mineral within it.

With a shaky voice, Davis said, "The two people who came with you—they walked into the vacuum chamber— and then they disappeared."

I pressed further, "Did you officially request the factory to lend us the vacuum chamber?"

His response was hesitant, "No—no, I didn't."

I quickly reassured him, "Then surely you wouldn't want this incident to become public knowledge?"

"Of course not," he replied hurriedly. "But how is this possible? Two people vanished. My God, where could they have gone?"

Where indeed? That was the haunting question echoing in my mind.

There was no answer forthcoming, but I realized a grave mistake on my part.

I had assumed that the pyramid's environment was a vacuum, leading me to believe that the mineral would emit "anti-transparent light" in a vacuum. But reality had shattered that assumption.

The pyramid's environment might mimic a vacuum, but it was not the same. This mineral, so unpredictable, emitted transparent light in normal air and "anti-transparent light" inside the pyramid. But in a true vacuum? I had no idea what it emitted, and now Liam and Nora were lost to us, vanished into the unknown.

The mineral, now exposed to ordinary air, failed to emit its characteristic transparent light, suggesting a change had occurred. My mind was a whirl of confusion, unable to form coherent speculations in the face of such an unprecedented event.

I spoke to Davis, "As long as neither of us speaks about this, no one will ever know what happened here."

He nodded, and with a heavy heart, I walked toward the vacuum chamber. The room held only remnants of the past, a stark reminder of the risks inherent in tampering with forces we barely understood.

Liam and Nora's fate was now a mystery, a sobering lesson in the unpredictable nature of such experiments.

When I approached the vacuum chamber, Davis's voice broke the silence. "Mr. Morris, can I ask you something?"

I paused, turning to face him. "What is it?"

His voice trembled with uncertainty, "Where did they go?"

I offered a bitter smile. "I don't know, I truly don't."

Stepping into the vacuum chamber, I examined the mineral, which now resembled a piece of tin. As I leaned closer, a sudden wave of heat emanated from it, startling me into a retreat. Everything appeared normal, but caution led me to prod the mineral with an iron rod. To my shock, it disintegrated into ash at the slightest touch.

Startled once more, I swiftly shut the box lid, gathered Liam and Nora's clothes, and exited the chamber.

I addressed Davis, "Goodbye. Even though your help led to unexpected consequences, I still appreciate it."

He remained rooted to the spot, overwhelmed by the bizarre events, words failing him.

I made my way outside, placing Liam and Nora's clothes in the car before settling into the driver's seat. Yet, I couldn't bring myself to drive. My thoughts were tangled in a chaotic web, and clarity eluded me.

With hands gripping the steering wheel, I sat for what felt like an eternity, wrestling with the implications until two possibilities emerged.

The first possibility was that the mineral released intense heat energy in a vacuum (light and heat are closely related). The heat, particularly sensitive to living tissue, could have vaporized Liam and Nora's bodies, reducing them to gas. This would explain the absence of anything but their clothes and the oxygen cylinders when the vacuum chamber was opened. The knocking I heard might have been the oxygen cylinder rolling against the door, and Davis's sensation of something passing could have been a rush of air.

The unsettling nature of the mineral's effects weighed heavily on my mind. Whether it emitted light or heat, its impact on living organisms was undeniable. This peculiarity — where transparent light could affect the human body but not clothing—filled me with dread.

If my first inference was correct, then Liam and Nora had been inadvertently harmed by my actions. The very thought made me break into a sweat, the possibility too horrifying to fully accept.

Desperately, I clung to another explanation: perhaps the mineral, in a vacuum, emitted an intense transparent light that rendered Liam and Nora instantly invisible. In their hearts, hope for restoration had turned to fear and despair. This might explain why they removed their clothes and eventually knocked on the door. Perhaps it was indeed their knocking I heard, not merely the sound of an oxygen cylinder. If so, as the door opened, they seized the opportunity to flee, their trust in me shattered by the unexpected outcome.

I fervently hoped this second scenario was the truth. It offered a shred of hope that they were still alive, albeit invisible, possibly regrouping and trying to find their way back.

Determining the truth between these scenarios proved impossible. I awaited any sign, a call from Liam or Nora, signaling their presence and perhaps seeking assistance to find Braque's hidden mineral. With it, they could return to the pyramid's unique atmosphere to regain visibility. Yet, no call came.

I remained vigilant, scanning for any unusual occurrences that might hint at their presence. But there was silence, leaving me in limbo, unsure if they existed in this world or if they viewed me as someone untrustworthy and deceitful, choosing to sever all ties.

The ash left from the mineral's disintegration was sent for analysis. The results were staggering—it was composed of elements unknown on Earth, possibly extraterrestrial in origin.

This conclusion, provided by a renowned polytechnic institute, solidified my belief in its authenticity.

I could only hope that the larger piece of mineral Braque had concealed would remain hidden forever, never to wreak havoc again.

The burden of the unknown lingered, a constant reminder of the fragile line between discovery and disaster, and the lives unintentionally caught in the balance.